# THE MUSIC OF CHANCE

Paul Auster was born in New Jersey in 1947. After attending Columbia University he lived in France for four years. Since 1974 he has published poems, essays, novels and translations. He lives in Brooklyn, New York.

# THE MUSIC
# OF CHANCE

Paul Auster

faber and faber
LONDON BOSTON

First published in the USA in 1990
by Viking Penguin, a division of Penguin Books USA Inc.
First published in Great Britain in 1991
by Faber and Faber Limited
3 Queen Square London WC1N 3AU
This export market edition first published in 1991

Printed in England by Clays Ltd, St Ives plc

A CIP record for this book is available from the British Library

ISBN 0-571-16674-1

4 6 8 10 9 7 5 3

# THE MUSIC
# OF CHANCE

# 1

---

For one whole year he did nothing but drive, traveling back and forth across America as he waited for the money to run out. He hadn't expected it to go on that long, but one thing kept leading to another, and by the time Nashe understood what was happening to him, he was past the point of wanting it to end. Three days into the thirteenth month, he met up with the kid who called himself Jackpot. It was one of those random, accidental encounters that seem to materialize out of thin air—a twig that breaks off in the wind and suddenly lands at your feet. Had it occurred at any other moment, it is doubtful that Nashe would have opened his mouth. But because he had already given up, because he figured there was nothing to lose anymore, he saw the stranger as a reprieve, as a last chance to do something for himself before it was too late. And just like that, he went ahead and did it. Without the slightest tremor of fear, Nashe closed his eyes and jumped.

It all came down to a question of sequence, the order of events.

If it had not taken the lawyer six months to find him, he never would have been on the road the day he met Jack Pozzi, and therefore none of the things that followed from that meeting ever would have happened. Nashe found it unsettling to think of his life in those terms, but the fact was that his father had died a full month before Thérèse walked out on him, and if he had had some inkling of the money he was about to inherit, he probably could have talked her into staying. Even if she hadn't stayed, there would have been no need to take Juliette out to Minnesota to live with his sister, and that alone would have kept him from doing what he did. But he still had his job with the fire department back then, and how was he supposed to take care of a two-year-old child when his work kept him out of the house at all hours of the day and night? If there had been some money, he would have hired a woman to live with them and look after Juliette, but if there had been any money, they wouldn't have been renting the bottom half of a dismal two-family house in Somerville, and Thérèse might never have run off in the first place. It wasn't that his salary was so bad, but his mother's stroke four years ago had emptied him out, and he was still sending monthly payments down to the rest home in Florida where she had died. Given all that, his sister's place had seemed like the only solution. At least Juliette would have a chance to live with a real family, to be surrounded by other kids and to breathe some fresh air, and that was a lot better than anything he could offer her himself. Then, out of the blue, the lawyer found him and the money fell into his lap. It was a colossal sum—close to two hundred thousand dollars, an almost unimaginable sum to Nashe—but by then it was already too late. Too many things had been set in motion during the past five months, and not even the money could stop them anymore.

He had not seen his father in over thirty years. The last time had been when he was two, and since then there had been no contact between them—not one letter, not one phone call, nothing.

According to the lawyer who handled the estate, Nashe's father had spent the last twenty-six years of his life in a small California desert town not far from Palm Springs. He had owned a hardware store, had played the stock market in his spare time, and had never remarried. He had kept his past to himself, the lawyer said, and it was only when Nashe Senior walked into his office one day to make out a will that he ever mentioned having any children. "He was dying of cancer," the voice on the telephone continued, "and he didn't know who else to leave his money to. He figured he might as well split it between his two kids—half for you and half for Donna."

"A peculiar way to make amends," Nashe said.

"Well, he was a peculiar one, your old man, no question about it. I'll never forget what he said when I asked him about you and your sister. 'They probably hate my guts,' he said, 'but it's too late to cry about that now. I only wish I could be around after I croak— just to see the look on their faces when they get the money.'"

"I'm surprised he knew where to find us."

"He didn't," the lawyer said. "And believe me, I've had one hell of a time tracking you down. It's taken me six months."

"It would have been a lot better for me if you'd made this call on the day of the funeral."

"Sometimes you get lucky, sometimes you don't. Six months ago, I still didn't know if you were alive or dead."

It wasn't possible to feel grief, but Nashe assumed that he would be touched in some other way—by something akin to sadness, perhaps, by a surge of last-minute angers and regrets. The man had been his father, after all, and that alone should have counted for a few somber thoughts about the mysteries of life. But it turned out that Nashe felt little else but joy. The money was so extraordinary to him, so monumental in its consequences, that it overwhelmed all the rest. Without pausing to consider the matter very carefully, he paid off his thirty-two-thousand-dollar debt to the

Pleasant Acres Nursing Home, went out and bought himself a new car (a red two-door Saab 900—the first unused car he had ever owned), and cashed in on the vacation time that he had accumulated over the past four years. The night before he left Boston, he threw a lavish party in his own honor, carried on with his friends until three o'clock in the morning, and then, without bothering to go to bed, climbed into the new car and drove to Minnesota.

That was where the roof started to cave in on him. In spite of all the celebrating and reminiscing that went on during those days, Nashe gradually understood that the situation was beyond repair. He had been away from Juliette for too long, and now that he had come back for her, it was as if she had forgotten who he was. He had thought the telephone calls would be enough, that talking to her twice a week would somehow keep him alive for her. But what do two-year-olds know about long-distance conversations? For six months, he had been nothing but a voice to her, a vaporous collection of sounds, and little by little he had turned himself into a ghost. Even after he had been in the house for two or three days, Juliette remained shy and tentative with him, shrinking back from his attempts to hold her as though she no longer fully believed in his existence. She had become a part of her new family, and he was little more than an intruder, an alien being who had dropped down from another planet. He cursed himself for having left her there, for having arranged things so well. Juliette was now the adored little princess of the household. There were three older cousins for her to play with, there was the Labrador retriever, there was the cat, there was the swing in the backyard, there was everything she could possibly want. It galled him to think that he had been usurped by his brother-in-law, and as the days wore on he had to struggle not to show his resentment. An ex–football player turned high school coach and math teacher, Ray Schweikert had always struck Nashe as something of a knucklehead, but there was no question that the guy had a way with kids. He was Mr. Good, the big-hearted American dad, and with Donna there to hold things together, the family was as solid as a rock. Nashe had some money now, but how had anything really changed? He tried to imagine how Juliette's life could be improved by going back to Boston with him, but he could not muster a single argument in his own defense. He wanted to be selfish, to stand on his rights, but his nerve kept failing him, and at last he gave in to the obvious truth. To wrench Juliette away from all this would do her more harm than good.

When he told Donna what he was thinking, she tried to talk him out of it, using many of the same arguments she had thrown at him twelve years before when he told her he was planning to quit college: Don't be rash, give it a little more time, don't burn your bridges behind you. She was wearing that worried big-sister look he had seen on her all through his childhood, and even now, three or four lifetimes later, he knew that she was the one person in the world he could trust. They wound up talking late into the night, sitting in the kitchen long after Ray and the kids had gone to bed, but for all of Donna's passion and good sense, it turned out just as it had twelve years before: Nashe wore her down until she started to cry, and then he got his way.

His one concession to her was that he would set up a trust fund for Juliette. Donna sensed that he was about to do something crazy (she told him as much that night), and before he ran through the entire inheritance, she wanted him to set aside a part of it, to put it in a place where it couldn't be touched. The following morning, Nashe spent two hours with the manager of the Northfield Bank and made the necessary arrangements. He hung around for the rest of that day and part of the next, and then he packed his bags and loaded up the trunk of his car. It was a hot afternoon in late July, and the whole family came out onto the front lawn to see him off. One after the other, he hugged and kissed the children, and when Juliette's turn came at the end, he hid his eyes from her by picking her up and crushing his face into her neck. Be a good girl, he said. Don't forget that Daddy loves you.

He had told them he was planning to go back to Massachusetts, but as it happened, he soon found himself traveling in the opposite direction. That was because he missed the ramp to the freeway—a common enough mistake—but instead of driving the extra twenty miles that would have put him back on course, he impulsively went up the next ramp, knowing full well that he had just committed himself to the wrong road. It was a sudden, unpremeditated decision, but in the brief time that elapsed between the two ramps, Nashe understood that there was no difference, that both ramps were finally the same. He had said Boston, but that was only because he had to tell them something, and Boston was the first word that entered his head. For the fact was that no one was expecting to see him there for another two weeks, and with so much time at his disposal, why bother to go back? It was a dizzying prospect—to imagine all that freedom, to understand how little it mattered what choice he made. He could go anywhere he wanted, he could do anything he felt like doing, and not a single person in the world would care. As long as he did not turn back, he could just as well have been invisible.

He drove for seven straight hours, paused momentarily to fill up the tank with gas, and then continued for another six hours until exhaustion finally got the better of him. He was in north-central Wyoming by then, and dawn was just beginning to lift over the horizon. He checked into a motel, slept solidly for eight or nine hours, and then walked over to the diner next door and put away a meal of steak and eggs from the twenty-four-hour breakfast menu. By late afternoon, he was back in the car, and once again he drove clear through the night, not stopping until he had gone halfway through New Mexico. After that second night, Nashe realized that he was no longer in control of himself, that he had fallen into the grip of some baffling, overpowering force. He was like a crazed animal, careening blindly from one nowhere to the next, but no matter how many resolutions he made to stop, he could not bring himself to do it. Every morning he would go to sleep telling himself that he had had enough, that there would be no more of it, and every afternoon he would wake up with the same desire, the same irresistible urge to crawl back into the car. He wanted that solitude again, that nightlong rush through the emptiness, that rumbling of the road along his skin. He kept it up for the whole two weeks, and each day he pushed himself a little farther, each day he tried to go a little longer than the day before. He covered the entire western part of the country, zigzagging back and forth from Oregon to Texas, charging down the enormous, vacant highways that cut through Arizona, Montana, and Utah, but it wasn't as though he looked at anything or cared where he was, and except for the odd sentence that he was compelled to speak when buying gas or ordering food, he did not utter a single word. When Nashe finally returned to Boston, he told himself that he was on the verge of a mental breakdown, but that was only because he couldn't think of anything else to account for what he had done. As he eventually discovered, the truth was far less dramatic. He was simply ashamed of himself for having enjoyed it so much.

Nashe assumed that it would stop there, that he had managed to work out the odd little bug that had been caught in his system, and now he would slip back into his old life. At first, everything seemed to go well. On the day of his return, they teased him at the fire house for not showing up with a tan ("What did you do, Nashe, spend your vacation in a cave?"), and by midmorning he was laughing at the usual wisecracks and dirty jokes. There was a big fire in Roxbury that night, and when the alarm came for a couple of backup engines, Nashe even went so far as to tell someone that he was glad to be home, that he had missed being away from all the action. But those feelings did not continue, and by the end of the week he found that he was growing restless, that he could not close his eyes at night without remembering the car. On his day off, he drove up to Maine and back, but that only seemed to make it worse, for it left him unsatisfied, itching for more time behind the wheel. He struggled to settle down again, but his mind kept wandering back to the road, to the exhilaration he had felt for those two weeks, and little by little he began to give himself up for lost. It wasn't that he wanted to quit his job, but with no more time coming to him, what else was he supposed to do? Nashe had been with the fire department for seven years, and it struck him as perverse that he should even consider such a possibility— to throw it away on the strength of an impulse, because of some nameless agitation. It was the only job that had ever meant anything to him, and he had always felt lucky to have stumbled into it. After quitting college, he had knocked around at a number of things for the next few years—bookstore salesman, furniture mover, bartender, taxi driver—and he had only taken the fire exam on a whim, because someone he had met in his cab one night was about to do it and he talked Nashe into giving it a try. That man was turned down, but Nashe wound up receiving the highest grade given that year, and all of a sudden he was being offered a job that he had last thought about when he was four years old. Donna laughed when he called and told her the news, but he went ahead and took the training anyway. There was no question that it was a curious choice, but the work absorbed him and continued to make him happy, and he had never second-guessed himself for sticking with it. Just a few months earlier, it would have been impossible for him to imagine leaving the department, but that was before his life had turned into a soap opera, before the earth had opened around him and swallowed him up. Maybe it was time for a change. He still had over sixty thousand dollars in the bank, and maybe he should use it to get out while he still could.

He told the captain that he was moving to Minnesota. It seemed like a plausible story, and Nashe did his best to make it sound convincing, going on at some length about how he had received an offer to go into business with one of his brother-in-law's friends (a partnership in a hardware store, of all things) and why he thought it would be a decent environment for his daughter to grow up in. The captain fell for it, but that did not prevent him from calling Nashe an asshole. "It's that bimbo wife of yours," he said. "Ever since she moved her pussy out of town, your brain's been fucked up, Nashe. There's nothing more pathetic than that. To see a good man go under because of pussy problems. Get a grip on yourself, fella. Forget those dimwit plans and do your job."

"Sorry, captain," Nashe said, "but I've already made up my mind."

"Mind? What mind? As far as I can tell, you don't have one anymore."

"You're just jealous, that's all. You'd give your right arm to trade places with me."

"And move to Minnesota? Forget it, pal. I can think of ten thousand things I'd rather do than live under a snowdrift nine months a year."

"Well, if you're ever passing through, be sure to stop by and say hello. I'll sell you a screwdriver or something."

"Make it a hammer, Nashe. Maybe I could use it to pound some sense into you."

Now that he had taken the first step, it wasn't difficult for him to push on to the end. For the next five days, he took care of business, calling up his landlord and telling him to look for a new tenant, donating furniture to the Salvation Army, cutting off his gas and electric service, disconnecting his phone. There was a recklessness and violence to these gestures that deeply satisfied him, but nothing could match the pleasure of simply throwing things away. On the first night, he spent several hours gathering up Thérèse's belongings and loading them into trash bags, finally getting rid of her in a systematic purge, a mass burial of each and every object that bore the slightest trace of her presence. He swooped through her closet and dumped out her coats and sweaters and dresses; he emptied her drawers of underwear, stockings, and jewelry; he removed all her pictures from the photo album; he threw out her makeup kits and fashion magazines; he disposed of her books, her records, her alarm clock, her bathing suits, her letters. That broke the ice, so to speak, and when he began to consider his own possessions the following afternoon, Nashe acted with the same brutal thoroughness, treating his past as if it were so much junk to be carted away. The entire contents of the kitchen went to a shelter for homeless people in South Boston. His books went to the high school girl upstairs; his baseball glove went to the little boy across the street; his record collection was sold off to a secondhand music store in Cambridge. There was a certain pain involved in these transactions, but Nashe almost began to welcome that pain, to feel ennobled by it, as if the farther he took himself away from the person he had been, the better off he would be in the future. He felt like a man who had finally found the courage to put a bullet through his head—but in this case the bullet was not death, it was life, it was the explosion that triggers the birth of new worlds.

He knew that the piano would have to go as well, but he let it wait until the end, not wanting to give it up until the last possible moment. It was a Baldwin upright that his mother had bought for him on his thirteenth birthday, and he had always been grateful to her for that, knowing what a struggle it had been for her to come up with the money. Nashe had no illusions about his playing, but he generally managed to put in a few hours at the instrument every week, sitting down to muddle through some of the old pieces he had learned as a boy. It always had a calming effect on him, as if the music helped him to see the world more clearly, to understand his place in the invisible order of things. Now that the house was empty and he was ready to go, he held back for an extra day to give a long farewell recital to the bare walls. One by one, he went through several dozen of his favorite pieces, beginning with *The Mysterious Barricades* by Couperin and ending with Fats Waller's *Jitterbug Waltz*, hammering away at the keyboard until his fingers grew numb and he had to give up. Then he called his piano tuner of the past six years (a blind man named Antonelli) and arranged to sell the Baldwin to him for four hundred and fifty dollars. By the time the movers came the next morning, Nashe had already spent the money on tapes for the cassette machine in his car. It was a fitting gesture, he felt—to turn one form of music into another—and the economy of the exchange pleased him. After that, there was nothing to hold him back anymore. He stayed around long enough to watch Antonelli's men wrestle the piano out of the house, and then, without bothering to say good-bye to anyone, he was gone. He just walked out, climbed into his car, and was gone.

Nashe did not have any definite plan. At most, the idea was to let himself drift for a while, to travel around from place to place and see what happened. He figured he would grow tired of it after a couple of months, and at that point he would sit down and worry about what to do next. But two months passed, and he still was not ready to give up. Little by little, he had fallen in love with his new life of freedom and irresponsibility, and once that happened, there were no longer any reasons to stop.

Speed was of the essence, the joy of sitting in the car and hurtling himself forward through space. That became a good beyond all others, a hunger to be fed at any price. Nothing around him lasted for more than a moment, and as one moment followed another, it was as though he alone continued to exist. He was a fixed point in a whirl of changes, a body poised in utter stillness as the world rushed through him and disappeared. The car became a sanctum of invulnerability, a refuge in which nothing could hurt him anymore. As long as he was driving, he carried no burdens, was unencumbered by even the slightest particle of his former life. That is not to say that memories did not rise up in him, but they no longer seemed to bring any of the old anguish. Perhaps the music had something to do with that, the endless tapes of Bach and Mozart and Verdi that he listened to while sitting behind the wheel, as if the sounds were somehow emanating from him and drenching the landscape, turning the visible world into a reflection of his own thoughts. After three or four months, he had only to enter the car to feel that he was coming loose from his body, that once he put his foot down on the gas and started driving, the music would carry him into a realm of weightlessness.

Empty roads were always preferable to crowded roads. They demanded fewer slackenings and decelerations, and because he did not have to pay attention to other cars, he could drive with the assurance that his thoughts would not be interrupted. He therefore tended to avoid large population centers, restricting himself to open, unsettled areas: northern New York and New England, the flat farm country of the heartland, the Western deserts. Bad weather was also to be shunned, for that interfered with driving as much as traffic did, and when winter came with its storms and inclemencies, he headed south, and with few exceptions stayed there until spring. Still, even under the best of conditions, Nashe knew that no road was entirely free of danger. There were constant perils to watch out for, and anything could happen at any moment. Swerves and potholes, sudden blowouts, drunken drivers, the briefest lapse of attention—any one of those things could kill you in an instant. Nashe saw a number of fatal accidents during his months on the road, and once or twice he came within a hair's breadth of crackups himself. He welcomed these close calls, however. They added an element of risk to what he was doing, and more than anything else, that was what he was looking for: to feel that he had taken his life into his own hands.

He would check into a motel somewhere, have dinner, and then go back to his room and read for two or three hours. Before turning in, he would sit down with his road atlas and plan out the next day's itinerary, choosing a destination and carefully charting his course. He knew that it was no more than a pretext, that the places had no meaning in themselves, but he followed this system until the end—if only as a way to punctuate his movements, to give himself a reason to stop before going on again. In September, he visited his father's grave in California, traveling to the town of Riggs one blistering afternoon just to see it with his own eyes. He wanted to flesh out his feelings with an image of some kind, even if that image was no more than a few words and numbers carved into a stone slab. The lawyer who had called about the money accepted his invitation to lunch, and afterward he showed Nashe the house where his father had lived and the hardware store he had run for those twenty-six years. Nashe bought some tools for his car there (a wrench, a flashlight, an air-pressure gauge), but he could never bring himself to use them, and for the rest of the year the package lay unopened in a remote corner of the trunk. On another occasion, he suddenly found himself weary of driving, and rather than push on for no purpose, he took a room at a small hotel in Miami Beach and spent nine straight days sitting by the pool and reading books. In November, he went on a gambling jag in Las Vegas, miraculously breaking even after four days of blackjack and roulette, and not long after that, he spent half a month inching through the deep South, stopping off in a number of Louisiana Delta towns, visiting a friend who had moved to Atlanta, and taking a boat ride through the Everglades. Some of these stops were unavoidable, but once Nashe found himself somewhere, he generally tried to take advantage of it and do some poking around. The Saab had to be cared for, after all, and with the odometer ticking off several hundred miles a day, there was much to be done: oil changes, lube jobs, wheel alignments, all the fine tunings and repairs that were necessary to keep him going. He sometimes felt frustrated at having to make these stops, but with the car placed in the hands of a mechanic for twenty-four or forty-eight hours, he had no choice but to sit tight until it was ready to roll again.

Early on, he had rented a mailbox in the Northfield post office, and at the beginning of every month Nashe passed through town to collect his credit-card bills and spend a few days with his daughter. That was the only part of his life that did not change, the one commitment he adhered to. He made a special visit for Juliette's birthday in mid-October (arriving with an armful of presents), and Christmas turned out to be a boisterous, three-day affair during which Nashe dressed up as Santa Claus and entertained everyone by playing the piano and singing songs. Less than a month after that, a second door unexpectedly opened to him. That was in Berkeley, California, and like most of the things that happened to him that year, it came about purely by chance. He had gone into a bookstore one afternoon to buy books for the next leg of his journey, and just like that he ran into a woman he had once known in Boston. Her name was Fiona Wells, and she found him standing in front of the Shakespeare shelf struggling to decide which one-volume edition he should take with him. They hadn't seen each other for a couple of years, but rather than greet him in any conventional way, she sidled up next to him, tapped her finger against one of the Shakespeares, and said, "Get this one, Jim. It has the best notes and the most readable print."

Fiona was a journalist who had once written a feature article about him for the *Globe*, "A Week in the Life of a Boston Fireman." It was the usual Sunday supplement claptrap, complete with photos and comments from his friends, but Nashe had been amused by her, had in fact liked her very much, and after she had been following him around for two or three days, he had sensed that she was beginning to feel attracted to him. Certain glances were given, certain accidental brushes of the fingers took place with increasing frequency—but Nashe had been a married man back then, and what might have happened between them did not. A few months after the article was published, Fiona took a job with the AP in San Francisco, and since then he had lost track of her.

She lived in a little house not far from the bookstore, and when she invited him there to talk about the old days in Boston, Nashe understood that she was still unattached. It was not quite four o'clock when they arrived, but they settled down immediately to hard drinks, breaking open a fresh bottle of Jack Daniel's to accompany their conversation in the living room. Within an hour, Nashe had moved next to Fiona on the couch, and not long after that he was putting his hand inside her skirt. There was a strange inevitability to it, he felt, as if their fluke encounter called for an extravagant response, a spirit of anarchy and celebration. They were not creating an event so much as trying to keep up with one, and by the time Nashe wrapped his arms around Fiona's naked body, his desire for her was so powerful that it was already verging on a feeling of loss—for he knew that he was bound to disappoint her in the end, that sooner or later a moment would come when he would want to be back in the car.

He spent four nights with her, and little by little he discovered that she was much braver and smarter than he had imagined. "Don't think I didn't want this to happen," she said to him on the last night. "I know you don't love me, but that doesn't mean I'm the wrong girl for you. You're a head case, Nashe, and if you've got to go away, then fine, you've got to go away. But just remember that I'm here. If you ever get the itch to crawl into someone's pants again, think about my pants first."

He could not help feeling sorry for her, but this feeling was also tinged with admiration—perhaps even something more than that:

a suspicion that she might be someone he could love, after all. For a brief moment, he was tempted to ask her to marry him, suddenly imagining a life of wisecracks and tender sex with Fiona, of Juliette growing up with brothers and sisters, but he couldn't manage to get the words out of his mouth. "I'll just be gone for a little while," he said at last. "It's time for my visit to Northfield. You're welcome to come along if you want to, Fiona."

"Sure. And what am I supposed to do about my job? Three sick days in a row is pushing it a bit far, don't you think?"

"I've got to be there for Juliette, you know that. It's important."

"Lots of things are important. Just don't disappear forever, that's all."

"Don't worry, I'll be back. I'm a free man now, and I can do whatever I bloody want."

"This is America, Nashe. The home of the goddamn free, remember? We can all do what we want."

"I didn't know you were so patriotic."

"You bet your bottom dollar, friend. My country right or wrong. That's why I'm going to wait for you to turn up again. Because I'm free to make a fool of myself."

"I told you I'll be back. I just made a promise."

"I know you did. But that doesn't mean you're going to keep it."

There had been other women before that, a series of short flings and one-night stands, but no one he had made any promises to. The divorced woman in Florida, for example, and the schoolteacher Donna had tried to set him up with in Northfield, and the young waitress in Reno—they had all vanished. Fiona was the only one who meant anything to him, and from their first chance meeting in January to the end of July, he rarely went longer than three weeks without visiting her. Sometimes he would call her from the road, and when she wasn't in, he would leave funny messages on her answering machine—just to remind her that he was thinking about her. As the months went by, Fiona's plump, rather awkward body became more and more precious to him: the large, almost unwieldy breasts; the slightly crooked front teeth; the excessive blond hair flowing crazily in a multitude of ringlets and curls. Pre-Raphaelite hair, she called it once, and even though Nashe had not understood the reference, the phrase seemed to capture something about her, to pinpoint some inner quality that turned her ungainliness into a form of beauty. She was so different from Thérèse—the dark and languid Thérèse, the young Thérèse with her flat belly and long, exquisite limbs—but Fiona's imperfections continued to excite him, since they made him feel their lovemaking as something more than just sex, something more than just the random coupling of two bodies. It became harder for him to end his visits, and the first hours back on the road were always filled with doubts. Where was he going, after all, and what was he trying to prove? It felt absurd that he should be traveling away from her— all for the purpose of spending the night in some lumpy motel bed at the edge of nowhere.

Still, he kept going, relentlessly moving around the continent, feeling more and more at peace with himself as time rolled on. If there was any drawback, it was simply that it would have to end, that he could not go on living this life forever. At first, the money had seemed inexhaustible to him, but after he had been traveling for five or six months, more than half of it had been spent. Slowly but surely, the adventure was turning into a paradox. The money was responsible for his freedom, but each time he used it to buy another portion of that freedom, he was denying himself an equal portion of it as well. The money kept him going, but it was also an engine of loss, inexorably leading him back to the place where he had begun. By the middle of spring, Nashe finally understood that the problem could no longer be ignored. His future was precarious, and unless he made some decision about when to stop, he would barely have a future at all.

He had spent most rashly in the beginning, indulging himself with visits to any number of first-class restaurants and hotels, drinking good wines and buying elaborate toys for Juliette and her cousins, but the truth was that Nashe did not have any pronounced craving for luxuries. He had always lived too close to the bone to think much about them, and once the novelty of the inheritance had worn off, he reverted to his old modest habits: eating simple food, sleeping in budget motels, spending next to nothing in the way of clothes. Occasionally he would splurge on music cassettes or books, but that was the extent of it. The real advantage of the money was not that it had bought him things: it was the fact that it had allowed him to stop thinking about money. Now that he was being forced to think about it again, he decided to make a bargain with himself. He would keep on going until there were twenty thousand dollars left, and then he would go back to Berkeley and ask Fiona to marry him. He wouldn't hesitate; this time he would really do it.

He managed to stretch it out until late July. Just when everything had fallen into place, however, his luck began to desert him. Fiona's ex-boyfriend, who had walked out of her life a few months before Nashe entered it, had apparently returned after a change of heart, and instead of jumping at Nashe's proposal, Fiona wept steadily for over an hour as she explained why he had to stop seeing her. I can't count on you, Jim, she kept saying. I just can't count on you.

At bottom, he knew that she was right, but that did not make it any easier to absorb the blow. After he left Berkeley, he was stunned by the bitterness and anger that took hold of him. Those fires burned for many days, and even when they began to diminish, he did not recover so much as lose ground, lapsing into a second, more prolonged period of suffering. Melancholy supplanted rage, and he could no longer feel much beyond a dull, indeterminate sadness, as if everything he saw were slowly being robbed of its color. Very briefly, he toyed with the idea of moving to Minnesota and looking for work there. He even considered going to Boston and asking for his old job back, but his heart wasn't in it, and he soon abandoned those thoughts. For the rest of July he continued to wander, spending as much time in the car as ever before, on some days even daring himself to push on past the point of exhaustion: going for sixteen or seventeen straight hours, acting as though he meant to punish himself into conquering new barriers of endurance. He was gradually coming to the realization that he was stuck, that if something did not happen soon, he was going to keep on driving until the money ran out. On his visit to Northfield in early August, he went to the bank and withdrew what remained of the inheritance, converting the entire balance into cash—a neat little stack of hundred-dollar bills that he stored in the glove compartment of his car. It made him feel more in control of the crisis, as if the dwindling pile of money were an exact replica of his inner state. For the next two weeks he slept in the car, forcing the most stringent economies on himself, but the savings were finally negligible, and he wound up feeling grubby and depressed. It was no good giving in like that, he decided, it was the wrong approach. Determined to improve his spirits, Nashe drove to Saratoga and checked into a room at the Adelphi Hotel. It was the racing season, and for an entire week he spent every afternoon at the track, gambling on horses in an effort to build up his bankroll again. He felt sure that luck would be with him, but aside from a few dazzling successes with long shots, he lost more often than he won, and by the time he managed to tear himself away from the place, another chunk of his fortune was gone. He had been on the road for a year and two days, and he had just over fourteen thousand dollars left.

Nashe was not quite desperate, but he sensed that he was getting there, that another month or two would be enough to push him into a full-blown panic. He decided to go to New York, but instead of traveling down the Thruway, he opted to take his time and wander along the back-country roads. Nerves were the real problem, he told himself, and he wanted to see if going slowly might not help him to relax. He set off after an early breakfast at the Spa City Diner, and by ten o'clock he was somewhere in the middle of Dutchess County. He had been lost for much of the time until then, but since it didn't seem to matter where he was, he hadn't bothered to consult a map. Not far from the village of Millbrook, he slowed down to twenty-eight or thirty. He was on a narrow two-lane road flanked by horse farms and meadows, and he had not seen another car for more than ten minutes. Coming to the top of a slight incline, with a clear view for several hundred yards ahead, he suddenly spotted a figure moving along the side of the road. It was a jarring sight in that bucolic setting: a thin, bedraggled man lurching forward in spasms, buckling and wobbling as if he were about to fall on his face. At first, Nashe took him for a drunk, but then he realized it was too early in the morning for anyone to be in that condition. Although he generally refused to stop for hitch-hikers, he could not resist slowing down to have a better look. The noise of the shifting gears alerted the stranger to his presence, and when Nashe saw him turn around, he immediately understood that the man was in trouble. He was much younger than he had appeared from the back, no more than twenty-two or twenty-three, and there was little doubt that he had been beaten. His clothes were torn, his face was covered with welts and bruises, and from the way he stood there as the car approached, he scarcely seemed to know where he was. Nashe's instincts told him to keep on driving, but he could not bring himself to ignore the young man's distress. Before he was aware of what he was doing, he had already stopped the car, had rolled down the window on the passenger side, and was leaning over to ask the stranger if he needed help. That was how Jack Pozzi stepped into Nashe's life. For better or worse, that was how the whole business started, one fine morning at the end of the summer.

# 2

Pozzi accepted the ride without saying a word, just nodded his head when Nashe told him he was going to New York, and scrambled in. From the way his body collapsed when it touched the seat, it was obvious that he would have gone anywhere, that the only thing that mattered to him was getting away from where he was. He had been hurt, but he also looked scared, and he behaved as though he were expecting some new catastrophe, some further attack from the people who were after him. Pozzi closed his eyes and groaned as Nashe put his foot on the accelerator, but even after they were traveling at fifty or fifty-five, he still did not say a word, had barely seemed to notice that Nashe was there. Nashe assumed he was in shock and did not press him, but it was a strange silence for all that, a disconcerting way for things to begin. Nashe wanted to know who this person was, but without some hint to go on, it was impossible to draw any conclusions. The evidence was contradictory, full of elements that did not add up. The clothes, for example, made little sense: powder blue leisure suit, Hawaiian shirt open at the collar, white loafers and thin white socks. It was garish, synthetic stuff, and even when such outfits had been in fashion (ten years ago? twenty years ago?), no one had worn them but middle-aged men. The idea was to look young and sporty, but on a young kid the effect was fairly ludicrous—as if he were trying to impersonate an older man who dressed to look younger than he was. Given the cheapness of the clothes, it seemed right that the kid should also be wearing a ring, but as far as Nashe could tell, the sapphire looked genuine, which didn't seem right at all. Somewhere along the line the kid must have had the money to pay for it. Unless he hadn't paid for it—which meant that someone had given it to him, or else that he had stolen it. Pozzi was no more than five-six or five-seven, and Nashe doubted that he weighed more than a hundred and twenty pounds. He was a wiry little runt with delicate hands and a thin, pointy face, and he could have been anything from a traveling salesman to a small-time crook. With blood dribbling out of his nose and his left temple gashed and swollen, it was hard to tell what kind of impression he normally made on the world. Nashe felt a certain intelligence emanating from him, but he couldn't be sure. For the moment, nothing was sure but the man's silence. That and the fact that he had been beaten to within several inches of his life.

After they had gone three or four miles, Nashe pulled into a Texaco station and eased the car to a halt. "I have to get some gas," he said. "If you'd like to clean up in the men's room, this would be a good time to do it. It might make you feel a little better."

There was no response. Nashe assumed that the stranger hadn't heard him, but just as he was about to repeat his suggestion, the man gave a slight, almost imperceptible nod. "Yeah," Pozzi said. "I probably don't look too good, do I?"

"No," Nashe said, "not too good. You look like you've just crawled out of a cement mixer."

"That's pretty much what I feel like, too."

"If you can't make it on your own, I'll be happy to lend you a hand."

"Naw, that's all right, buddy, I can do it. Just watch. Ain't nothing I can't do when I put my mind to it."

Pozzi opened the door and began to extricate himself from the seat, grunting as he tried to move, clearly flabbergasted by the sharpness of the pain. Nashe came around to steady him, but the kid waved him off, shuffling toward the men's room with slow, cautious steps, as if willing himself not to fall down. In the meantime, Nashe filled the gas tank and checked the oil, and when his passenger still had not returned, he went into the garage and bought a couple of cups of coffee from the vending machine. A good five minutes elapsed, and Nashe began to wonder if the kid hadn't blacked out in the bathroom. He finished his coffee, stepped outside onto the tarmac, and was about to go knock on the door when he caught sight of him. Pozzi was moving in the direction of the car, looking somewhat more presentable after his session at the sink. At least the blood had been washed from his face, and with his hair slicked back and the torn jacket discarded, Nashe realized that he would probably mend on his own, that there would be no need to take him to a doctor.

He handed the second cup of coffee to the kid and said, "My name is Jim. Jim Nashe. Just in case you were wondering."

Pozzi took a sip of the now tepid drink and winced with displeasure. Then he offered his right hand to Nashe. "I'm Jack Pozzi," he said. "My friends call me Jackpot."

"I guess you hit the jackpot, all right. But maybe not the one you were counting on."

"You've got your best of times, and you've got your worst of times. Last night was one of the worst."

"At least you're still breathing."

"Yeah. Maybe I got lucky, after all. Now I get a chance to see how many more dumb things can happen to me."

Pozzi smiled at the remark, and Nashe smiled back, encouraged to know that the kid had a sense of humor. "If you want my advice," Nashe said, "I'd get rid of that shirt, too. I think its best days are behind it."

Pozzi looked down at the dirty, blood-stained material and fingered it wistfully, almost with affection. "I would if I had another one. But I figured this was better than showing off my beautiful body to the world. Common decency, you know what I mean? People are supposed to wear clothes."

Without saying a word, Nashe walked to the back of the car, opened the trunk, and started looking through one of his bags. A moment later, he extracted a Boston Red Sox T-shirt and tossed it to Pozzi, who caught it with his free hand. "You can wear this," Nashe said. "It's way too big for you, but at least it's clean."

Pozzi put his coffee cup on the roof of the car and examined the shirt at arm's length. "The Boston Red Sox," he said. "What are you, a champion of lost causes or something?"

"That's right. I can't get interested in things unless they're hopeless. Now shut up and put it on. I don't want you smearing blood all over my goddamn car."

Pozzi unbuttoned the torn Hawaiian shirt and let it drop to his feet. His naked torso was white, skinny, and pathetic, as if his body hadn't been out in the sun for years. Then he pulled the T-shirt over his head and opened his hands, palms up, presenting himself for inspection. "How's that?" he asked. "Any better?"

"Much better," Nashe said. "You're beginning to resemble something human now."

The shirt was so large on Pozzi that he almost drowned in it. The cloth dangled halfway down his legs, the short sleeves hung over his elbows, and for a moment or two it looked as if he had been turned into a scrawny twelve-year-old boy. For reasons that were not quite clear to him, Nashe felt moved by that.

They headed south on the Taconic State Parkway, figuring to make it down to the city in two or two and a half hours. As Nashe soon learned, Pozzi's initial silence had been an aberration. Now that the kid was out of danger, he began to show his true colors, and it wasn't long before he was talking his head off. Nashe didn't ask for the story, but Pozzi told it to him anyway, acting as though the words were a form of repayment. You rescue a man from a difficult situation, and you've earned the right to hear how he got himself into it.

"Not one dime," he said. "They didn't leave us with a single fucking dime." Pozzi let that cryptic remark hang in the air for a moment, and when Nashe said nothing, he started again, scarcely pausing to catch his breath for the next ten or fifteen minutes. "It's four o'clock in the morning," he continued, "and we've been sitting at the table for seven straight hours. There's six of us in the room, and the other five are your basic chumps, chipsters of the first water. You give your right arm to get into a game with monkeys like that—the rich boys from New York who play for a little weekend excitement. Lawyers, stockbrokers, corporate hot shots. Losing doesn't bother them as long as they get their thrills. Good game, they say to you after you've won, good game, and then they shake your hand and offer you a drink. Give me a steady dose of guys like that and I could retire before I'm thirty. They're the best. Solid Republicans, with their Wall Street jokes and goddamn dry martinis. The old boys with the five-dollar cigars. True-blue American assholes.

"So there I am playing with these pillars of the community, having myself a real good time. Nice and steady, raking in my share of pots, but not trying to show off or anything—just playing it nice and steady, keeping them all in the game. You don't kill the goose that lays the golden egg. They play every month, those dumbbells, and I'd like to get invited back. It was hard enough swinging the invitation for last night. I must have worked on it for half a year, and so I was on my best behavior, all polite and deferential, talking like some faggot who goes to the country club every afternoon to play the back nine. You've got to be an actor in this business, at least if you want to move in on the real action. You want to make them feel good you're emptying their coffers, and you can't do that unless you show them you're an okay kind of guy. Always say please and thank you, smile at their dumb-ass jokes, be modest and dignified, a real gentleman. Gee, tonight must be my lucky night, George. By golly, Ralph, the cards sure are coming my way. All that kind of crap.

"Anyway, I got there with a little more than five grand in my pocket, and by four o'clock I'm almost up to nine. The game's going to break up in about an hour, and I'm getting ready to roll. I've figured those mugs out, I'm so on top of it I can tell what cards they're holding just by looking at their eyes. I figure I'll go for one more big win, walk out with twelve or fourteen thousand, and call it a good night's work.

"I'm sitting on a solid hand, jacks full, and the pot's beginning to build. The room is quiet, we're all concentrating on the bets, and then, out of nowhere, the door flies open and in burst these four huge motherfuckers. 'Don't move,' they shout, 'don't move or you're dead'—yelling at the top of their lungs, pointing goddamn shotguns in our faces. They're all dressed in black, and they've got these stockings pulled down over their heads so you can't tell what they look like. It was the ugliest thing I ever saw—four creatures from the black lagoon. I was so scared, I thought I'd shit in my pants. Down on the floor, one of them says, lie down flat on the floor and no one will get hurt.

"People tell you about stuff like that—hijacking poker games, it's an old hustle. But you never think it's going to happen to you. And the worst part of it was, we're sitting there playing with cash.

All that dough is sitting right there on the table. It's a dumb thing to do, but those rich creeps like it that way, it makes them feel important. Like desperadoes in some half-assed western movie—the big showdown at the Last Gasp Saloon. You're supposed to play with chips, everybody knows that. The whole idea is to forget about the money, to concentrate on the goddamn game. But that's how those lawyers play, and there's nothing I can do about their rinky-dink house rules.

"There's forty, maybe fifty thousand dollars' worth of legal tender sunning itself on the table. I'm spread out on the floor and can't see a thing, but I can hear them stuffing money into bags, going around the table and sweeping it off—whoosh, whoosh, making quick work of it. I figure it's going to be over soon, and maybe they won't turn their guns on us. I'm not thinking about the money anymore, I just want to get out of there with my hide intact. Fuck the money, I say to myself, just don't shoot me. It's weird how fast things can happen. One minute, I'm about to raise the guy on my left, thinking what a smart, high-class dude I am, and the next minute I'm flat on the ground, hoping I don't get my brains blown out. I'm digging my face into the goddamn shag carpet and praying like a son of a bitch those robbers are going to split before I open my eyes again.

"Believe it or not, my prayers are answered. The robbers do just what they say they're going to do, and three or four minutes later they're gone. We hear their car drive away, and we all stand up and start breathing again. My knees are knocking together, I'm shaking like a palsy victim, but it's over, and everything is all right. At least that's what I think. As it turns out, the real fun hasn't even started yet.

"George Whitney got it going. He's the guy who owns the house, one of those hot-air balloons who walks around in green plaid pants and white cashmere sweaters. Once we've had a drink and settled down a little, big George says to Gil Swanson—that's the lugger who worked out the invitation for me—'It's just like I told you, Gil,' he says, 'you can't bring riffraff into a game like this.' 'What are you talking about, George?' Gil says, and George says, 'Figure it out for yourself, Gil. We play every month for seven years and nothing ever goes wrong. Then you tell me about this punk kid who's supposed to be a good player and twist my arm to bring him up, and look what happens. I had eight thousand dollars sitting on that table, and I don't take kindly to a bunch of thugs walking off with it.'

"Before Gil has a chance to say anything, I walk right up to George and open my big mouth. I probably shouldn't have done that, but I'm pissed off, and it's all I can do not to punch him in the face. 'What the fuck does that mean?' I say to him. 'It means that you set us up, you little slimeball,' he says, and then he starts poking me in the chest with his finger, pushing me back into the corner of the room. He keeps poking at me with that fat finger of his, and all the while he's still talking. 'I'm not going to let you and your hoodlum friends get away with a thing like that,' he says. 'You're going to pay for it, Pozzi. I'll see that you get what's coming to you.' On and on, jabbing with that finger of his and yammering in my face, and finally I just swat his arm away and tell him to step back. He's a big one, this George, maybe six-two or six-three. Fifty years old, but he's in good shape, and I know there'll be trouble if I try to tangle with him. 'Hands off, pig,' I say to him, 'just keep your hands off me and step back.' But the bastard is going crazy and won't stop. He grabs me by the shirt, and at that point I lose my cool and send my fist straight into his gut. I try to run away, but I don't get three feet before another one of those lawyers grabs hold of me and pins my arms behind my back. I try to break away from him, but before I can get my arms free, big George is in front of me again and letting me have it in the stomach. It was awful, man, a real Punch-and-Judy show, a bloodbath in living color. Every time I broke away, another one of them would catch me. Gil was the only one who wasn't part of it, but there wasn't much he could do against the four others. They kept working me over. For a moment there I thought they were going to kill me, but after a while they started to run out of gas. Those turds were strong, but they didn't have much stamina, and I finally squirmed loose and made it to the door. A couple of them went after me, but there was no way I was going to let them catch me again. I tore ass out of there and headed for the woods, running for all I was worth. If you hadn't picked me up, I'd probably still be running now."

Pozzi sighed with disgust, as if to expel the whole miserable episode from his mind. "At least there's no permanent damage," he continued. "The old bones will mend, but I can't say I'm too thrilled about losing the money. It couldn't have come at a worse time. I had big plans for that little bundle, and now I'm wiped out, now I have to start all over again. Shit. You play fair and square, you win, and you wind up losing anyway. There's no justice. Day after tomorrow, I was supposed to be in one of the biggest games of my life, and now it's not going to happen. Ain't a fucking chance in hell I can raise the kind of money I need by then. The only games I know about this weekend are nickel-and-dime stuff, a total washout. Even if I got lucky, I couldn't earn more than a couple of grand. And that's probably stretching it."

It was this last statement that finally induced Nashe to open his mouth. A small idea had flickered through him, and by the time the words came to his lips, he was already struggling to keep his voice under control. The entire process couldn't have taken longer than a second or two, but that was enough to change everything, to send him hurtling over the edge of a cliff. "How much money do you need for this game?" he asked.

"Nothing under ten thousand," Pozzi said. "And that's rock bottom. I couldn't walk in with a penny less than that."

"Sounds like an expensive proposition."

"It was the chance of a lifetime, pal. A goddamn invitation to Fort Knox."

"If you'd won, maybe. But the fact is you could have lost. There's always that risk, isn't there?"

"Sure there's a risk. We're talking poker here, that's the name of the game. But there's no way I could have lost. I've already played with those clowns once. It would have been a piece of cake."

"How much were you expecting to win?"

"A ton. A whole fucking ton."

"Give me a rough estimate. A ballpark figure."

"I don't know. Thirty or forty thousand, it's hard to guess. Maybe fifty."

"That's a lot of money. A lot more than your friends were playing for last night."

"That's what I'm trying to tell you. These guys are millionaires. And they don't know the first thing about cards. I mean, they're ignoramuses, those two. You sit down with them, and it's like playing with Laurel and Hardy."

"Laurel and Hardy?"

"That's what I call them, Laurel and Hardy. One's fat and the other's thin, just like old Stan and Ollie. They're genuine pea-brains, my friend, a pair of born chumps."

"You sound awfully sure of yourself. How do you know they're not a couple of hustlers?"

"Because I checked them out. Six or seven years ago, they shared a ticket in the Pennsylvania state lottery and won twenty-seven million dollars. It was one of the biggest payoffs of all time. Guys with that kind of dough aren't going to bother hustling a small-time operator like me."

"You're not making this up?"

"Why should I make it up? The fat one's name is Flower, and the skinny guy is called Stone. The weird thing is that they both have the same first name—William. But Flower goes by Bill, and Stone calls himself Willie. It's not as confusing as it sounds. Once you're with them, you don't have any trouble telling them apart."

"Like Mutt and Jeff."

"Yeah, that's right. They're a regular comedy team. Like those funny little buggers on TV, Ernie and Bert. Only these guys are called Willie and Bill. It has a nice ring to it, doesn't it? Willie and Bill."

"How did you happen to meet them?"

"I ran into them in Atlantic City last month. There's a game I sometimes go to down there, and they sat in on it for a while. After twenty minutes, they were both down five thousand dollars. I never saw such stupid betting in my life. They thought they could bluff their way through anything—like they were the only ones who knew how to play, and the rest of us were just dying to fall for their Humpty-Dumpty tricks. A couple of hours later, I went over to one of the casinos to horse around, and there they were again, standing at the roulette wheel. The fat one came up to me—"

"Flower."

"—right, Flower. He came up to me and said, I like your style, son, you play a mean hand of poker. And then he went on to say that if I ever felt like getting into a friendly little game with them, I was more than welcome to drop by their house. So that's how it happened. I told him sure, I'd love to play with them some time, and last week I called up and arranged the game for this coming Monday. That's why I'm so burned about what happened last night. It would have been a beautiful experience, an honest-to-goodness walk down Jackpot Lane."

"You just said 'their house.' Does that mean they live together?"

"You're pretty sharp, aren't you? Yeah, that's what I said— 'their house.' It sounds a little strange, but I don't think they're a pair of fruits or anything. They're both in their fifties, and they both used to be married. Stone's wife died, and Flower and his wife are divorced. They've each got a couple of kids, and Stone's even a grandfather. He used to be an optometrist before he won the lottery, and Flower used to be an accountant. Real ordinary middle-class guys. They just happen to live in a twenty-room mansion and get one point three-five million tax-free dollars every year."

"I guess you've been doing your homework."

"I told you, I checked them out. I don't like to get into games when I don't know who I'm playing with."

"Do you do anything besides play poker?"

"No, that's it. I just play poker."

"No job? Nothing to back you up if you hit a dry spell?"

"I worked in a department store once. That was the summer after I got out of high school, and they put me in the men's shoe department. It was the pits, let me tell you, the absolute worst. Getting down on your hands and knees like some kind of dog, having to breathe in all those dirty sock smells. It used to make me want to barf. I quit after three weeks, and I haven't had a regular job since."

"So you do all right for yourself."

"Yeah, I do all right. I have my ups and downs, but there's never been anything I couldn't handle. The main thing is I do what I want. If I lose, it's my ass that loses. If I win, the money's mine to keep. I don't have to take shit from anyone."

"You're your own boss."

"Right. I'm my own boss. I call my own shots."

"You must be a pretty good player, then."

"I'm good, but I've still got a ways to go. I'm talking about the great ones—your Johnny Moseses, your Amarillo Slims, your Doyle Brunsons. I want to get into the same league as those guys. You ever hear about Binion's Horseshoe Club in Vegas? That's where they play the World Series of Poker. In a couple of years, I think

I'll be ready for them. That's what I want to do. Build up enough cash to buy into that game and go head to head with the best."

"That's all very nice, kid. It's good to have dreams, they help to keep a person going. But that's for later, what you might call long-range planning. What I want to know is what you're going to do today. We'll be getting to New York in about an hour, and then what's going to happen to you?"

"There's this guy I know in Brooklyn. I'll give him a buzz when we hit town and see if he's in. If he is, he'll probably put me up for a while. He's a crazy son of a bitch, but we get along okay. Crappy Manzola. It's a hell of a name, isn't it? He got it when he was a kid because he had such crappy, rotten teeth. He's got a beautiful set of false teeth now, but everyone still calls him Crappy."

"And what happens if Crappy isn't there?"

"The fuck if I know. I'll think of something."

"In other words, you don't have a clue. You're just going to wing it."

"Don't worry about me, I can take care of myself. I've been in worse places than this before."

"I'm not worried. It's just that something has occurred to me, and I have a feeling it might interest you."

"Such as?"

"You told me you needed ten thousand dollars to play cards with Flower and Stone. What if I knew someone who would be willing to put up the money for you? What kind of arrangement would you be willing to make with him in return?"

"I'd pay him back as soon as the game was over. With interest."

"This person isn't a moneylender. He'd probably be thinking more along the lines of a business partnership."

"And what are you, some kind of a venture capitalist or something?"

"Forget about me. I'm just a guy who drives a car. What I want to know is what kind of offer you'd be willing to make. I'm talking about percentages."

"Shit, I don't know. I'd pay him back the ten grand, and then I'd give him a fair share of the profits. Twenty percent, twenty-five percent, something like that."

"That sounds a bit stingy to me. After all, this person is the one who's taking the risk. If you don't win, he's the one who loses, not you. See what I mean?"

"Yeah, I see what you mean."

"I'm talking about an even split Fifty percent for you, fifty percent for him. Minus the ten thousand, of course. How does that strike you? Do you think it's fair?"

"I suppose I could live with it. If that's the only way I get to play with those jokers, it's probably worth it. But where do you fit into this? As far as I can tell, it's just the two of us talking in this car. Where's this other guy supposed to be? The one with the ten thousand dollars."

"He's around. It won't be hard to find him."

"Yeah, that's what I figured. And if this guy just happens to be sitting next to me right now, what I'd like to know is why he wants to get involved in a thing like this. I mean, he doesn't know me from a hole in the wall."

"No reason. He just feels like it."

"That's not good enough. There's got to be a reason. I won't go for it unless I know."

"Because he needs the money. That should be pretty obvious."

"But he's already got ten thousand dollars."

"He needs more than that. And he's running out of time. This is probably the last chance he's going to get."

"Yeah, okay, I can buy that. It's what you would call a desperate situation."

"But he's not stupid either, Jack. He doesn't throw his money away on grifters. So before I talk business with you, I've got to make sure you're the real thing. You might be a hell of a card player, but you also might be a bullshit artist. Before there's any deal, I've got to see what you can do with my own eyes."

"No problem, partner. Once we get to New York, I'll show you my stuff. No problem at all. You'll be so impressed, your mouth will drop open. I guarantee it. I'll make the eyes fall out of your fucking head."

# 3

---

Nashe understood that he was no longer behaving like himself. He could hear the words coming out of his mouth, but even as he spoke them, he felt they were expressing someone else's thoughts, as if he were no more than an actor performing on the stage of some imaginary theater, repeating lines that had been written for him in advance. He had never felt this way before, and the wonder of it was how little it disturbed him, how easily he slipped into playing his part. The money was the only thing that mattered, and if this foul-mouthed kid could get it for him, then Nashe was willing to risk everything to see that it happened. It was a crazy scheme, perhaps, but the risk was a motivation in itself, a leap of blind faith that would prove he was finally ready for anything that might happen to him.

At that point, Pozzi was simply a means to an end, the hole in the wall that would get him from one side to the other. He was an opportunity in the shape of a human being, a card-playing specter whose one purpose in the world was to help Nashe win back his freedom. Once that job was finished, they would go their separate ways. Nashe was going to use him, but that did not mean he found Pozzi entirely objectionable. In spite of his wise-ass posturing, there was something fascinating about this kid, and it was hard not to grant him a sort of grudging respect. At least he had the courage of his convictions, and that was more than could be said of most people. Pozzi had taken the plunge into himself; he was improvising his life as he went along, trusting in pure wit to keep his head above water, and even after the thrashing he had just been given, he did not seem demoralized or defeated. The kid was rough around the edges, at times even obnoxious, but he exuded a confidence that Nashe found reassuring. It was still too early to know if Pozzi could be believed, of course, but considering how little time there had been for him to invent a story, considering the farfetched plausibility of the whole situation, it seemed doubtful that he was anything other than what he claimed to be. Or so Nashe assumed. One way or the other, it wouldn't take long for him to find out.

The important thing was to appear calm, to rein in his excitement and convince Pozzi that he knew what he was doing. It wasn't exactly that he wanted to impress him, but he instinctively felt that he had to keep the upper hand, to match the kid's bravura with a quiet, unflinching confidence of his own. He would play the old man to Pozzi's upstart, using the advantage he had in size and age to give off an aura of hard-earned wisdom, a steadiness that would counterbalance the kid's nervous, impulsive manner. By the time they came to the northern reaches of the Bronx, Nashe had already settled on a plan of action. It would mean paying out a little more than he would have liked, perhaps, but in the long run he figured it would be money well spent.

The trick was not to say anything until Pozzi started asking questions, and then, when he did ask them, to be ready with good answers. That was the surest way to control the situation: to keep the kid slightly off balance, to create the illusion that he was always one step ahead of him. Without saying a word, Nashe steered the car onto the Henry Hudson Parkway, and when Pozzi finally asked him where they were going (as they drove past Ninety-sixth Street), Nashe said: "You're all worn out, Jack. You need some food and sleep, and I could go for a little lunch myself. We'll check into the Plaza and take it from there."

"You mean the Plaza Hotel?" Pozzi said.

"That's right, the Plaza Hotel. I always stay there when I'm in New York. Any objections?"

"No objections. I was just wondering, that's all. Sounds like a good idea to me."

"I thought you'd like it."

"Yeah, I like it. I like to do things in style. It's good for the soul."

They parked the car in an underground lot on East Fifty-eighth Street, removed Nashe's bags from the trunk, and then walked around the corner to the hotel. Nashe asked for two single rooms with a connecting bath, and as he signed the register at the desk, he watched Pozzi out of the corner of his eye, noting the small, satisfied smirk on the kid's face. That look pleased him, for it seemed to indicate that Pozzi was sufficiently awed by his good fortune to appreciate what Nashe was doing for him. It all boiled down to a question of staging. Just two hours before, Pozzi's life had been in ruins, and now he was standing inside a palace, trying not to gawk at the opulence that surrounded him. Had the contrast been less striking, it would not have produced the desired effect, but as it was, Nashe had only to look at the kid's twitching mouth to know that he had made his point.

They were given rooms on the seventh floor ("Lucky seven," as Pozzi remarked in the elevator), and once the bellboy had been tipped and they were settled in, Nashe dialed room service and ordered lunch. Two steaks, two salads, two baked potatoes, two bottles of Beck's. Meanwhile, Pozzi was marching into the bathroom to take a shower, closing the door behind him but not bothering to lock it. Nashe took that as another good sign. He listened for a moment or two as the water sizzled against the tub, then changed into a clean white shirt and dug out the money he had transferred from the glove compartment to one of his suitcases (fourteen thousand dollars wrapped in a small plastic shopping bag). Without saying anything to Pozzi, he slipped out of the room, took the elevator down to the ground floor, and deposited thirteen thousand dollars in the hotel safe. Before going back up, he made a little detour and stopped in at the newsstand to buy a deck of cards.

Pozzi was sitting in his own room when Nashe returned. The two bathroom doors were open, and Nashe could see the kid sprawled out in an armchair, his body wrapped in two or three white towels. The Saturday-afternoon kung fu movie was playing on the television, and when Nashe poked his head in to say hello, Pozzi pointed to the set and said that maybe he should start taking lessons from Bruce Lee. "The little dude's no bigger than I am," he said, "but look at the way he handles those fuckers. If I knew how to do that stuff, last night never would have happened."

"Are you feeling any better?" Nashe asked.

"My body's all sore, but I don't think anything's broken."

"I guess you'll live, then."

"Yeah, I guess so. I might not be able to play the violin anymore, but it looks like I'm going to live."

"The food will be here any minute. You can put on a pair of my pants if you like. After we eat, I'll take you out to buy some new clothes."

"That's probably a good idea. I was just thinking it might not be so hot to push this Roman senator act too far."

Nashe tossed Pozzi a pair of blue jeans to go with the Red Sox T-shirt, and once again the kid seemed to shrink down to the size of a little boy. In order not to trip over himself, he rolled up the bottoms of the pants to his ankles. "You've sure got a handsome wardrobe," he said as he walked into Nashe's room, holding up the jeans by the waist. "What are you, the Boston cowboy or something?"

"I was going to let you borrow my tux, but then I figured I'd better wait and see what your table manners are like. I wouldn't want it to get ruined just because you can't keep ketchup from dribbling out of your mouth."

The food was wheeled in on a rattling cart, and the two of them sat down to lunch. Pozzi worked on his steak with relish, but after several minutes of steady chewing and swallowing, he put down his knife and fork as if he had suddenly lost interest. He leaned back in his chair and looked around the room. "It's funny how you start to remember things," he said in a subdued voice. "I've been in this hotel before, you know, but I haven't thought about it for a long time. Not for years."

"You must have been pretty young if it happened so long ago," Nashe said.

"Yeah, I was just a kid. My father brought me here one weekend in the fall. I must have been eleven, maybe twelve."

"Just the two of you? What about your mother?"

"They were divorced. They split up when I was a baby."

"And you lived with her?"

"Yeah, we lived in Irvington, New Jersey. That's where I grew up. A sad, crummy little town."

"Did you see much of your father?"

"I barely even knew who he was."

"And then he showed up one day and took you to the Plaza."

"Yeah, more or less. I saw him once before that, though. The first time was a strange business, I don't think I've ever been so spooked by anything. I was eight years old then, and one day in the middle of the summer I'm sitting on the front steps of our

house. My mother was off at work, and I'm sitting there by myself
sucking on this orange Popsicle and looking across the street. Don't
ask me how I remember it was orange, I just do. It's like I'm still
holding the damn thing in my hand now. It was a hot day, and
I'm sitting there with my orange Popsicle, thinking maybe I'll get
on my bike when I'm finished and go over to my friend Walt's
house and get him to turn on the hose in the backyard. The Popsicle
is just starting to melt on my leg, and all of a sudden this big white
Cadillac comes inching down the street. It was a hell of a car. All
new and spanking clean, with spiderweb hubcaps and whitewall
tires. The guy behind the wheel looks like he's lost. Slowing down
in front of every house, craning his neck out the window to check
the addresses. So I'm watching this with the dumb Popsicle drip-
ping all over me, and then the car stops and the guy shuts off the
motor. Right in front of my house. The guy gets out and starts
coming up the walk—dressed in this flashy white suit and smiling
this big, friendly smile. At first I thought it was Billy Martin, he
looked just like him. You know, the baseball manager. And I think
to myself: why is Billy Martin coming to see me? Does he want to
sign me up as his new batboy or something? Jesus, the shit that
goes flying through your head when you're a kid. Well, he gets a
little closer, and I see that it's not Billy Martin after all. So now
I'm really confused, and to be honest with you, a little bit scared.
I ditch the Popsicle in the bushes, but before I can decide what
else I'm going to do, the guy's already in front of me. 'Hey there,
Jack,' he says. 'Long time no see.' I don't know what he's talking
about, but since he knows my name, I figure he's a friend of my
mother's or something. So I tell him my mother's at work, trying
to be polite, but he says yeah, he knows that, he just talked with
her over at the restaurant. That's where my mother worked, she
was a waitress back then. And so I say to him: 'You mean you
came here to see me?' And he says: 'You got it, kid. I figured it
was about time we caught up on each other's news. The last time

I saw you, you were still in diapers.' The whole conversation is making less and less sense to me now, and the only thing I can think of is that this guy must be my Uncle Vince, the one who ran off to California when my mother was still a kid. 'You're Uncle Vince, aren't you?' I say to him, but he just shakes his head and smiles. 'Hold onto your hat, little guy,' he says, or something like that, 'but believe it or not, you're looking at your father.' The thing is, I don't believe it for a second. 'You can't be my father,' I say to him. 'My father got killed in Vietnam.' 'Yeah, well,' the guy says, 'that's what everyone thought. But I wasn't really killed, see. I escaped. They had me there as a prisoner, but I dug my way out and escaped. It's taken me a long time to get here.' It's starting to get a little more convincing now, but I still have my doubts. 'Does that mean you're going to live with us now?' I say to him. 'Not exactly,' he says, 'but that shouldn't stop us from getting to know each other.' That seems all wrong, and now I'm pretty sure that he's trying to trick me. 'You can't be my father,' I say again. 'Fathers don't go away. They live at home with their families.' 'Some fathers,' the guy says, 'but not all of them. Look. If you don't believe me, I'll prove it to you. Your name's Pozzi, right? John Anthony Pozzi. And your father's name has to be Pozzi, too. Right?' I just nod my head at what he's saying, and then he reaches into his pocket and pulls out his wallet. 'Look at this, kid,' he says, and then he takes the driver's license out of the wallet and hands it to me. 'Read what it says on that piece of paper.' And so I read it to him: 'John Anthony Pozzi.' And I'll be damned if the whole story isn't written there in black and white."

Pozzi paused for a moment and took a sip of beer. "I don't know," he continued. "When I think about it now, it's like it happened in a dream or something. I can remember parts of it, but the rest just blurs over in my mind, like maybe it never really happened. I remember that my old man took me out for a spin in his Caddy, but I don't know how long it lasted, I can't even remember what we talked about. But I remember the air conditioning in the car and the smell of the leather upholstery, I remember feeling annoyed that my hands were all sticky from the Popsicle I'd been eating. The main thing, I guess, was that I was still scared. Even though I'd seen the driver's license, I started doubting it all over again. Something funny's going on, I kept telling myself. This guy might say he's my father, but that doesn't mean he's telling the truth. It could be a trick of some kind, a hoax. All this is going through my head as we drive around town, and then all of a sudden we're back in front of my house. It's like the whole thing took about half a second. My old man doesn't even get out of the car. He just reaches into his pocket, pulls out a hundred-dollar bill, and slaps it into my hand. 'Here, Jack,' he says, 'a little something so you'll know I'm thinking about you.' Shit. It was more money than I'd ever seen in my life. I didn't even know they made things like hundred-dollar bills. So I get out of the car with this C-note in my hand, and I remember thinking to myself, Yeah, I guess this means he's my father, after all. But before I can think of anything to say, he's squeezing my shoulder and saying good-bye to me. 'See you around, kid,' he says, or something like that, and then he starts up the car and drives off."

"A funny way to meet your father," Nashe said.

"You're telling me."

"But what about when you came here to the Plaza?"

"That didn't happen until three or four years later."

"And you didn't see him in all that time?"

"Not once. It was like he just vanished again. I kept asking my mother about him, but she was pretty tight-lipped about it, she didn't want to say much. Later on, I found out that he'd spent a few years in the can. That's why they got divorced, she told me. He'd been up to no good."

"What did he do?"

"Got himself involved in a boiler-room scam. You know, selling stocks in a dummy corporation. One of those high-class swindles."

"He must have done all right after he got out. Well enough to drive a Cadillac anyway."

"Yeah, I suppose so. I think he wound up in Florida selling real estate. Struck it rich in condo land."

"But you're not sure."

"I'm not sure of anything. I haven't heard from the guy in a long time. He could be dead now for all I know."

"But he showed up again three or four years later."

"Out of the blue, just like the first time. I'd given up on him by then. Four years is a long time to wait when you're a kid. It feels like fucking forever."

"And what did you do with the hundred dollars?"

"It's funny you should ask that. At first I was going to spend it. You know, buy a fancy new baseball glove or something, but nothing ever seemed quite right, I could never bring myself to part with it. So I wound up saving it all those years. I kept it in a little box in my underwear drawer, and every night I would take it out and look at it—just to make sure it was really there."

"And if it was there, that meant you had really seen your father."

"I never thought of it that way. But yeah, that's probably it. If I held on to the money, then maybe that meant my father would be coming back."

"A little boy's logic."

"You're so dumb when you're a kid, it's pathetic. I can't believe I used to think like that."

"We all did. It's part of growing up."

"Yeah, well, it was all pretty complicated. I never showed the money to my mother, but every now and then I would take it out of the box and let my friend Walt hold it. It made me feel good, I don't know why. Like if I saw him touching it, then I knew I wasn't making it up. But the funny thing was, after about six months

I got it into my head that the money was fake, that it was a counterfeit bill. It might have been something that Walt said, I can't say for sure, but I do remember thinking that if the money was fake, then the guy who gave it to me couldn't have been my father."

"Around and around."

"Yeah. Around and around and around. One day, Walt and I got to talking about it, and he said the only way we'd ever find out was if we took it to the bank. I didn't want to let it out of my room, but since I figured it was counterfeit anyway, it probably didn't matter. So off we go the bank, all scared that someone's going to rob us, creeping along like we're on some goddamn dangerous mission. The teller at the bank turned out to be a nice guy. Walt says to him, 'My friend here wants to know if this is a real hundred-dollar bill,' and the teller takes it and looks it over real careful. He even put the thing under a magnifying glass just to make sure."

"And what did he say?"

" 'It's real, boys,' he says. 'A genuine U.S. Treasury note.' "

"So the man who gave it to you was really your father."

"Correct. But where does that leave me now? If this guy is really my father, then why doesn't he come back and see me? At least he could write a letter or something. But instead of getting pissed off about it, I start making up stories to explain why he's not in touch. I figure, shit, I figure he's some kind of James Bond character, one of those secret agents working for the government and he can't blow his cover by coming to see me. After all, by now I believe all that bullshit about escaping from a prison camp in Vietnam, and if he can do that, he must have been one hell of a fucking macho man, right? A stud and a half. Christ, I must have been a goddamn moron to think like that."

"You had to invent something. It's not possible to leave it blank. The mind won't let you."

"Maybe. But I sure spun myself a ton of crap. I was up to my neck in it."

"What happened when he finally turned up again?"

"He called first this time and spoke to my mother. I remember that I was already in bed upstairs, and she came into my room and told me about it. 'He wants to spend the weekend with you in New York,' she said, and it wasn't hard to see that she was burned. 'The son of a bitch has got his nerve, doesn't he?' she kept saying. 'That son of a bitch has got his nerve.' So Friday afternoon he pulls up in front of the house in another Cadillac. This one was black, and I remember that he was wearing one of those snappy camel-hair coats and smoking a big cigar. It had nothing to do with James Bond. He looked like some guy who'd stepped out of an Al Capone movie."

"It was winter this time."

"The dead of winter, and it was freezing out. We drove through the Lincoln Tunnel, checked into the Plaza, and then went out to Gallagher's on Fifty-second Street. I still remember the place. It was like walking into a slaughterhouse. Hundreds of raw steaks hanging in the window, it's enough to turn you into a vegetarian. But the dining room is okay. The walls are covered with photos of politicians and sports guys and movie stars, and I admit that I was pretty impressed. That was the whole idea of the weekend, I think. My father wanted to impress me, and he wound up doing a good job of it. After dinner, we went to the fights at the Garden. The next day, we went back there for a college basketball doubleheader, and on Sunday we drove up to the Stadium to see the Giants play the Redskins. And don't think we sat in the rafters either. Fifty-yard line, friend, the best seats in the house. Yeah, I was impressed, I was fucking bowled over by it. And everywhere we went, there's my old man peeling off bills from this fat roll he carried in his pocket. Tens, twenties, fifties—he didn't even bother to look. He gave out tips like it was nothing, you know what I mean?

Ushers, headwaiters, bellboys. They all had their hands out, and he just flicked off the bucks like there was no tomorrow."

"You were impressed. But did you have a good time?"

"Not really. I mean, if this was the way people lived, then where had I been all these years? Do you know what I'm saying?"

"I think so."

"It was hard to talk to him, and most of the time I felt embarrassed, all tied up in knots. He kind of bragged to me the whole weekend—telling me about his business deals, trying to make me think what a great guy he was, but I really didn't know what the fuck he was talking about. He also gave me a lot of advice. 'Promise me you'll finish high school'—he said that two or three times—'promise me you'll finish high school so you don't turn out to be a bum.' I'm this little runt in the sixth grade, and what do I know about high school and shit like that? But he made me promise, and so I gave him my word that I would. It got to be a little creepy. But the worst thing was when I told him about the hundred dollars he'd given me the last time. I thought he'd like to hear how I hadn't spent it, but it really kind of shocked him, I could see it in his face, he acted like I'd insulted him or something. 'Holding on to money is for saps,' he said. 'It's just a lousy piece of paper, kid, and it won't do a goddamn thing for you sitting in a box.'"

"Tough guy talk."

"Yeah, he wanted to show me what a tough guy he was. But maybe it didn't work out like he thought it would. When I got back home on Sunday night, I remember feeling pretty shook up. He gave me another hundred-dollar bill, and the next day I went out and spent it after school—just like that. He said spend it, and so that's what I did. But the funny thing was, I didn't feel like using the money on myself. I went to this jewelry store in town and bought a pearl necklace for my mother. I still remember what it cost. A hundred and eighty-nine dollars, counting the tax."

"And what did you do with the other eleven dollars?"

"I bought her a big box of chocolates. One of those fancy red boxes shaped like a heart."

"She must have been happy."

"Yeah, she broke down and cried when I gave the stuff to her. I was glad I did it. It made me feel good."

"And what about high school? Did you stick to your promise?"

"What do you think I am, a dumbbell or something? Of course I finished high school. I did okay, too. Had a B-minus average and played on the basketball team. I was a regular Mr. Hot Shot."

"What did you do, play on stilts?"

"I was the point guard, man, and I did all right out there, let me tell you. They called me the Mouse. I was so quick, I could pass the ball between guys' legs. One game, I set a school record with fifteen assists. I was one tough little hombre out there."

"But you didn't get any college scholarship offers."

"I got a few nibbles, but nothing that really interested me. Besides, I figured I could do better for myself playing poker than taking some business administration course at Bullshit Tech."

"So you found a job in a department store."

"Temporarily. But then my old man came through with a graduation present. He sent me a check for five thousand dollars. How do you like that? I don't see the fucker for six or seven years, and then he remembers my high school graduation. Talk about mixed reactions. I could have died I was so happy. But I also felt like kicking the son of a bitch in the balls."

"Did you send him a thank-you note?"

"Sure I did. It's sort of required, isn't it? But the guy never answered me. I haven't heard a peep from him since."

"Worse things have happened, I suppose."

"Shit, I don't care anymore. It's probably all for the best."

"And that was the beginning of your career."

"You got it, pal. That was the beginning of my glorious career, my uninterrupted march to the heights of fame and fortune."

After that conversation, Nashe noticed a shift in his feelings toward Pozzi. A certain softening set in, a gradual if reluctant admission that there was something inherently likable about the kid. That did not mean that Nashe was prepared to trust him, but for all his wariness, he sensed a new and growing impulse to watch out for him, to take on the role of Pozzi's guide and protector. Perhaps it had something to do with his size, the undernourished, almost stunted body—as if his smallness suggested something not yet completed—but it also might have come from the story he had told about his father. All during Pozzi's reminiscences, Nashe had inevitably thought about his own boyhood, and the curious correspondence he found between their two lives had struck a chord in him: the early abandonment, the unexpected gift of money, the abiding anger. Once a man begins to recognize himself in another, he can no longer look on that person as a stranger. Like it or not, a bond is formed. Nashe understood the potential trap of such thinking, but at that point there was little he could do to prevent himself from feeling drawn to this lost and emaciated creature. The distance between them had suddenly narrowed.

Nashe decided to put off the card test for the moment and attend to Pozzi's wardrobe. The stores would be closing in a few hours, and there was no point in making the kid walk around in his baggy clown costume for the rest of the day. Nashe realized that he probably should have been more hard-nosed about it, but Pozzi was clearly exhausted, and he did not have the heart to force him into an immediate showdown. That was a mistake, of course. If poker was a game of endurance, of quick thinking under pressure, what better moment to test someone's abilities than when his mind was clouded over with exhaustion? In all probability, Pozzi would flunk the test, and the money Nashe was about to shell out on clothes for him would be wasted. Given that impending disappointment, however, Nashe was in no rush to get down to business. He wanted to savor his anticipation a bit longer, to delude himself into believing there was still some cause for hope. Besides, he was looking forward to the little shopping excursion he had planned. A few hundred dollars wouldn't make much difference in the long run, and the thought of watching Pozzi stroll through Saks Fifth Avenue was a pleasure he didn't want to deny himself. It was a situation ripe with comic possibilities, and if nothing else, he might come out of it with the memory of a few laughs. When it came right down to it, even that was more than he had expected to accomplish when he woke up that morning in Saratoga.

Pozzi started bitching the moment they entered the store. The men's department was filled with faggot clothes, he said, and he'd rather walk around in his bath towels than be caught in any of this preppie vomit. It might be all right if your name was Dudley L. Dipshit the Third and you lived on Park Avenue, but he was Jack Pozzi from Irvington, New Jersey, and he was damned if he was going to wear one of those pink alligator shirts. Back where he came from, they'd kick your ass if you showed up in a thing like that. They'd tear you apart, and they'd flush the pieces down the toilet. As he rattled on with his abuse, Pozzi kept looking at the women who walked by, and if any of them happened to be young or attractive, he would stop talking and make a stab at eye contact, or twist his head around on his neck to watch the sway of their buttocks as they disappeared down the aisle. He winked at a couple of them, and another one who inadvertently brushed his arm he even managed to address. "Hey, babe," he said. "Got any plans tonight?"

"Stay calm, Jack," Nashe warned him once or twice. "Just stay calm. They'll throw you out of here if you keep it up."

"I'm calm," Pozzi said. "Can't a guy check out the local talent?"

At bottom, it was almost as if Pozzi were carrying on because he knew that Nashe expected it of him. It was a self-conscious performance, a whirlwind of predictable antics that he was offering up as an expression of thanks to his new friend and benefactor, and if he had sensed that Nashe wanted him to stop, he would have stopped without another word. At least that was what Nashe concluded later, for once they began studying the clothes in earnest, the kid showed a surprising lack of resistance to his arguments. The implication was that Pozzi somehow understood that he was being given the opportunity to learn something, and that in turn implied that Nashe had already won his respect.

"It's like this, Jack," Nashe said. "Two days from now, you're going up against a couple of millionaires. And you won't be playing in some ratty pool hall, you'll be in their house as an invited guest. They're probably planning to feed you and put you up for the night. You don't want to make a bad impression, do you? You don't want to walk in there looking like some ignorant hood. I saw the kinds of clothes you like to wear. They're a tip-off, Jack, they give you away as a cheap know-nothing. You see a man in threads like that and you say to yourself, there's a walking advertisement for Losers Anonymous. They've got no style, no class. When we were in the car, you told me you have to be an actor in your line of work. Well, an actor needs a costume. You might not like these clothes, but rich people wear them, and you want to show the world you've got some taste, that you're a man of discretion. It's time to grow up, Jack. It's time to start taking yourself seriously."

Little by little, Nashe wore him down, and in the end they walked out of the store with five hundred dollars' worth of bourgeois sobriety and restraint, an outfit of such conventionality as to make its wearer invisible in any crowd: navy blue blazer, light gray slacks, penny loafers, and a white cotton shirt. Since the weather was still warm, Nashe said, they could dispense with a tie, and Pozzi went along with that omission, saying that enough was enough. "I already feel like a creep," he said. "There's no point in trying to strangle me, too."

It was close to five o'clock when they returned to the Plaza. After depositing the packages on the seventh floor, they went back downstairs for a drink in the Oyster Bar. After one beer, Pozzi suddenly seemed crushed with fatigue, as if he were fighting to keep his eyes open. Nashe sensed that he was also in pain, and rather than force him to hold out any longer, he called for the check.

"You're fading fast," he said. "It's probably time you went upstairs and took a nap."

"I feel like shit," Pozzi said, not bothering to protest. "Saturday night in New York, but it doesn't look like I'm going to make it."

"It's dreamland for you, friend. If you wake up in time, you can have a late supper, but it might be a good idea just to sleep on through till morning. There's no question you'll feel a whole lot better then."

"Gotta stay in shape for the big fight. No fucking around with the broads. Keep your pecker in your pants and steer clear of the greasy food. Road work at five, sparring at ten. Think mean. Think mean and lean."

"I'm glad you catch on so quickly."

"We're talking championship bout here, Jimbo, and the Kid needs his rest. When you're in training, you've got to be ready to make every sacrifice."

So they went upstairs again, and Pozzi crawled into bed. Before he switched off the light, Nashe made him swallow three aspirins and then left a glass of water and the aspirin bottle on the night table. "If you happen to wake up," he said, "take a few more of these. They'll help dull the pain."

"Thanks, Mom," Pozzi said. "I hope you don't mind if I skip my prayers tonight. Just tell God I was too sleepy, okay?"

Nashe left through the bathroom, shut both doors, and sat down on his bed. He suddenly felt at a loss, not knowing what to do with himself for the rest of the evening. He considered going out and having dinner somewhere, but in the end he decided against it. He didn't want to stray too far from Pozzi. Nothing was going to happen (he was more or less certain of that), but at the same time he felt it would be wrong to take anything for granted.

At seven o'clock, he ordered a sandwich and a beer from room service and turned on the television. The Mets were playing in Cincinnati that night, and he followed the game through to the ninth inning, shuffling and reshuffling the new cards as he sat on the bed, playing one hand of solitaire after another. At ten thirty, he switched off the television and climbed into bed with a paperback copy of Rousseau's *Confessions*, which he had started reading during his stay in Saratoga. Just before he fell asleep, he came to the passage in which the author is standing in a forest and throwing stones at trees. If I hit that tree with this stone, Rousseau says to himself, then all will go well with my life from now on. He throws the stone and misses. That one didn't count, he says, and so he picks up another stone and moves several yards closer to the tree. He misses again. That one didn't count either, he says, and then he moves still closer to the tree and finds another stone. Again he misses. That was just the final warm-up toss, he says, it's the next one that really counts. But just to make sure, he walks right up to the tree this time, positioning himself directly in front of the target. He is no more than a foot away from it by now, close enough to touch it with his hand. Then he lobs the stone squarely against the trunk. Success, he says to himself, I've done it. From this moment on, life will be better for me than ever before.

Nashe found the passage amusing, but at the same time he was too embarrassed by it to want to laugh. There was something terrible about such candor, finally, and he wondered where Rousseau had found the courage to reveal such a thing about himself, to admit to such naked self-deception. Nashe turned off the lamp, closed his eyes, and listened to the hum of the air conditioner until he couldn't hear it anymore. At some point during the night, he dreamt of a forest in which the wind passed through the trees with the sound of shuffling cards.

The next morning, Nashe continued to delay the test. It had almost become a point of honor by then, as if the real test were with himself and not with Pozzi's ability at cards. The point was to see how long he could live in a state of uncertainty: to act as though he had forgotten about it and in that way use the power of silence to force Pozzi into making the first move. If Pozzi said nothing, then that would mean the kid was nothing but talk. Nashe liked the symmetry of that conundrum. No words would mean it was all words, and all words would mean it was only air and bluff and deception. If Pozzi was serious, he would have to bring up the subject sooner or later, and as time went on, Nashe found himself more and more willing to wait. It was a bit like trying to breathe and hold your breath at the same time, he decided, but now that he had started the experiment, he knew that he was going to carry on with it to the very end.

Pozzi seemed considerably revived from his long night's sleep. Nashe heard him turn on the shower just before nine o'clock, and twenty minutes later he was standing in his room, once again wearing the outfit of white towels.

"How's the senator feeling this morning?" Nashe said.

"Better," Pozzi said. "The bones still ache, but Jackus Pozzius is back in business."

"Which means that a little breakfast is probably in order."

"Make it a big breakfast. The old pit is crying out for sustenance."

"Sunday brunch, then."

"Brunch, lunch, I don't care what you call it. I'm famished."

Nashe ordered breakfast to be sent up to the room, and another hour went by with no mention of the test. Nashe began to wonder if Pozzi wasn't playing the same game that he was: refusing to be the first to talk about it, digging in for a war of nerves. But no sooner did he begin to think this than he discovered that he was wrong. After they had eaten, Pozzi went back to his room to dress. When he returned (wearing the white shirt, the gray slacks, and the loafers—which made him look quite presentable, Nashe thought) he wasted no time in getting down to it. "I thought you wanted to see what kind of poker player I was," he said. "Maybe we should buy a deck of cards somewhere and get started."

"I have the cards," Nashe said. "I was just waiting until you were ready."

"I'm ready. I've been ready from the word go."

"Good. Then it looks like we've come to the moment of truth. Sit down, Jack, and show me your stuff."

They played seven-card stud for the next three hours, using torn-up pieces of Plaza stationery to stand in as chips. With only two of them in the game, it was difficult for Nashe to measure the full scope of Pozzi's talents, but even under those distorted circumstances (which magnified the role of luck and made full-scale betting all but impossible), the kid beat him soundly, nibbling away at Nashe's paper chips until the whole pile was gone. Nashe was no master, of course, but he was far from inept. He had played nearly every week during his two years at Bowdoin College, and after he joined the fire department in Boston, he had sat in on enough games to know that he could hold his own against most decent players. But the kid was something else, and it did not take Nashe long to understand that. He seemed to concentrate better, to analyze situations more quickly, to be more sure of himself than anyone Nashe had faced in the past. After the first wipeout, Nashe suggested that he play with two hands instead of one, but the results were essentially the same. If anything, Pozzi made faster work of it than the first time. Nashe won his share of hands, but the take from those wins was always small, significantly smaller than the sums that Pozzi's winning hands invariably produced. The kid had an unerring knack for knowing when to fold and when to stay in, and he never pushed a losing hand too far, often dropping out after only the third or fourth card had been dealt. In the beginning, Nashe stole a few hands with wild bluffs, but after twenty or thirty minutes, that strategy started to backfire on him. Pozzi had him figured out, and in the end it was almost as though he could read Nashe's mind, as though he were sitting inside his head and watching him think. This encouraged Nashe, since he wanted Pozzi to be good, but it was a disturbing sensation for all that, and the unpleasantness of it lingered for some time afterward. He began to play too conservatively, relying on caution at every turn, and from then on Pozzi took control of the game, bluffing and manipulating him almost at will. The kid did not gloat, however. He played with dead seriousness, showing no trace of his customary sarcasm and humor. It was not until Nashe called it quits that he seemed to return to himself—suddenly leaning back in his chair and breaking into a broad, satisfied smile.

"Not bad, kid," Nashe said. "You beat the pants off me."

"I told you," Pozzi said. "I don't fuck around when it comes to poker. Nine times out of ten, I'm going to come out on top. It's like a law of nature."

"Let's just hope that tomorrow is one of those nine times."

"Don't worry, I'm going to kill those suckers. I guarantee it. They're not half as good as you are, and you saw what I just did to you."

"Total destruction."

"That's right. It was a nuclear holocaust in here. A goddamn Hiroshima."

"Are you willing to shake on the deal we made in the car?"

"A fifty-fifty split? Yeah, I'm willing to do that."

"Minus the initial ten thousand, of course."

"Minus the ten grand. But there's still the other stuff to con-sider."

"What other stuff?"

"The hotel. The food. The clothes you bought for me yesterday."

"Don't worry about it. Those things are write-offs, what you might call a normal business expense."

"Shit. You don't have to do that."

"I don't have to do anything. But I did it, didn't I? It's my present to you, Jack, and we'll leave it at that. If you want to, you can think of it as a bonus for getting me in on the action."

"A finder's fee."

"Exactly. A commission for services rendered. Now all you have to do is pick up the phone and see if Laurel and Hardy are still expecting you. We wouldn't want to go there for nothing. And make sure they give you good directions. It wouldn't be nice to show up late."

"I'd better mention that you're coming with me. Just so they know what to expect."

"Tell them your car is in the shop for repairs and you're getting a ride with a friend."

"I'll tell them you're my brother."

"Let's not exaggerate."

"Sure, I'll tell them you're my brother. That way they won't ask any questions."

"All right, tell them whatever you want. Just don't make it too complicated. You don't want to start off with your foot in your mouth."

"Don't worry, pal, you can trust me. I'm the Jackpot Kid, re-member? It doesn't matter what I say. As long as I'm the one who says it, everything is going to turn out right."

They set off for the town of Ockham at one thirty the following afternoon. The game was not scheduled to begin until dark, but Flower and Stone were expecting them at four. "It's like they can't do enough for us," Pozzi said. "First they're going to give us tea. Then we get a tour of the house. And before we sit down to play cards, we're all going to have dinner. How do you like that? Tea! I can't fucking believe it."

"There's a first time for everything," Nashe said. "Just remember to behave yourself. No slurping. And when they ask you how many lumps of sugar you want, just say one."

"They might be jerks, those two, but their heart seems to be in the right place. If I wasn't such a greedy son of a bitch, I'd almost begin to feel sorry for them."

"You're the last person I'd expect to feel sorry for a couple of millionaires."

"Well, you know what I mean. First they wine and dine us, and then we walk off with their money. You've got to feel sorry for bozos like that. Just a little bit anyway."

"I wouldn't push it too far. No one goes into a game expecting to lose, not even millionaires with good manners. You never can tell, Jack. For all we know, they're sitting down there in Pennsylvania feeling sorry for us."

The afternoon turned out to be warm and hazy, with thick clouds massing overhead and a threat of rain in the air. They drove through the Lincoln Tunnel and began following a series of New Jersey highways in the direction of the Delaware River. For the first forty-five minutes, neither one of them said very much. Nashe drove, and Pozzi looked out the window and studied the map. If nothing else, Nashe felt certain that he had come to a turning point, that no matter what happened in the game that night, his days on the road had come to an end. The mere fact that he was in the car with Pozzi now seemed to prove the inevitability of that end. Something was finished, and something else was about to begin, and for the moment Nashe was in between, floating in a place that was neither here nor there. He knew that Pozzi stood a good chance of winning, that the odds were in fact better than good, but the thought of winning struck him as too easy, as something that would happen too quickly and naturally to bear any permanent consequences. He therefore kept the possibility of defeat uppermost in his thoughts, telling himself it was always better to prepare for the worst than to be caught by surprise. What would he do if things went badly? How would he act if the money were lost? The strange thing was not that he was able to imagine this possibility but that he could do so with such indifference and detachment, with so little inner pain. It was as if he finally had no part in what was about to happen to him. And if he was no longer involved in his own fate, where was he, then, and what had become of him? Perhaps he had been living in limbo for too long, he thought, and now that he needed to find himself again, there was nothing to catch hold of anymore. Nashe suddenly felt dead inside, as if all his feelings had been used up. He wanted to feel afraid, but not even disaster could terrify him.

After they had been on the road for a little less than an hour, Pozzi started to talk again. They were traveling through a thunderstorm at that point (somewhere between New Brunswick and Princeton), and for the first time in the three days they had been together, he seemed to show some curiosity about the man who had rescued him. Nashe was caught with his guard down, and because he had not been prepared for Pozzi's bluntness, he found himself talking more openly than he would have expected, unburdening himself of things he normally would not have shared with anyone. As soon as he saw what he was doing, he almost cut himself short, but then he decided that it didn't matter. Pozzi would be gone from his life by the next day, and why bother to hold anything back from someone he would never see again?

"And so, Professor," the kid said, "what are you going to do with yourself after we strike it rich?"

"I haven't decided yet," Nashe said. "First thing tomorrow, I'll probably go see my daughter and spend a few days with her. Then I'll sit down and make some plans."

"So you're a daddy, huh? I hadn't figured you for one of those family guys."

"I'm not. But I have this little girl in Minnesota. She'll be turning four in a couple of months."

"And no wife in the picture?"

"There used to be one, but not anymore."

"Is she out there in Michigan with the kid?"

"Minnesota. No, the girl lives with my sister. With my sister and brother-in-law. He used to play defensive back for the Vikings."

"No kidding? What's his name?"

"Ray Schweikert."

"Can't say I ever heard of him."

"He only lasted a couple of seasons. The poor lummox smashed up his knee in training camp and that was the end of him."

"And what about the wife? Did she croak on you or something?"

"Not exactly. She's probably still alive somewhere."

"A disappearing act, huh?"

"I guess you could call it that."

"You mean she walked out on you and didn't take the kid? What kind of bimbo would do a thing like that?"

"I've often asked that question myself. At least she left me a note."

"That was nice of her."

"Yeah, it filled me with immense gratitude. The only trouble was that she put it on the kitchen counter. And since she hadn't bothered to clean up after breakfast, the counter was wet. By the time I got home that evening, the thing was soaked through. It's hard to read a letter when the ink is blurred. She even mentioned the name of the guy she ran off with, but I couldn't make it out. Gorman or Corman, I think it was, but I still don't know which."

"I hope she was good-looking anyway. There had to be something to make you want to marry her."

"Oh, she was good-looking all right. The first time I saw Thérèse, I thought she was about the most beautiful woman I'd ever seen. I couldn't keep my hands off her."

"A good piece of ass."

"That's one way of putting it. It just took me a while to realize that all her brains were down there, too."

"It's an old story, pal. You let your dick do your thinking for you, and that's what happens. Still, if it was my wife, I would have dragged her back and pounded some sense into her."

"There wouldn't have been any point. Besides, I had my work to do. I couldn't just take off and go looking for her."

"Work? You mean you have a job?"

"Not anymore. I quit about a year ago."

"What did you do?"

"I put out fires."

"A troubleshooter, huh? Company calls you in when there's a problem, and then you go around the office looking for holes to plug. That's top-level management. You must have made some good money."

"No, I'm talking about real fires. The kind you put out with hoses—the old hook-and-ladder routine. Axes, burning buildings, people jumping out of windows. The stuff you read about in the paper."

"You're pulling my leg."

"It's true. I was with the Boston fire department for close to seven years."

"You sound pretty proud of yourself."

"I suppose I am. I was good at what I did."

"If you liked it so much, then why did you quit?"

"I got lucky. All of a sudden, my ship came in."

"You win the Irish Sweepstakes or something?"

"It was more like the graduation present you told me about."

"But bigger."

"One would hope so."

"And now? What are you up to now?"

"Right now I'm sitting in this car with you, little man, hoping you're going to come through for me tonight."

"A regular soldier of fortune."

"That's it. I'm just following my nose and waiting to see what turns up."

"Welcome to the club."

"Club? What club is that?"

"The International Brotherhood of Lost Dogs. What else? We're letting you in as a certified, card-carrying member. Serial number zero zero zero zero."

"I thought that was your number."

"It is. But it's your number, too. That's one of the beauties of the Brotherhood. Everyone who joins gets the same number."

By the time they came to Flemington, the thunderstorm had passed. Sunlight broke through the dispersing clouds, and the wet land shimmered with a sudden, almost supernatural clarity. The trees stood out more sharply against the sky, and even the shadows seemed to cut more deeply into the ground, as if their dark, intricate outlines had been etched with the precision of scalpels. In spite of the storm, Nashe had made good time, and they were running somewhat ahead of schedule. They decided to stop for a cup of coffee, and once they were in town, they took further advantage of the occasion to empty their bladders and buy a carton of cigarettes. Pozzi explained that he normally didn't smoke, but he liked to have cigarettes on hand whenever he played cards. Tobacco was a useful prop, and it helped to prevent his opponents from watching him too closely, as if he could literally hide his thoughts behind a cloud of smoke. The important thing was to remain inscrutable, to build a wall around yourself and not let anyone in. The game was more than just betting on your cards, it was studying your opponents for weaknesses, reading their gestures for possible tics and telltale responses. Once you were able to detect a pattern, the advantage swung heavily in your favor. By the same token, the good player always did everything in his power to deny that advantage to anyone else.

Nashe paid for the cigarettes and handed them to Pozzi, who tucked the oblong box of Marlboros under his arm. Then the two of them left the store and took a brief stroll down the main street, threading their way through the small knots of summer tourists who had reemerged with the sun. After going a couple of blocks, they came upon an old hotel with a plaque on the facade that informed them that this was where the reporters covering the Lindbergh kidnapping trial had stayed back in the 1930s. Nashe told Pozzi that Bruno Hauptmann had probably been innocent, that new evidence seemed to suggest that the wrong man had been executed for the crime. He then went on the talk about Lindbergh, the all-American hero, and how he had turned fascist during the war, but Pozzi seemed bored with his little lecture, and so they turned around and headed back to the car.

It wasn't difficult to find the bridge at Frenchtown, but once they crossed the Delaware into Pennsylvania, the route became less certain. Ockham was no more than fifteen miles from the river, but they had to make a number of complicated turns to get there, and they wound up crawling along the narrow, twisting roads for close to forty minutes. If not for the storm, it would have gone somewhat faster, but the low ground was clogged with mud, and once or twice they had to climb out of the car to remove fallen branches that were blocking their way. Pozzi kept referring to the directions he had scribbled down while talking to Flower on the phone, calling out each landmark as it came into view: a covered bridge, a blue mailbox, a gray stone with a black circle painted on it. After a while, it began to feel as if they were traveling through a maze, and when they finally approached the last turn, they both admitted that they would have been hard-pressed to find their way back to the river.

Pozzi had never seen the house before, but he had been told that it was a large and impressive place, a mansion with twenty rooms surrounded by more than three hundred acres of property. From the road, however, there was nothing to suggest the wealth that lay behind the barrier of trees. A silver mailbox with the names FLOWER and STONE written on it stood beside an unpaved road that led through a dense tangle of woods and shrubs. It looked uncared-for, as if it might have been the entrance to an old, broken-down farm. Nashe swung the Saab onto the bumpy, rut-grooved path and inched his way forward for five or six hundred yards—far enough to make him wonder if the path would ever end. Pozzi said nothing, but Nashe could feel his apprehension, a sullen, sulking sort of silence that seemed to say that he, too, was beginning to doubt the venture. At last, however, the road began to climb, and when the ground leveled off a few minutes later, they could see a tall iron gate fifty yards ahead. They drove on, and once they reached the gate, the upper portion of the house became visible through the bars: an immense brick structure looming in the near distance, with four chimneys jutting into the sky and sunlight bouncing off the pitched slate roof.

The gate was closed. Pozzi jumped out of the car to open it, but after giving two or three tugs on the handle, he turned to Nashe and shook his head, indicating that it was locked. Nashe put the car into neutral, applied the emergency brake, and climbed out to see what should be done. The air suddenly seemed cooler to him, and a strong breeze was blowing across the ridge, rustling the foliage with the first faint sign of fall. As Nashe put his feet on the ground and stood up, an overpowering sense of happiness washed through him. It lasted only an instant, then gave way to a brief, almost imperceptible feeling of dizziness, which vanished the moment he began walking toward Pozzi. After that, his head seemed curiously emptied out, and for the first time in many years, he fell into one of those trances that had sometimes afflicted him as a boy: an abrupt and radical shift of his inner bearings, as if the world around him had suddenly lost its reality. It made him feel like a shadow, like someone who had fallen asleep with his eyes open.

After examining the gate for a moment, Nashe discovered a small white button lodged in one of the stone pillars that supported the ironwork. He assumed that it was connected to a bell in the house and pushed against it with the tip of his index finger. Hearing no sound, he pushed once again for good measure, just to make sure it wasn't supposed to ring outside. Pozzi scowled, growing impatient with all the delays, but Nashe just stood there in silence, breathing in the smells of the dank earth, enjoying the stillness that surrounded them. About twenty seconds later, he caught sight of a man jogging in their direction from the house. As the figure approached, Nashe concluded that it could not have been either Flower or Stone, at least not from the way Pozzi had described them. This was a stocky man of no particular age, dressed in blue work pants and a red flannel shirt, and from his clothes Nashe guessed that he was a hireling of some sort—the gardener, or perhaps the keeper of the gate. The man spoke to them through the bars, still panting from his exertions.

"What can I do for you, boys?" he said. It was a neutral question, neither friendly nor hostile, as if it were the same question he asked every visitor who came to the house. As Nashe studied the man more closely, he was struck by the remarkable blueness of his eyes, a blue so pale that the eyes almost seemed to vanish when the light hit them.

"We're here to see Mr. Flower," Pozzi said.

"You the two from New York?" the man said, looking past them at the Saab idling on the dirt road.

"You got it," Pozzi said. "Straight from the Plaza Hotel."

"What about the car, then?" the man asked, running a set of thick, sturdy fingers through his sandy-gray hair.

"What about it?" Pozzi said.

"I was wondering," the man said. "You come from New York, but the tags on the car say Minnesota, 'land of ten thousand lakes.' Seems to me like that's somewhere in the opposite direction."

"You got a problem or something, chief?" Pozzi said. "What the fuck difference does it make where the car comes from?"

"You don't have to get huffy, fella," the man replied. "I'm just doing my job. A lot of people come prowling around here, and we can't have no uninvited guests sneaking through the gates."

"We've got an invitation," Pozzi said, trying to control his temper. "We're here to play cards. If you don't believe me, go ask your boss. Flower or Stone, it doesn't matter which. They're both personal friends of mine."

"His name is Pozzi," Nashe added. "Jack Pozzi. You must have been told he was expected."

The man stuck his hand into his shirt pocket, removed a small scrap of paper, cupped it in his palm, and studied it briefly at arm's length. "Jack Pozzi," he repeated. "And what about you, fella?" he said, looking at Nashe.

"I'm Nashe," Nashe said. "Jim Nashe."

The man put the scrap of paper back in his pocket and sighed. "Don't let nobody in without a name," he said. "That's the rule. You shoulda told me straight off. There wouldn't have been no problem then."

"You didn't ask," Pozzi said.

"Yeah," the man mumbled, almost talking to himself. "Well, maybe I forgot."

Without saying another word, he opened both doors of the gate, then gestured to the house behind him. Nashe and Pozzi returned to the car and drove on through.

# 4

---

The doorbell chimed with the opening notes of Beethoven's Fifth Symphony. They both grinned stupidly in surprise, but before either one of them could make a remark about it, the door was opened by a black maid dressed in a starched gray uniform and she was ushering them into the house. She led them across the black-and-white checkered floor of a large entrance hall that was cluttered with several pieces of broken statuary (a naked wood nymph missing her right arm, a headless hunter, a horse with no legs that floated above a stone plinth with an iron shaft connected to its belly), took them through a high-ceilinged dining room with an immense walnut table in its center, down a dimly lit corridor whose walls were decorated with a series of small landscape paintings, and then knocked on a heavy wooden door. A voice answered from within and the maid pushed the door open, stepping aside to allow Nashe and Pozzi to enter. "Your guests are here," she said, barely looking into the room, and then she closed the door and made a quick, silent exit.

It was a large, almost self-consciously masculine room. Standing on the threshold during those first instants, Nashe noticed the dark wood paneling on the walls, the billiard table, the worn Persian rug, the stone fireplace, the leather chairs, the ceiling fan turning overhead. More than anything else, it made him think of a movie set, a mock-up of a British men's club in some turn-of-the-century colonial outpost. Pozzi had started it, he realized. All the talk about Laurel and Hardy had planted a suggestion of Hollywood in his mind, and now that Nashe was there, it was difficult for him not to think of the house as an illusion.

Flower and Stone were both dressed in white summer suits. One was standing by the fireplace smoking a cigar, and the other was sitting in a leather chair holding a glass that could have contained either water or gin. The white suits no doubt contributed to the colonial atmosphere, but once Flower spoke, welcoming them into the room with his rough but not unpleasant American voice, the illusion was shattered. Yes, Nashe thought, one was fat and the other was thin, but that was as far as the similarity went. Stone had a taut, emaciated look to him that recalled Fred Astaire more insistently than the long-faced, weeping Laurel, and Flower was more burly than rotund, with a jowly face that resembled some ponderous figure like Edward Arnold or Eugene Pallette rather than the corpulent yet light-footed Hardy. But for all those quibbles, Nashe understood what Pozzi had meant.

"Greetings, gentlemen," Flower said, coming toward them with an outstretched hand. "Delighted you could make it."

"Hi, there, Bill," Pozzi said. "Good to see you again. This here's my big brother, Jim."

"Jim Nashe, isn't it?" Flower said amiably.

"That's right," Nashe said. "Jack and I are half-brothers. Same mother, different fathers."

"I don't know who's responsible for it," Flower said, nodding in Pozzi's direction, "but he's one hell of a little poker player."

"I got him started when he was just a kid," Nashe said, unable to resist the line. "When you see talent, there's an obligation to encourage it."

"You bet," Pozzi said. "Jim was my mentor. He taught me everything I know."

"But he beats the living daylights out of me now," Nashe said. "I don't even dare to sit down at the same table with him anymore."

By then, Stone had extricated himself from his chair and was walking toward them, drink still in hand. He introduced himself to Nashe, shook hands with Pozzi, and a moment later the four of them were sitting around the empty fireplace waiting for the refreshments to arrive. Since Flower did most of the talking, Nashe assumed that he was the dominant one of the pair, but for all the big man's warmth and blustery humor, Nashe found himself more attracted to the silent, bashful Stone. The small man listened attentively to what the others said, and while he made few comments of his own (stumbling inarticulately when he did, acting almost embarrassed by the sound of his voice), there was a stillness and serenity in his eyes that Nashe found deeply sympathetic. Flower was all agitation and lunging goodwill, but there was something crude about him, Nashe felt, some edge of anxiety that made him appear to be at odds with himself. Stone, on the other hand, was a simpler and gentler sort of person, a man without airs who sat comfortably inside his own skin. But those were only first impressions, Nashe realized. As he continued to watch Stone sip away at the clear liquid in his glass, it occurred to him that the man might also be drunk.

"Willie and I have always loved cards," Flower was saying. "Back in Philadelphia, we used to play poker every Friday night. It was a ritual with us, and I don't think we missed more than a handful of games in ten years. Some people go to church on Sunday, but for us it was Friday-night poker. God, how we used to love our weekends back then! Let me tell you, there's no better medicine than a friendly card game for sloughing off the cares of the workaday world."

"It's relaxing," Stone said. "It helps to get your mind off things."

"Precisely," Flower said. "It helps to open the spirit to other possibilities, to wipe the slate clean." He paused for a moment to pick up the thread of his story. "Anyway," he continued, "for many years Willie and I had our offices in the same building on Chestnut Street. He was an optometrist, you know, and I was an accountant, and every Friday we'd close up shop promptly at five. The game was always at seven, and week in and week out we always spent those two hours in precisely the same way. First, we'd swing around to the corner newsstand and buy a lottery ticket, and then we'd go across the street to Steinberg's Deli. I would always order a pastrami on rye, and Willie would have the corned beef. We did that for a long time, didn't we, Willie? Nine or ten years, I would say."

"At least nine or ten," Stone said. "Maybe eleven or twelve."

"Maybe eleven or twelve," Flower said with satisfaction. By now it was clear to Nashe that Flower had told this story many times in the past, but that did not prevent him from savoring the opportunity to do so again. Perhaps it was understandable. Good fortune is no less bewildering than bad, and if millions of dollars had literally tumbled down on you from the sky, perhaps you would have to go on telling the story in order to convince yourself it had really happened. "In any case," Flower went on, "we stuck to this routine for a long time. Life continued, of course, but the Friday nights remained sacred, and in the end they proved stronger than anything else. Willie's wife died; my wife left me; a host of disappointments threatened to break our hearts. But through it all, those poker sessions in Andy Dugan's office on the fifth floor continued like clockwork. They never failed us, we could count on them through thick and thin."

"And then," Nashe interrupted, "you suddenly struck it rich."

"Just like that," Stone said. "A bolt from the blue."

"It was almost seven years ago," Flower said, trying not to stray from the narrative. "October fourth, to be precise. No one had hit the winning number for several weeks, and the jackpot had grown to an all-time high. Over twenty million dollars, if you can believe it, a truly astonishing sum. Willie and I had been playing for years, and until then we hadn't won so much as a penny, not one plug nickel for all the hundreds of dollars we had spent. Nor did we ever expect to. The odds are always the same, after all, no matter how many times you play. Millions and millions to one, the longest of long shots. If anything, I think we bought those tickets just so we could talk about what we would do with the money if we ever happened to win. That was one of our favorite pastimes: sitting in Steinberg's Deli with our sandwiches and spinning out stories about how we would live if our luck suddenly turned. It was a harmless little game, and it made us happy to let our thoughts run free like that. You might even call it therapeutic. You imagine another life for yourself, and it keeps your heart pounding."

"It's good for the circulation," Stone said.

"Precisely," Flower said. "It puts some juice in the old ticker."

At that moment, there was a knock on the door, and the maid wheeled in a tray of iced drinks and tea sandwiches. Flower paused in his telling as the snacks were distributed, but once the four of them had settled back into their chairs, he immediately started up again.

"Willie and I always went partners on a single ticket," he said. "It was more enjoyable that way, since it didn't put us in competition with each other. Imagine if one of us had won! It would have been unthinkable for him not to share the prize money with the other, and so rather than have to go through all that, we simply split the ticket half and half. One of us would choose the first number, the other would choose the second, and then we would go on taking turns until all the holes had been punched out. We came close a few times, missed the jackpot by only a digit or two. A loss was a loss, but I must say that we found those *almosts* rather exciting."

"They spurred us on," Stone said. "They made us believe that anything was possible."

"On the day in question," Flower continued, "seven years ago this October fourth, Willie and I punched out the holes a little more deliberately than usual. I can't say why that was, but for some reason we actually discussed the numbers we were going to pick. I've dealt with numbers all my life, of course, and after a while you begin to feel that each number has a personality of its own. A twelve is very different from a thirteen, for example. Twelve is upright, conscientious, intelligent, whereas thirteen is a loner, a shady character who won't think twice about breaking the law to get what he wants. Eleven is tough, an outdoorsman who likes tramping through woods and scaling mountains; ten is rather simpleminded, a bland figure who always does what he's told; nine is deep and mystical, a Buddha of contemplation. I don't want to bore you with this, but I'm sure you understand what I mean. It's all very private, but every accountant I've ever talked to has always said the same thing. Numbers have souls, and you can't help but get involved with them in a personal way."

"So there we were," Stone said, "holding the lottery ticket in our hands, trying to decide which numbers to bet on."

"And I looked at Willie," Flower said, "and I said 'Primes.' And Willie looked back at me and said 'Of course.' Because that was precisely what he was going to say to me. I got the word out of my mouth a split second faster than he did, but the same thought had also occurred to him. Prime numbers. It was all so neat and elegant. Numbers that refuse to cooperate, that don't change or divide, numbers that remain themselves for all eternity. And so we picked out a sequence of primes and then walked across the street and had our sandwiches."

"Three, seven, thirteen, nineteen, twenty-three, thirty-one," Stone said.

"I'll never forget it," Flower said. "It was the magic combination, the key to the gates of heaven."

"But it shocked us just the same," Stone said. "For the first week or two, we didn't know what to think."

"It was chaos," Flower said. "Television, newspapers, magazines. Everyone wanted to talk to us and take our pictures. It took a while for that to die down."

"We were celebrities," Stone said. "Genuine folk heroes."

"Still," Flower said, "we never came out with any of those ludicrous remarks you hear from other winners. The secretaries who say they're going to keep their jobs, the plumbers who swear they'll go on living in their tiny apartments. No, Willie and I were never so stupid. Money changes things, and the more money you have, the greater those changes are going to be. Besides, we already knew what we were going to do with our winnings. We had talked about it so much, it was hardly a mystery to us. Once the hubbub blew over, I sold my share of the firm, and Willie did the same with his business. At that point, we didn't have to think about it. It was a foregone conclusion."

"But that was only the beginning," Stone said.

"True enough," Flower said. "We didn't rest on our laurels. With more than a million coming in every year, we could pretty much do whatever we wanted. Even after we bought this place, there was nothing to stop us from using the money to make more money."

"Bucks County!" Stone said, letting out a brief guffaw.

"Bingo," Flower said, "a perfect bull's-eye. No sooner did we become rich than we started to become very rich. And once we were very rich, we became fabulously rich. I knew my way around investments, after all. I had been handling other people's money for so many years, it was only natural that I should have learned a trick or two along the way. But to be honest with you, we never expected things to work out as well as they did. First it was silver. Then it was Eurodollars. Then it was the commodities market. Junk bonds, superconductors, real estate. You name it, and we've turned a profit on it."

"Bill has the Midas touch," Stone said. "A green thumb to end all green thumbs."

"Winning the lottery was one thing," Flower said, "but you'd think that would have been the end of it. A once-in-a-lifetime miracle. But good luck has continued to come our way. No matter what we do, everything seems to turn out right. So much money pours in now, we give half of it to charity—and still we have more than we know what to do with. It's as though God has singled us out from other men. He's showered us with good fortune and lifted us to the heights of happiness. I know this might sound presumptuous to you, but at times I feel that we've become immortal."

"You might be raking it in," Pozzi said, finally entering the conversation, "but you didn't do so hot when you played me at poker."

"That's true," Flower said. "Very true. In these past seven years, it's the one time our luck has failed us. Willie and I made many blunders that night, and you thrashed us soundly. That's why I was so eager to arrange a rematch."

"What makes you think it's going to be any different this time?" Pozzi said.

"I'm glad you asked that question," Flower said. "After you beat us last month, Willie and I felt humiliated. We had always thought of ourselves as fairly respectable poker players, but you proved to us that we were wrong. So, rather than roll over and give up, we decided to get better at it. We've been practicing day and night. We even took lessons from someone."

"Lessons?" Pozzi said.

"From a man named Sid Zeno," Flower said. "Have you ever heard of him?"

"Sure, I've heard of Sid Zeno," Pozzi said. "He lives out in Vegas. He's getting on in years now, but he used to be one of the top half dozen players in the game."

"He still has an excellent reputation," Flower said. "So we had him flown out here from Nevada, and he wound up spending a week with us. I think you'll find our performance much improved this time, Jack."

"I hope so," Pozzi said, obviously not impressed, but still trying to remain polite. "It would be a shame to spend all that money on lessons and not get anything out of it. I'll bet you old Sid charged a pretty penny for his services."

"He didn't come cheap," Flower said. "But I think he was worth it. At one point, I asked him if he had ever heard of you, but he confessed that he didn't know your name."

"Well, Sid's a little out of touch these days," Pozzi said. "Besides, I'm still at the beginning of my career. The word hasn't spread yet."

"I suppose you could say that Willie and I are at the beginning of our careers, too," Flower said, standing up from his seat and lighting a new cigar. "If nothing else, the game should be exciting tonight. I'm looking forward to it immensely."

"Me too, Bill," Pozzi said. "It's going to be a gas."

They began the tour of the house on the ground floor, walking through one room after another as Flower talked to them about the furniture, the architectural improvements, and the paintings that hung on the walls. By the second room, Nashe noticed that the big man rarely neglected to mention what each thing had cost, and as the catalogue of expenses continued to grow, he found that he was developing a distinct antipathy to this boorish creature who seemed so full of himself, who exulted so shamelessly in his fussy accountant's mind. As before, Stone said almost nothing, piping in an occasional non sequitur or redundant remark, a perfect yes-man in the thrall of his larger and more aggressive friend. The whole scene was beginning to get Nashe down, and eventually he could think of little else but how absurd it was for him to be there, enumerating the odd conjunctions of chance that had put him in this particular house at this particular moment, as if for no other purpose than to listen to the bombastic prattle of a fat, overstuffed stranger. If not for Pozzi, he might have slipped into a serious funk. But there was the kid, tripping happily from room to room, seething with sarcastic politeness as he pretended to be following what Flower said. Nashe could not help admiring him for his spirit, for his ability to make the most of the situation. When Pozzi flashed him a quick wink of amusement in the third or fourth room, he felt almost grateful to him, as if he were a morose king drawing courage from the pranks of his court jester.

Things picked up considerably once they climbed to the second floor. Rather than show them the bedrooms that stood behind the six closed doors in the main hallway, Flower took them to the end of the corridor and opened a seventh door that led to what he referred to as the "east wing." This door was almost invisible, and until Flower put his hand on the knob and started to open it, Nashe had not noticed it was there. Covered with the same wallpaper that ran the length of the corridor (an ugly, old-fashioned fleur-de-lys pattern in muted pinks and blues), the door was so skillfully cam-ouflaged that it seemed to melt into the wall. The east wing, Flower explained, was where he and Willie spent most of their time. It was a new section of the house that they had built shortly after moving in (and here he gave the precise amount it had cost, a figure which Nashe promptly tried to forget), and the contrast between the dark, somewhat musty old house and this new wing was impressive, even startling. The moment they stepped across the sill, they found themselves standing under a large, many-faceted glass roof. Light poured down from above, inundating them with the brightness of the late afternoon. It took Nashe's eyes a moment to adjust, but then he saw that this was only a passageway. Directly in front of them there was another wall, a freshly painted white wall with two closed doors in it.

"One half belongs to Willie," Flower said, "and the other half is mine."

"It looks like a greenhouse up here," Pozzi said. "Is that what you fellows do, grow plants or something?"

"Not quite," Flower said. "But we cultivate other things. Our interests, our passions, the garden of our minds. I don't care how much money you have. If there's no passion in your life, it's not worth living."

"Well put," Pozzi said, nodding his head with feigned seriousness. "I couldn't have phrased it better myself, Bill."

"It doesn't matter which part we visit first," Flower said, "but I know that Willie is especially eager to show you his city. Maybe we should start by going through the door on the left."

Without waiting to hear Stone's opinion on the matter, Flower opened the door and gestured for Nashe and Pozzi to go in. The room was much larger than Nashe had imagined it would be, a place almost barnlike in its dimensions. With its high transparent ceiling and pale wooden floor, it seemed to be all openness and light, as if it were a room suspended in the middle of the air. Running along the wall immediately to their left was a series of benches and tables, the surfaces of which were cluttered with tools, scraps of wood, and an odd assortment of metal bric-a-brac. The only other object in the room was an enormous platform that stood in the center of the floor, covered with what seemed to be a miniature scale-model rendering of a city. It was a marvelous thing to behold, with its crazy spires and lifelike buildings, its narrow streets and microscopic human figures, and as the four of them approached the platform, Nashe began to smile, astounded by the sheer invention and elaborateness of it all.

"It's called the City of the World," Stone said modestly, almost struggling to get the words out of his mouth. "It's only about half-finished, but I guess you can get some idea of what it's supposed to look like."

There was a slight pause as Stone searched for something more to say, and in that brief interval Flower jumped in and started talking again, acting like one of those proud, overbearing fathers who always pushes his son into playing the piano for the guests. "Willie has been at it for five years now," he said, "and you have to admit that it's amazing, a stupendous achievement. Just look at the city hall over there. It took him four months to do that building alone."

"I like working on it," Stone said, smiling tentatively. "It's the way I'd like the world to look. Everything in it happens at once."

"Willie's city is more than just a toy," Flower said, "it's an artistic vision of mankind. In one way, it's an autobiography, but in another way, it's what you might call a utopia—a place where the past and future come together, where good finally triumphs over evil. If you look carefully, you'll see that many of the figures actually represent Willie himself. There, in the playground, you see him as a child. Over there, you see him grinding lenses in his shop as a grown man. There, on the corner of that street, you see the two of us buying the lottery ticket. His wife and parents are buried in the cemetery over here, but there they are again, hovering as angels over that house. If you bend down, you'll see Willie's daughter holding his hand on the front steps. That's what you might call the private backdrop, the personal material, the inner component. But all these things are put in a larger context. They're merely an example, an illustration of one man's journey through the City of the World. Look at the Hall of Justice, the Library, the Bank, and the Prison. Willie calls them the Four Realms of Togetherness, and each one plays a vital role in maintaining the harmony of the city. If you look at the Prison, you'll see that all the prisoners are working happily at various tasks, that they all have smiles on their faces. That's because they're glad they've been punished for their crimes, and now they're learning how to recover the goodness within them through hard work. That's what I find so inspiring about Willie's city. It's an imaginary place, but it's also realistic. Evil still exists, but the powers who rule over the city have figured out how to transform that evil back into good. Wisdom reigns here, but the struggle is nevertheless constant, and great vigilance is required of all the citizens—each of whom carries the entire city within himself. William Stone is a great artist, gentlemen, and I consider it a tremendous honor to count myself among his friends."

As Stone blushed and looked down at the floor, Nashe pointed to a blank area of the platform and asked what his plans for that section were. Stone looked up, stared at the empty space for a moment, and then smiled in contemplation of the work that lay ahead of him.

"The house we're standing in now," he said. "The house, and then the grounds, the fields, and the woods. Over to the right"— and here he pointed in the direction of the far corner—"I'm thinking about doing a separate model of this room. I'd have to be in it, of course, which means that I would also have to build another City of the World. A smaller one, a second city to fit inside the room within the room."

"You mean a model of the model?" Nashe said.

"Yes, a model of the model. But I have to finish everything else first. It would be the last element, a thing to add at the very end."

"Nobody could make anything so small," Pozzi said, looking at Stone as though he were insane. "You'd go blind trying to do a thing like that."

"I have my lenses," Stone said. "All the small work is done under magnifying glasses."

"But if you did a model of the model," Nashe said, "then theoretically you'd have to do an even smaller model of that model. A model of the model of the model. It could go on forever."

"Yes, I suppose it could," Stone said, smiling at Nashe's remark. "But I think it would be very difficult to get past the second stage, don't you? I'm not just talking about the construction, I'm also talking about time. It's taken me five years to get this far. It will probably take another five years to finish the first model. If the model of the model is as difficult as I think it's going to be, that would take another ten years, maybe even another twenty years. I'm fifty-six now. If you add it up, I'm going to be pretty old when I finish anyway. And nobody lives forever. At least that's what I think. Bill might have other ideas about that, but I wouldn't bet much money on them. Sooner or later, I'm going to leave this world like everyone else."

"You mean," Pozzi said, his voice rising with incredulity, "you mean you're planning to work on this thing for the rest of your life?"

"Oh yes," Stone said, almost shocked that anyone could have thought otherwise. "Of course I am."

There was a brief silence as this remark sank in, and then Flower put his arm around Stone's shoulder and said: "I don't pretend to have any of Willie's artistic talent. But perhaps that's all for the best. Two artists in the household might be taking it a bit far.

Someone has to attend to the practical side of things, eh Willie? It takes all kinds of people to make a world."

Flower's rambling chatter continued as they left Stone's workshop, returned to the passageway, and approached the other door. "As you will see, gentlemen," he was saying, "my interests lie in another direction altogether. By nature, I suppose you could call me an antiquarian. I like to track down historical objects that have some value or significance, to surround myself with tangible remnants of the past. Willie makes things; I like to collect them."

Flower's half of the east wing was entirely different from Stone's. Instead of one large open area, his was divided into a network of smaller rooms, and if not for the glass dome perched overhead, the atmosphere might have been oppressive. Each of the five rooms was choked with furniture, overspilling bookcases, rugs, potted plants, and a multitude of knickknacks, as though the idea was to reproduce the thick, tangled feeling of a Victorian parlor. As Flower explained, however, there was a certain method to the apparent disorder. Two of the rooms were devoted to his library (first editions of English and American authors in one; his collection of history books in the other), a third room was given over to his cigars (a climate-controlled chamber with a dropped ceiling that housed his stock of hand-rolled masterpieces: cigars from Cuba and Jamaica, from the Canary Islands and the Philippines, from Sumatra and the Dominican Republic), and a fourth room served as the office in which he conducted his financial affairs (an oldfashioned room like the others, but with several pieces of modern equipment in it as well: telephone, typewriter, computer, fax machine, stock ticker, file cabinets, and so on). The last room was twice the size of any of the others, and as it was also significantly less cluttered, Nashe found it almost pleasant by contrast. This was the place where Flower kept his historical memorabilia. Long rows of glassed-in display cabinets occupied the center of the room, and the walls were fitted with mahogany shelves and cupboards with protective glass doors. Nashe felt as if he had walked into a museum. When he looked over at Pozzi, the kid gave him a goofy grin and rolled his eyes, making it perfectly clear that he was already bored to death.

Nashe did not think the collection dull so much as curious. Neatly mounted and labeled, each object sat under the glass as though proclaiming its own importance, but in fact there was little to get excited about. The room was a monument to trivia, packed with articles of such marginal value that Nashe wondered if it were not some kind of joke. But Flower seemed too proud of himself to understand how ridiculous it was. He kept referring to the pieces as "gems" and "treasures," oblivious to the possibility that there might be people in the world who did not share his enthusiasm, and as the tour continued over the next half hour, Nashe had to fight back an impulse to feel sorry for him.

In the long run, however, the impression that lingered of that room was quite different from what Nashe had imagined it would be. In the weeks and months that followed, he often found himself thinking back to what he had seen there, and it stunned him to realize how many of the objects he could remember. They began to take on a luminous, almost transcendent quality for him, and whenever he stumbled across one of them in his mind, he would unearth an image so distinct that it seemed to glow like an apparition from another world. The telephone that had once sat on Woodrow Wilson's desk. A pearl earring worn by Sir Walter Raleigh. A pencil that had fallen from Enrico Fermi's pocket in 1942. General McClellan's field glasses. A half-smoked cigar filched from an ashtray in Winston Churchill's office. A sweatshirt worn by Babe Ruth in 1927. William Seward's Bible. The cane used by Nathaniel Hawthorne after he broke his leg as a boy. A pair of spectacles worn by Voltaire. It was all so random, so misconstrued, so utterly beside the point. Flower's museum was a graveyard of shadows, a demented shrine to the spirit of nothingness. If those objects continued to call out to him, Nashe decided, it was because they were impenetrable, because they refused to divulge anything about themselves. It had nothing to do with history, nothing to do with the men who had once owned them. The fascination was simply for the objects as material things, and the way they had been wrenched out of any possible context, condemned by Flower to go on existing for no reason at all: defunct, devoid of purpose, alone in themselves now for the rest of time. It was the isolation that haunted Nashe, the image of irreducible separateness that burned down into his memory, and no matter how hard he struggled, he never managed to break free of it.

"I've begun to branch out into new areas," Flower said. "The things you see here are what you might call snippets, dwarf mementoes, motes of dust that have slipped through the cracks. I've started a new project now, and in the end it will make all this look like child's play." The fat man paused for a moment, put a match to his dead cigar, and then puffed until his face was surrounded by smoke. "Last year Willie and I went on a trip to England and Ireland," he said. "We haven't done much traveling, I'm afraid to say, and this glimpse of life abroad gave us enormous pleasure. The best thing about it was discovering how many old things there are in that part of the world. We Americans are always tearing down what we build, destroying the past in order to start over again, rushing headlong into the future. But our cousins on the other side of the pond are more attached to their history, it comforts them to know that they belong to a tradition, to age-old habits and customs. I won't bore you by going into my love of the past. You have only to look around you to know how much it means to me. While I was over there with Willie, visiting the ancient sites and monuments, it occurred to me that I had the opportunity to do something grand. We were in the west of Ireland then, and one day as we were motoring around the countryside, we came upon a fifteenth-century castle. It was no more than a heap of stones, really, sitting forlornly in a little valley or glen, and it was so sad and neglected that my heart went out to it. To make a long story short, I decided to buy it and have it shipped back to America. That took some time, of course. The owner was an old codger by the name of Muldoon, Patrick Lord Muldoon, and he was naturally quite reluctant to sell. Some persuasion was required on my part, but money talks, as they say, and in the end I got what I wanted. The stones of the castle were loaded onto trucks—lorries, as they call them over there—and transported to a ship in Cork. Then they were sent across the ocean, once again loaded onto lorries—trucks, as we call them over here, ha!—and brought to our little spot in the Pennsylvania woods. Amazing, isn't it? The whole thing cost a bundle, I can assure you, but what do you expect? There were over ten thousand stones, and you can imagine what that kind of cargo must have weighed. But why worry when money is no object? The castle arrived less than a month ago, and even as we speak, it's sitting on this property—over there in a meadow at the northern edge of our land. Just think, gentlemen. A fifteenth-century Irish castle destroyed by Oliver Cromwell. An historical ruin of major significance, and Willie and I own it."

"You're not planning to rebuild the thing, are you?" Nashe asked. For some reason, the idea struck him as grotesque. Instead of the castle, he kept seeing the bent old figure of Lord Muldoon, wearily submitting to the blunderbuss of Flower's fortune.

"We thought about it, Willie and I," Flower said, "but we finally dismissed it as impractical. Too many pieces are missing."

"A hodgepodge," Stone said. "In order to rebuild it, we'd have to mix in new materials with the old. And that would defeat the purpose."

"So you have ten thousand stones sitting in a meadow," Nashe said, "and you don't know what to do with them."

"Not anymore," Flower said. "We know exactly what we're going to do with them. Don't we, Willie?"

"Absolutely," Stone said, suddenly beaming with pleasure. "We're going to build a wall."

"A monument, to be more precise," Flower said. "A monument in the shape of a wall."

"How fascinating," Pozzi said, his voice oozing with unctuous contempt. "I can't wait to see it."

"Yes," Flower said, failing to catch the kid's mocking tone, "it's an ingenious solution, if I do say so myself. Rather than try to reconstruct the castle, we're going to turn it into a work of art. To my mind, there's nothing more mysterious or beautiful than a wall. I can already see it: standing out there in the meadow, rising up like some enormous barrier against time. It will be a memorial to itself, gentlemen, a symphony of resurrected stones, and every day it will sing a dirge for the past we carry within us."

"A Wailing Wall," Nashe said.

"Yes," Flower said, "a Wailing Wall. A Wall of Ten Thousand Stones."

"Who's going to put it together for you, Bill?" Pozzi asked. "If you need a good contractor, I might be able to help you out. Or are you and Willie planning to do it yourselves?"

"I think we're a bit too old for that now," Flower said. "Our handyman will hire the workers and oversee the day-to-day operations. I think you've already met him. His name is Calvin Murks. He's the man who let you through the gate."

"And when do things get started?" Pozzi asked.

"Tomorrow," Flower said. "We have a little job of poker to take care of first. Once that's out of the way, the wall is our next project. To tell you the truth, we've been too busy preparing for tonight to give it much attention. But tonight is nearly upon us now, and then it's on to the next thing."

"From cards to castles," Stone said.

"Precisely," Flower answered. "And from talk to food. Believe it or not, my friends, I think it's time for dinner."

Nashe no longer knew what to think. At first he had taken Flower and Stone for a pair of amiable eccentrics—a trifle daft, perhaps, but essentially harmless—but the more he saw of them and listened to what they said, the more uncertain his feelings had become. Sweet little Stone, for example, whose manner was so humble and benign, turned out to spend his days constructing a model of some bizarre, totalitarian world. Of course it was charming, of course it was deft and brilliant and admirable, but there was a kind of warped, voodoo logic to the thing, as if under all the cuteness and intricacy one was supposed to feel a hint of violence, an atmosphere of cruelty and revenge. With Flower, too, everything was ambiguous, difficult to pin down. One moment, he seemed perfectly sensible; the next moment, he sounded like a lunatic, rambling on like an out-and-out madman. There was no question that he was gracious, but even his joviality seemed forced, suggesting that if he did not bombard them with all that pedantic, overly articulate talk, the mask of fellowship might somehow slip from his face. To show what? Nashe had not formed any definite opinion, but he knew that he was feeling more and more unsettled. If nothing else, he told himself, he would have to watch carefully, he would have to stay on his guard.

The dinner turned out to be a ridiculous affair, a low-level farce that seemed to nullify Nashe's doubts and prove that Pozzi had been right all along: Flower and Stone were no more than grown-up children, a pair of half-wit clowns who did not deserve to be taken seriously. By the time they came downstairs from the east wing, the huge walnut table in the dining room had been set for four. Flower and Stone took their usual seats at the two ends, and Nashe and Pozzi sat across from each other in the middle. The initial surprise occurred when Nashe glanced down at his placemat. It was a plastic novelty item that appeared to date from the 1950s, and its vinyl surface was emblazoned with a full-color photograph of Hopalong Cassidy, the old cowboy star from the Saturday matinees. Nashe's first thought was to interpret it as a piece of self-conscious kitsch, a little stab at humor on the part of his hosts, but then the food was brought in, and the meal turned out to be no more than a kiddie banquet, a dinner fit for six-year-olds: hamburger patties on white, untoasted buns, bottles of Coke with plastic straws sticking out of them, potato chips, corn on the cob, and a ketchup dispenser in the shape of a tomato. Except for the absence of paper hats and noisemakers, it reminded Nashe of the birthday parties he had attended as a small boy. He kept looking at Louise, the black maid who served the food, searching her expression for something that would give away the joke, but she never cracked a smile, going about her business with all the solemnity of a waitress in a four-star restaurant. To make matters worse, Flower ate with his paper napkin tucked under his chin (presumably to avoid splattering his white suit), and when he saw that Stone had eaten only half his hamburger, he actually leaned forward with a gluttonous light in his eye and asked his friend if he could finish it for him. Stone was only too happy to comply, but rather than pass his entire plate, he simply picked up the half-eaten hamburger, handed it to Pozzi, and asked him to give it to Flower. From the look on Pozzi's face at that moment, Nashe thought he was about to throw it at the fat man, yelling something like *Catch!* or *Think fast!* as the food sailed through the air. For dessert, Louise brought out four dishes of raspberry Jell-O, each one topped with a little mound of whipped cream and a maraschino cherry.

The strangest thing about the dinner was that no one said anything about it. Flower and Stone acted as though it were perfectly normal for adults to eat this way, and neither one of them offered any apologies or explanations. At one point, Flower mentioned that they always had hamburgers on Monday night, but that was the extent of it. Otherwise, the conversation flowed along as it had before (which is to say, Flower discoursed at length and the others listened to him), and by the time they were crunching on the last of the potato chips, the talk had come around to poker. Flower enumerated all the reasons why the game was so attractive to him— the sense of risk, the mental combat, the absolute purity of it— and for once Pozzi seemed to be paying more than halfhearted attention to him. Nashe himself said nothing, knowing that he had little to add to the subject. Then the meal was over, and the four of them were finally standing up from the table. Flower asked if anyone would care for a drink, and when both Nashe and Pozzi declined, Stone rubbed his hands together and said, "Then maybe we should go into the other room and break out the cards." And just like that, the game began.

# 5

They played in the same room where the tea had been served. A large folding table had been set up in an open area between the sofa and the windows, and when he saw that blank wooden surface and the empty chairs poised around it, Nashe suddenly understood how much was at stake for him. This was the first time he had seriously confronted what he was doing, and the force of that awareness came very abruptly—with a surging of his pulse and a frantic pounding in his head. He was about to gamble his life on that table, he realized, and the insanity of that risk filled him with a kind of awe.

Flower and Stone went about their preparations with a dogged, almost grim sense of purpose, and as Nashe watched them count out the chips and examine the sealed packages of cards, he understood that nothing was going to be simple, that Pozzi's triumph was by no means certain. The kid had stepped outside to fetch his cigarettes from the car, and when he entered the room he was already smoking, puffing away at his Marlboro with short, nervous drags. The festive atmosphere of just a short while ago seemed to vanish in that smoke, and the whole room was suddenly tense with anticipation. Nashe wished that he were going to be playing a more active role in what happened, but that was the bargain he had struck with Pozzi: once the first card was dealt, he would be shunted off to the sidelines, and from then on there would be nothing for him to do but watch and wait.

Flower walked to the far end of the room, opened a safe in the wall beside the billiard table, and asked Nashe and Pozzi to come over and look inside it. "As you can see for yourselves," he said, "it's perfectly empty. I thought we could use it as our bank. Cash for chips, and the cash goes here. Once we've finished playing, we'll open the safe again and distribute the money according to what happens. Does either of you object to that?" Neither one of them did, and Flower continued. "In the interests of fairness," he said, "it seems to me that we should all go in for the same amount. The verdict will be more decisive that way, and since Willie and I aren't just playing for money, we'll be happy to go along with any amount you choose. What do you say, Mr. Nashe? How much were you planning to spend on backing your brother?"

"Ten thousand dollars," Nashe said. "If it's no problem for you, I think I'd like to turn the whole amount into chips before we start."

"Excellent," Flower said. "Ten thousand dollars, a good round sum."

Nashe hesitated for a moment, and then he said: "A dollar for every stone in your wall."

"Indeed," Flower answered, with a touch of condescension in his voice. "And if Jack does his job, maybe you'll have enough to build a castle when you're finished."

"A castle in Spain, perhaps," Stone suddenly chimed in. Then, grinning at his own witticism, he unexpectedly lowered himself to the floor, reached under the billiard table, and pulled out a small satchel. Still crouching on the rug, he opened the bag and started removing thousand-dollar bundles of cash, smacking each one onto the felt surface above him. When he had counted out twenty of these bundles, he zipped up the bag, shoved it back under the table, and climbed to his feet. "Here you are," he said to Flower. "Ten thousand for you and ten thousand for me."

Flower asked Nashe and Pozzi if they would like to count the money themselves, and Nashe was surprised when the kid said yes. As Pozzi meticulously thumbed through each bundle, Nashe slipped ten one-thousand-dollar bills out of his wallet and laid them gently on the billiard table. He had gone to a bank early that morning in New York and converted his horde of hundreds into these monstrous notes. It was not for the convenience so much as to spare himself embarrassment when the time came to purchase the chips—realizing that he did not want to be placed in the position of having to dump wads of rumpled cash onto a stranger's floor. There was something clean and abstract about doing it this way, he found, a sense of mathematical wonder in seeing his world reduced to ten small pieces of paper. He still had a bit left over, of course, but twenty-three hundred dollars didn't amount to much. He had kept this reserve in more modest denominations, stuffing the money into two envelopes and then placing each envelope in an inside breast pocket of his sport jacket. For the time being, that was all he had: twenty-three hundred dollars and a pile of plastic poker chips. If the chips were lost, he wouldn't be able to get very far. Three or four weeks, maybe, and then he'd barely have a pot to piss in.

After a short discussion, Flower, Stone, and Pozzi settled on the ground rules of the game. They would play seven-card stud from start to finish, with no wild cards or jokers—straight hardball all the way, as Pozzi put it. If Pozzi pulled ahead early, the other two would be allowed to replenish their stakes to a maximum of thirty thousand dollars. There would be a five-hundred-dollar limit on bets, and the game would keep going until one player was wiped out. If all three of them managed to stay in, they would call a stop to it after twenty-four hours, no questions asked. Then, like diplomats who had just concluded a peace treaty, they shook hands and walked over to the billiard table to collect their chips.

Nashe took a seat behind Pozzi's right shoulder. Neither Flower nor Stone mentioned it, but he knew that it would be bad form to wander around the room while they were playing. He was an interested party, after all, and he had to avoid doing anything that might look suspicious. If he happened to be in a place where he could glimpse their hands, they might think that he and Pozzi were cheats, communicating through a code of private signals: coughs, for example, or eye blinks, or scratches of the head. The possibilities for deception were infinite. They all knew that, and therefore no one bothered to say a word.

The first few hands were undramatic. The three of them played cautiously, circling like boxers in the early rounds of a fight, testing each other with jabs and head-feints, gradually settling into the feel of the ring. Flower lit up a fresh cigar, Stone chewed on a stick of Doublemint gum, and Pozzi kept a cigarette burning between the fingers of his left hand. Each was pensive and withdrawn, and Nashe began to be a little surprised by the lack of talk. He had always associated poker with a kind of freewheeling roughhouse chatter, an exchange of foul-mouthed jokes and friendly insults, but these three were all business, and it wasn't long before Nashe felt an atmosphere of genuine antagonism insinuate itself into the room. The sounds of the game took over for him, as if everything else had been erased: the clinking of the chips, the noise of the stiff cards being shuffled before each hand, the dry announcements of bets and raises, the plunges into total silence. Eventually, Nashe started taking cigarettes from Pozzi's pack on the table—lighting up unconsciously, not realizing that he was smoking for the first time in over five years.

He was hoping for an early blowout, a massacre, but in the first two hours Pozzi merely held his own, winning about a third of the pots and making little if any headway. The cards weren't coming to him, and any number of times he was forced to fold after betting on the initial three or four cards of a hand, occasionally using his bad luck to bluff out a victory, but clearly not wanting to push that tactic too far. Fortunately, the bets were rather low in the beginning, with no one daring to go in for more than one fifty or two hundred on any given round, and that helped to keep the damage to a minimum. Nor did Pozzi show any signs of panic. Nashe was reassured by that, and as time went on, he sensed that the kid's patience was going to pull them through. Still, it meant giving up on his dream of rapid annihilation, and that was something of a disappointment. It was going to be an intense, grueling affair, he realized, which proved that Flower and Stone were no longer the same players they had been when Pozzi saw them in Atlantic City. Perhaps the lessons with Sid Zeno were responsible for the change. Or perhaps they had always been good and had used that other game to lure Pozzi into this one. Of the two possibilities, Nashe found the second far more disturbing than the first.

Then things took a turn for the better. Just before eleven o'clock, the kid hauled in a three-thousand-dollar pot with aces and queens, and for the next hour he went on a tear, winning three out of every four hands, playing with such assurance and cunning that Nashe could see the other two begin to sag, as if their wills were buckling, visibly giving way to the attack. Flower bought another ten thousand dollars' worth of chips at midnight, and fifteen minutes later Stone sprang for another five. The room was filled with smoke by then, and when Flower finally inched open one of the windows, Nashe was startled by the din of crickets singing in the grass outside. Pozzi was sitting on twenty-seven thousand dollars at that point, and for the first time all evening, Nashe allowed his mind to wander away from the game, feeling that his concentration was somehow no longer required. Everything was under control now, and there could be no harm in drifting off a little, in indulging himself with an occasional reverie about the future. Incongruous as it seemed to him later, he even started to think about settling down somewhere, of moving out to Minnesota and buying a house with the money he was going to win. Costs were low in that part of the country, and he didn't see why there wouldn't be enough for a down payment. After that, he'd talk to Donna about having Juliette live with him again, and then maybe he'd pull some strings in Boston to work out a job with the local fire department. The fire engines in Northfield were pale green, he remembered, and it amused him to think about that, wondering how many other things would be different in the Midwest and how many would be the same.

They opened a new deck of cards at one o'clock, and Nashe took advantage of the interruption to excuse himself to go to the bathroom. He fully intended to come right back, but once he flushed the toilet and stepped back into the darkened hallway, he could not help noticing how pleasurable it felt to be stretching his legs. He was tired from sitting in a cramped position for so many hours, and since he was already on his feet, he decided to take a little stroll through the house to get a second wind. In spite of his exhaustion, he was filled with happiness and excitement, and he did not feel ready to return yet. For the next three or four minutes, he groped his way through the unlit rooms that Flower had shown them before dinner, bumping blindly into doorframes and pieces of furniture until he found himself in the front hall. A lamp was on at the top of the stairs, and as he lifted his eyes to look at it, he suddenly remembered Stone's workshop in the east wing. Nashe hesitated to go up there without permission, but the urge to see the model again was too strong to resist. Brushing aside his qualms, he grabbed hold of the bannister and started up the stairs two at a time.

He spent close to an hour looking at the City of the World, examining it in a way that had not been possible before—without the distraction of pretending to be polite, without Flower's commentaries buzzing in his ears. This time he was able to sink himself into the details, moving slowly from one area of the model to another, studying the minute architectural flourishes, the painstaking application of colors, the vivid, sometimes startling expressions on the faces of the tiny, one-inch figures. He saw things that had entirely escaped him during the first visit, and many of these discoveries turned out to be marked by wicked flashes of humor: a dog pissing against a fireplug in front of the Hall of Justice; a group of twenty men and women marching down the street, all of them wearing glasses; a masked robber slipping on a banana peel in a back alley. But these funny bits only made the other elements seem more ominous, and after a while Nashe found himself concentrating almost exclusively on the prison. In one corner of the exercise yard, the inmates were talking in small groups, playing basketball, reading books; but then, with a kind of horror, he saw a blindfolded prisoner standing against the wall just behind them, about to be executed by a firing squad. What did this mean? What crime had this man committed, and why was he being punished in this terrible way? For all the warmth and sentimentality depicted in the model, the overriding mood was one of terror, of dark dreams sauntering down the avenues in broad daylight. A threat of punishment seemed to hang in the air—as if this were a city at war with itself, struggling to mend its ways before the prophets came to announce the arrival of a murderous, avenging God.

Just as he was about to switch off the light and leave the room, Nashe turned around and walked back to the model. Fully conscious of what he was about to do, and yet with no sense of guilt, feeling no compunctions whatsoever, he found the spot where Flower and Stone were standing in front of the candy store (arms flung around each other's shoulders, looking at the lottery ticket with their heads bowed in concentration), lowered his thumb and middle finger to the place where their feet joined the floor, and gave a little tug. The figures were glued fast, and so he tried again, this time with a swift, impulsive jerk. There was a dull snap, and a moment later he was holding the two wooden men in the palm of his hand. Scarcely bothering to look at them, he shoved the souvenir into his pocket. It was the first time that Nashe had stolen anything since he was a small boy. He was not sure why he had done it, but the last thing he was looking for just then was a reason. Even if he could not articulate it to himself, he knew that it had been absolutely necessary. He knew that in the same way he knew his own name.

When Nashe took his seat behind Pozzi again, Stone was shuffling the cards, getting ready to deal the next hand. It was past two o'clock by then, and one look at the table was enough to tell Nashe that everything had changed, that tremendous battles had been fought in his absence. The kid's mountain of chips had dwindled to one-third its former size, and if Nashe's calculations were correct, that meant they were back where they had been at the start, perhaps even a thousand or two in the hole. It didn't seem possible. Pozzi had been flying high, on the brink of sewing up the whole business, and now they seemed to have him on the run, pushing hard to break his confidence, to crush him once and for all. Nashe could barely imagine what had happened.

"Where the fuck have you been?" Pozzi said, whispering with pent-up fury.

"I took a nap on the sofa in the living room," Nashe lied. "I couldn't help it. I was exhausted."

"Shit. Don't you know better than to walk out on me like that? You're my lucky charm, asshole. As soon as you left, the goddamn roof started to collapse."

Flower interrupted at that point, too pleased with himself not to jump in and offer his own version of what had taken place. "We've had some big hands," he said, trying not to gloat. "Your brother went for broke on a full house, but Willie came through on the last card and beat him out with four sixes. Then, just a few hands later, there was a dramatic showdown, a duel to the death. In the end, my three kings prevailed over your brother's three jacks. You've missed some excitement, young man, I can tell you that. This is poker as it was meant to be played."

Curiously enough, Nashe did not feel alarmed by these drastic reversals. If anything, Pozzi's slump had a galvanizing effect on him, and the more frustrated and confused the kid became, the more Nashe's confidence seemed to grow, as if it were precisely this sort of crisis that he had been searching for all along.

"Maybe it's time to inject a few vitamins into my brother's stake," he said, smiling at the pun. He reached into his jacket pockets and pulled out the two envelopes of money. "Here's twenty-three hundred dollars," he said. "Why don't we buy some more chips, Jack? It's not much, but at least it will give you a little more room to work with."

Pozzi knew that it was the last money Nashe had in the world, and he hesitated to accept it. "I'm still hanging in there," he said. "Let's give it a few more hands and see what happens."

"Don't worry about it, Jack," Nashe said. "Take the money now. It'll change the mood, help to get you going again. You've just hit a lull, that's all, but you'll come roaring back. It happens all the time."

But Pozzi didn't come roaring back. Even with the new chips, things continued to go against him. He won the occasional hand, but those victories were never large enough to shore up his eroding funds, and every time his cards seemed to offer some promise, he would bet too much and wind up losing, squandering his resources on luckless, desperation efforts. By the time dawn came, he was down to eighteen hundred dollars. His nerves were shot, and if Nashe still had any hopes of winning, he had only to study Pozzi's trembling hands to know that the hour of miracles had passed. The birds were waking up outside, and as the first glimmers of light entered the room, Pozzi's bruised and pale face seemed ghastly in its whiteness. He was turning into a corpse before Nashe's eyes.

Still, the show wasn't over yet. On the next hand, Pozzi was dealt two kings in the hole and the ace of hearts up, and when the fourth card was another king—the king of hearts—Nashe sensed that the tide was about to turn again. The betting was heavy, however, and before the fifth card was even dealt, the kid had just three hundred dollars left. Flower and Stone were running him out of the game: he wasn't going to have enough to see him to the end of the hand. Without even thinking, Nashe stood up and said to Flower, "I want to make a proposition."

"A proposition?" Flower said. "What are you talking about?"

"We're almost out of chips."

"Fine. Then go ahead and buy some more."

"We would, but we've also run out of cash."

"Then I suppose that means the game is over. If Jack can't stay in for the rest of the hand, then we'll have to put an end to it. Those were the rules we agreed on before."

"I know that. But I want to propose something else, something other than cash."

"Please, Mr. Nashe, no IOUs. I don't know you well enough to offer credit."

"I'm not asking for credit. I want to put up my car as collateral."

"Your car? And what kind of car is that? A second-hand Chevy?"

"No, it's a good car. A year-old Saab in perfect condition."

"And what am I supposed to do with it? Willie and I already have three cars in the garage. We're not in the market for another one."

"Sell it, then. Give it away. What difference does it make? It's the only thing I have to offer. Otherwise, the game has to stop. And why put an end to it when we don't have to?"

"And how much do you think this car of yours is worth?"

"I don't know. I paid sixteen thousand dollars for it. It's probably worth at least half that now, maybe even ten."

"Ten thousand dollars for a used car? I'll give you three."

"That's absurd. Why don't you go outside and have a look at it before you make an offer?"

"Because I'm in the middle of a hand now. I don't want to break my concentration."

"Then give me eight, and we'll call it a deal."

"Five. That's my final offer. Five thousand dollars."

"Seven."

"No, five. Take it or leave it, Mr. Nashe."

"All right, I'll take it. Five thousand for the car. But don't worry. We'll deduct it from our winnings at the end. I wouldn't want you to be stuck with something you don't want."

"We'll see about that. In the meantime, let's count out the chips and get on with it. I can't stand these interruptions. They destroy all the pleasure."

Pozzi had been given an emergency transfusion, but that did not mean he was going to live. He would pull through the present crisis, perhaps, but the long-term prospects were still cloudy, touch-and-go at best. Nashe had done everything he could, however, and that in itself was a consolation, even a point of pride. But he also knew that the blood bank was exhausted. He had gone much farther than he thought he would, as far as it was possible for him to go, but still it might not be far enough.

Pozzi had the two kings in the hole, with the king and ace of hearts showing. Flower's two up cards were a six of diamonds and a seven of clubs—a possible straight, perhaps, but still weak when compared to the three kings the kid was already holding. Stone's hand was a potential threat, however. Two eights were showing, and from the way he had led off the betting on the fourth card (coming on strong, with consecutive raises of three hundred and four hundred dollars), Nashe suspected that good things were hidden in his hole cards. Another pair, perhaps, or even the third and fourth eights. Nashe pinned his hopes on Pozzi drawing the fourth king, but he wanted it to come at the end, face-down on the seventh deal. In the meantime, he thought, give him two more hearts. Even better, give him the queen and jack of hearts. Make it look as though he's risking everything on a possible straight flush—and then stun them with the four kings at the end.

Stone dealt the fifth cards. Flower received a five of spades; Pozzi got his heart. It wasn't the queen or jack, but it was almost as good: the eight of hearts. The flush was still intact, and Stone no longer had a chance of drawing the fourth eight. As Stone dealt himself the three of clubs, Pozzi turned to Nashe and smiled for the first time in several hours. All of a sudden, things were looking hopeful.

In spite of the three, Stone opened by betting the limit, the full five hundred. This puzzled Nashe somewhat, but then he decided it had to be a bluff. They were trying to squeeze out the kid, and with so much money in reserve, they could afford to take a few wild punches. Flower stayed in with his possible straight, and then Pozzi saw the five hundred and raised another five hundred, which Stone and Flower both matched.

Flower's sixth card turned out to be the jack of diamonds, and the moment he saw it skidding across the table, he let out a sigh of disappointment. Nashe assumed that he was dead. Then, as if by magic, Pozzi came up with the three of hearts. When Stone drew the nine of spades, however, Nashe suddenly began to worry that Pozzi's cards were too strong. But Stone bet high again, and even after Flower dropped out, the hand was alive and well, still growing as they moved into the home stretch.

Stone and Pozzi went head to head on their sixth cards, going back and forth in a flurry of raises and counterraises. By the time they were done, Pozzi had just fifteen hundred dollars left to use on the last deal. Nashe had figured that ransoming the car would buy them at least another hour or two, but the betting had become so furious that everything had suddenly boiled down to the one hand. The pot was enormous. If Pozzi won, he would be off and running again, and this time Nashe sensed that there would be no stopping him. But he had to win. If he lost, that would be the end of it.

Nashe knew that it would be too much to hope for the fourth king. The odds against it were simply too great. But no matter what happened, Stone would have to assume that Pozzi was holding a flush. The four exposed hearts had seen to that, and since the kid was playing with his back to the wall, his big bets would seem to eliminate the possibility of a bluff. Even if the seventh card was a dud, the three kings would probably do the trick anyway. It was a good hand, Nashe thought, a solid hand, and from the looks of things on the table, the chances of Stone beating it were slim.

Pozzi drew the four of clubs. In spite of everything, Nashe could not help feeling a bit let down. Not so much for the king, perhaps, but at least for the absence of another heart. *Heart failure*, he said to himself, not sure if it was meant entirely in jest, and then Stone dealt himself the last card and they were ready to square off and finish the hand.

It all happened very quickly. Stone, still leading with his two eights, went in for five hundred. Pozzi saw the five hundred, then raised another five hundred. Stone saw Pozzi's raise, hesitated for a second or two with the chips in his hand, and clinked down another five hundred. Then, with only five hundred left at that point, the kid pushed his remaining chips into the center of the table. "All right, Willie," he said. "Let's see what you've got."

Stone's face gave away nothing. One by one, he turned over his hole cards, but even after all three of them were showing, it would have been difficult to tell whether he had won or lost. "I have these two eights," he said. "And then I have this ten" (turning it over), "and then I have this other ten" (turning it over), "and then I have this third eight" (turning over the seventh and last card).

"A full house!" Flower roared, pounding his fist on the table. "What can you do to answer that, Jack?"

"Not a thing," Pozzi said, not bothering to turn over his cards. "He's got me beat." The kid stared down at the table for several moments, as if trying to absorb what had happened. Then, mustering his courage, he wheeled around and grinned at Nashe. "Well, old buddy," he said. "It looks like we have to walk home."

As he spoke those words, Pozzi's face was filled with such embarrassment that Nashe could only feel sorry for him. It was odd, but the fact was that he felt worse for the kid than he felt for himself. Everything was lost, and yet the only feeling inside him was one of pity.

Nashe clapped Pozzi on the shoulder, as if to reassure him, and then he heard Flower burst out laughing. "I hope you boys have comfortable shoes," the fat man said. "It's a good eighty or ninety miles back to New York, you know."

"Cool your jets, Tubby," Pozzi said, finally forgetting his manners. "We owe you five thousand bucks. We'll give you a marker, you give us the car, and we'll pay you back within a week."

Flower, unruffled by the insult, burst out laughing again. "Oh no," he said. "That's not the deal I made with Mr. Nashe. The car belongs to me now. If you don't have any other way of getting home, then you'll just have to walk. That's the way it goes."

"What kind of bullshit poker player are you, Hippo-Face?" Pozzi said. "Of course you'll take our marker. That's the way it works."

"I said it before," Flower answered calmly, "and I'll say it again. No credit. I'd be a fool to trust a pair like you. The minute you drove away from here, my money would be gone."

"All right, all right," Nashe said, hastily trying to improvise a solution. "We'll cut for it. If I win, you give us back the car. Just like that. One cut, and it's finished."

"No problem," Flower said. "But what happens if you don't win?"

"Then I owe you ten thousand dollars," Nashe said.

"You should think carefully, my friend," Flower said. "This hasn't been your lucky night. Why make things worse for yourself?"

"Because we need the car to get out of here, asshole," Pozzi said.

"No problem," Flower repeated. "But just remember that I warned you."

"Shuffle the cards, Jack," Nashe said, "and then hand them to Mr. Flower. We'll give him the first try."

Pozzi opened a new deck, discarded the jokers, and shuffled as Nashe had asked him to. With exaggerated ceremony, he leaned forward and slapped the cards down in front of Flower. The fat man didn't hesitate. He had nothing to lose, after all, and so he promptly reached for the cards, lifting half the deck between his thumb and middle finger. A moment later he was holding up the seven of hearts. Stone shrugged when he saw it, and Pozzi clapped his hands—just once, very fiercely, celebrating the mediocre draw.

Then Nashe was holding the deck in his hands. He felt utterly blank inside, and for a brief moment he marveled at how ridiculous this little drama was. Just before he cut, he thought to himself: This is the most ridiculous moment of my life. Then he winked at Pozzi, lifted the cards, and came up with the four of diamonds.

"A four!" Flower yelled, slapping his hand against his forehead in disbelief. "A four! You couldn't even beat my seven!"

Everything went silent after that. A long moment passed, and then, in a voice that sounded more weary than triumphant, Stone finally said: "Ten thousand dollars. It looks like we've hit the magic number again."

Flower leaned back in his chair, puffed on his cigar for several moments, and studied Nashe and Pozzi as though he were seeing them for the first time. His expression made Nashe think of a high school principal sitting in his office with a couple of delinquent kids. His face did not reflect anger so much as puzzlement, as if he had just been presented with a philosophical problem that had no apparent answer. A punishment would have to be meted out, that was certain, but for the moment he seemed to have no idea what to suggest. He didn't want to be harsh, but neither did he want to be too lenient. He needed something to fit the crime, a fair punishment that would have some educational value to it— not punishment for its own sake, but something creative, something that would teach the culprits a lesson.

"I think we have a dilemma here," he said at last.

"Yes," Stone said. "A real dilemma. What you might call a situation."

"These two fellows owe us money," Flower continued, acting as though Nashe and Pozzi were no longer there. "If we let them leave, they'll never pay us back. But if we don't let them leave, they won't have a chance to come up with the money they owe us."

"I guess you'll just have to trust us, then," Pozzi said. "Isn't that right, Mr. Butterball?"

Flower ignored Pozzi's remark and turned to Stone. "What do you think, Willie?" he said. "It's something of a quandary, isn't it?"

As he listened to this conversation, Nashe suddenly remembered Juliette's trust fund. It probably wouldn't be difficult to withdraw ten thousand dollars from it, he thought. A call to the bank in Minnesota could get things started, and by the end of the day the money would be sitting in Flower and Stone's account. It was a practical solution, but once he worked out the sequence in his head, he rejected it, appalled at himself for even considering such a thing. The equation was too terrible: to pay off his gambling debts by stealing from his daughter's future. No matter what happened, it was out of the question. He had brought this problem down on himself, and now he would have to take his medicine. Like a man, he thought. He would have to take it like a man.

"Yes," Stone said, mulling over Flower's last comment, "it's a difficult one, all right. But that doesn't mean we won't think of something." He lapsed into thought for ten or twenty seconds, and then his face gradually began to brighten. "Of course," he said, "there's always the wall."

"The wall?" Flower said. "What do you mean by that?"

"The wall," Stone repeated. "Someone has to build it."

"Ah . . . ," Flower said, catching on at last. "The wall! A brilliant idea, Willie. By God, I think you've really surpassed yourself this time."

"Honest work for an honest wage," Stone said.

"Exactly," Flower said. "And little by little the debt will be paid off."

But Pozzi was not having any of it. The instant he realized what they were proposing, his mouth literally dropped open in astonishment. "You've got to be kidding," he said. "If you think I'm going to do that, you're out of your minds. There's no way. There's absolutely no fucking way." Then, starting to lift himself out of his chair, he turned to Nashe and said, "Come on, Jim, let's get out of here. These two guys are full of shit."

"Take it easy, kid," Nashe said. "There's no harm in listening. We've got to work out something, after all."

"No harm!" Pozzi shouted. "They belong in the nuthouse, can't you see that? They're one-hundred-percent bonkers."

Pozzi's agitation had a curiously calming effect on Nashe, as if the more vehemently the kid acted, the more clearheaded Nashe found it necessary to become. There was no doubt that things had taken a strange turn, but Nashe realized that he had somehow been expecting it, and now that it was happening, there was no panic inside him. He felt lucid, utterly in control of himself.

"Don't worry about it, Jack," he said. "Just because they make us an offer, that doesn't mean we have to accept. It's a question of manners, that's all. If they have something to tell us, then we owe them the courtesy of hearing them out."

"It's a waste of time," Pozzi muttered, sinking back into his chair. "You don't negotiate with madmen. Once you start to do that, your brain gets all fucked up."

"I'm glad you brought your brother along with you," Flower said, letting out a sigh of disgust. "At least there's one reasonable man we can talk to."

"Shit," Pozzi said. "He's not my brother. He's just some guy I met on Saturday. I barely even know him."

"Well, whether you're related to him or not," Flower said, "you're lucky to have him here. For the fact is, young man, you're staring at a heap of trouble. You and Nashe owe us ten thousand dollars, and if you try to walk out without paying, we'll call the police. It's as simple as that."

"I already said we'd listen to you," Nashe interrupted. "You don't have to make threats."

"I'm not making threats," Flower said. "I'm just presenting you with the facts. Either you show some cooperation and we work out an amicable arrangement, or we take more drastic measures. There are no other alternatives. Willie has come up with a solution, a perfectly ingenious solution in my opinion, and unless you have something better to offer, I think we should get down to brass tacks."

"The specifics," Stone said. "Hourly wage, living quarters, food. The practical details. It's probably best to get those things settled before we start."

"You can live right out there in the meadow," Flower said.

"There's a trailer on the premises already—what they call a mobile home. It hasn't been used for some time, but it's in perfectly good condition. Calvin lived there a few years ago while we were building his cottage for him. So there's no problem about putting you up. All you have to do is move in."

"It has a kitchen," Stone added. "A fully equipped kitchen. A refrigerator, a stove, a sink, all the modern conveniences. A well for water, electrical hookup, baseboard heating. You can do your cooking there and eat whatever you want. Calvin will keep you stocked with supplies, whatever you ask him for he'll bring. Just give him a shopping list every day, and he'll go into town and get what you need."

"We'll provide you with work clothes, of course," Flower said, "and if there's anything else you want, all you have to do is ask. Books, newspapers, magazines. A radio. Extra blankets and towels. Games. Whatever you decide. We don't want you to be uncomfortable, after all. In the final analysis, you might even enjoy yourselves. The work won't be too strenuous, and you'll be outdoors in this beautiful weather. It will be a working holiday, so to speak, a short, therapeutic respite from your normal lives. And every day you'll see another section of the wall go up. That will be immensely satisfying, I think: to see the tangible fruits of your labor, to be able to step back and see the progress you've made. Little by little, the debt will be paid off, and when the time comes for you to go, not only will you walk out of here free men, but you'll have left something important behind you."

"How long do you think it will take?" Nashe said.

"That depends," Stone answered. "You'll get so much per hour. Once your total earnings come to ten thousand dollars, you'll be free to go."

"What if we finish the wall before we've earned ten thousand dollars?"

"In that case," Flower said, "we'll consider the debt paid in full."

"And if we don't finish, what are you planning to pay us?"

"Something commensurate with the task. A normal wage for workers on this kind of job."

"Such as?"

"Five, six dollars an hour."

"That's too low. We won't even consider it for less than twelve."

"This isn't brain surgery, Mr. Nashe. It's unskilled labor. Piling one stone on top of another. It doesn't require much study to do that."

"Still, we're not going to do it for six dollars an hour. If you can't do any better than that, you might as well call the police."

"Eight, then. My final offer."

"It's still not good enough."

"Stubborn, aren't you? And what if I went up to ten? What would you say to that?"

"Let's figure it out, and then we'll see."

"Fine. It won't take but a second. Ten dollars apiece comes to twenty dollars an hour for the two of you. If you put in an average of ten hours of work—just to keep the figures simple—then you'll be earning two hundred dollars a day. Two hundred into ten thousand is fifty. Which means it will take you approximately fifty days. If it's late August now, that comes out to some time in the middle of October. Not so long. You'll be finished just as the leaves are beginning to turn."

Bit by bit, Nashe found himself giving in to the idea, gradually accepting the wall as the only solution to his predicament. Exhaustion might have played a part in it—the lack of sleep, the inability to think anymore—but somehow he thought not. Where was he going to go, anyway? His money was gone, his car was gone, his life was in a shambles. If nothing else, perhaps those fifty days would give him a chance to take stock, to sit still for the first time in over a year and ponder his next move. It was almost a relief to have the decision taken out of his hands, to know that he had finally stopped running. The wall would not be a punishment so much as a cure, a one-way journey back to earth.

The kid was beside himself, however, and all during the conversation he kept emitting disgruntled, petulant noises, aghast at Nashe's acquiescence and the insane haggling over money. Before Nashe had a chance to shake hands on a deal with Flower, Pozzi grabbed hold of his arm and announced that he had to talk to him in private. Then, not bothering to wait for a response, he yanked Nashe out of his chair and dragged him into the hall, slamming the door shut with his foot.

"Come on," he said, still pulling on Nashe's arm. "Let's go. It's time to leave."

But Nashe shrugged off Pozzi's hand and stood his ground. "We can't leave," he said. "We owe them money, and I'm not in the mood to get hauled off to jail."

"They're just bluffing. There's no way they'd get the fuzz involved in this."

"You're wrong, Jack. Guys with money like that can do anything they want. The minute those two called, the cops would jump. We'd be picked up before we were half a mile from here."

"You sound scared, Jimbo. Not a good sign. It makes you look ugly."

"I'm not scared. I'm just being smart."

"Crazy, you mean. Keep it up, pal, and pretty soon you'll be as crazy as they are."

"It's less than two months, Jack, no big deal. They'll feed us, give us a place to live, and before you know it, we'll be gone. Why worry about it? We might even have some fun."

"Fun? You call lifting stones fun? It sounds like a goddamn chain gang to me."

"It can't kill us. Not fifty days of it. Besides, the exercise will probably do us some good. Like lifting weights. People pay good money to do that in health clubs. We've already paid our membership fee, so we might as well take advantage of it."

"How do you know it will be only fifty days?"

"Because that's the agreement."

"And what if they don't stick to the agreement?"

"Look, Jack, don't worry so much. If we run into any problems, we'll take care of them."

"It's a mistake to trust those fuckers, I'm telling you."

"Then maybe you're right, maybe you should go now. I'm the one who got us into this mess, so the debt is my responsibility."

"I'm the one who lost."

"You lost the money, but I'm the one who cut for the car."

"You mean you'd stay here and do it alone?"

"That's what I'm saying."

"Then you really are crazy, aren't you?"

"What difference does it make what I am? You're a free man, Jack. You can walk out now, and I won't hold it against you. That's a promise. No hard feelings."

Pozzi looked at Nashe for a long moment, wrestling with the choice he had just been given, searching Nashe's eyes to see if he had meant what he had said. Then, very slowly, a smile began to form on the kid's face, as if he had just understood the punch line to an obscure joke. "Shit," he said. "Do you really think I'd leave you alone, old man? If you did that work yourself, you'd probably drop dead of a heart attack."

Nashe had not been expecting it. He had assumed that Pozzi would jump at his offer, and during those moments of certainty, he had already begun to imagine what it would be like to live out in the meadow alone, trying to resign himself to that solitude, coming to a point of such resolve that he was almost beginning to welcome it. But now that the kid was in, he felt glad. As they walked back into the room to announce their decision, it fairly stunned him to realize how glad he was.

They spent the next hour putting it all in writing, drawing up a document that stated the terms of their agreement in the clearest possible language, with clauses that covered the amount of the debt, the conditions of repayment, the hourly wage, and so on. Stone typed it out twice, and then all four of them signed at the bottom of both copies. After that, Flower announced that he was going off to look for Murks and make the necessary arrangements concerning the trailer, the work site, and the purchase of supplies. It would take several hours, he said, and in the meantime they were welcome to have breakfast in the kitchen if they were hungry. Nashe asked a question about the design of the wall, but Flower told him not to trouble himself about that. He and Stone had already finished the blueprints, and Murks knew exactly what had to be done. As long as they followed Calvin's instructions, nothing could go wrong. On that confident note, the fat man left the room, and Stone led Nashe and Pozzi to the kitchen, where he asked Louise to cook up some breakfast for them. Then, mumbling a brief, awkward good-bye, the thin man vanished as well.

The maid clearly resented having to prepare the meal, and as she went about the business of beating eggs and frying bacon, she took out her displeasure by refusing to address a word to either one of them—muttering a string of invective under her breath, acting as if the task were an insult to her dignity. Nashe realized how thoroughly things had changed for them. He and Pozzi had been stripped of their status, and henceforth they would no longer be treated as invited guests. They had been reduced to the level of hired hands, tramps who come begging for leftovers at the back door. It was impossible not to notice the difference, and as he sat there waiting for his food, he wondered how Louise had caught on so quickly to their demotion. The day before, she had been perfectly polite and respectful; now, just sixteen hours later, she could barely hide her contempt for them. And yet neither Flower nor Stone had said a word to her. It was as if some secret communiqué had been broadcast silently through the house, informing her that he and Pozzi no longer counted, that they had been relegated to the category of nonpersons.

But the food was excellent, and they both ate with considerable appetite, wolfing down extra helpings of toast along with numerous cups of coffee. Once their stomachs were full, however, they lapsed into a state of drowsiness, and for the next half hour they struggled to keep their eyes open by smoking more of Pozzi's cigarettes. The long night had finally caught up with them, and neither one seemed capable of talking anymore. Eventually, the kid dozed off in his chair, and for a long time after that Nashe just stared into space, seeing nothing as his body gave in to a deep and languorous exhaustion.

Murks arrived a few minutes past ten, bursting into the kitchen with a clatter of work boots and jangling keys. The noise immediately brought Nashe back to life, and he was out of his chair before Murks reached the table. Pozzi slept on, however, oblivious to the commotion around him.

"What's the matter with him?" Murks said, gesturing with his thumb at Pozzi.

"He had a rough night," Nashe said.

"Yeah, well, from what I heard, things didn't go too good for you either."

"I don't need as much sleep as he does."

Murks pondered the remark for a moment, and then he said, "Jack and Jim, huh? And which one are you, fella?"

"Jim."

"I guess that makes your friend Jack."

"Good thinking. After that, the rest is easy. I'm Jim Nashe, and he's Jack Pozzi. It shouldn't take long for you to get the hang of it."

"Yeah, I remember. Pozzi. What's he, some kind of Spaniard or something?"

"More or less. He's a direct descendant of Christopher Columbus."

"No kidding?"

"Would I make up something like that?"

Again, Murks fell silent, as if trying to absorb this curious bit of information. Then, looking at Nashe with his pale blue eyes, he abruptly changed the subject. "I took your stuff out of the car and put it in the jeep," he said. "The bags and all those tapes. I figured you might as well have it with you. They said you're going to be here for a while."

"And what about the car?"

"I drove it over to my place. If you want, you can sign the registration papers tomorrow. There's no rush."

"You mean they gave the car to you?"

"Who else? They didn't want it, and Louise just bought a new car last month. It seems like a good one to me. Handles real nice."

Murks's statement hit him like a fist in the stomach, and for a moment or two Nashe actually felt himself fighting back tears. It had not occurred to him to think about the Saab, and now, all of a sudden, the sense of loss was absolute, as if he had just been told his closest friend was dead. "Sure," he said, making a great effort not to show his feelings. "Just bring the papers around to me tomorrow."

"Good. We'll be plenty busy today anyway. There's lots to do. Got to get you boys settled in first, and then I'll show you the plans and walk you around the place. You wouldn't believe how many stones there are. It's about like a mountain is what it is, an honest-to-goodness mountain. I ain't never seen so many stones in all my life."

# 6

There was no road from the house to the meadow, so Murks drove the jeep straight through the woods. He was apparently an old hand at it, and he charged along at a frenetic pace—maneuvering around the trees with abrupt, hairpin turns, bouncing recklessly over stones and exposed roots, yelling at Nashe and Pozzi to duck clear of hanging branches. The jeep made a tremendous racket, and birds and squirrels scattered as they approached, bolting helter-skelter through the leaf-covered darkness. After Murks had roared along in this way for fifteen minutes or so, the sky suddenly brightened, and they found themselves on a grassy verge studded with low-lying bushes and thin shoots. The meadow was just ahead of them. The first thing Nashe noticed was the trailer— a pale green structure propped up on several rows of cinder blocks—and then, all the way at the other end of the field, he saw the remains of Lord Muldoon's castle. Contrary to what Murks had told them, the stones did not form a mountain so much as a series of mountains—a dozen haphazard piles jutting up from the ground at different angles and elevations, a chaos of towering rubble strewn about like a set of children's blocks. The meadow itself was much larger than Nashe had expected. Surrounded by woods on all four sides, it seemed to cover an area roughly equivalent to three or four football fields: it was an immense territory of short, stubbled grass, as flat and silent as the bottom of a lake. Nashe turned around and looked for the house, but it was no longer visible. He had imagined that Flower and Stone would be standing at a window watching them through a telescope or a pair of binoculars, but the woods were mercifully in the way. Just knowing that he would be hidden from them was something to be thankful for, and in those first moments after climbing from the jeep, he began to sense that he had already won back a measure of his freedom. Yes, the meadow was a desolate place; but there was also a certain forlorn beauty to it, an air of remoteness and calm that could almost be called soothing. Not knowing what else to think, Nashe tried to take heart from that.

The trailer turned out to be not half bad. It was hot and dusty inside, but the dimensions were spacious enough for two people to live there in reasonable comfort: a kitchen, a bathroom, a living room, and two small bedrooms. The electricity worked, the toilet flushed, and water ran into the sink when Murks turned the faucet. The furnishings were sparse, and what there was had a dull and impersonal look to it, but it was no worse than what you found in your average cheap motel. There were towels in the bathroom, the kitchen was stocked with cookware and eating utensils, there was bedding on the beds. Nashe felt relieved, but Pozzi didn't say much of anything, walking through the tour as though his mind were somewhere else. Still brooding about poker, Nashe thought. He decided to leave the kid alone, but it was hard not to wonder how long it would take him to get over it.

They aired out the place by opening the windows and turning on the fan, and then they sat down to study the blueprints in the kitchen. "We're not talking about anything fancy here," Murks said, "but that's probably just as well. This thing's going to be a monster, and there's no point in trying to make it pretty." He carefully removed the plans from a cardboard cylinder and spread them out on the table, weighting down each corner with a coffee cup. "What you got here is your basic wall," he continued. "Two thousand feet long and twenty feet high—ten rows of a thousand stones each. No twists or turns, no arches or columns, no frills of any sort. Just your basic, no-nonsense wall."

"Two thousand feet," Nashe said. "That's more than a third of a mile long."

"That's what I'm trying to tell you. This baby is a giant."

"We'll never finish," Pozzi said. "There's no way two men can build that sucker in fifty days."

"The way I understand it," Murks said, "you don't have to. You just put in your time, do as much as you can, and that's it."

"You got it, gramps," Pozzi said. "That's it."

"We'll see how far you get," Murks said. "They say faith can move mountains. Well, maybe muscles can do it, too."

The plans showed the wall cutting a diagonal line between the northeast and southwest corners of the meadow. As Nashe discovered after studying the diagram, this was the only way a two-thousand-foot wall could fit within the boundaries of the rectangular field (which was roughly twelve hundred feet wide and eighteen hundred feet long). But just because the diagonal was a mathematical necessity, that did not make it a bad choice. To the extent that he bothered to think about it, even Nashe admitted that a slant was preferable to a square. The wall would have a greater visual impact that way—splitting the meadow into triangles rather than boxes—and for whatever it was worth, it pleased him that no other solution was possible.

"Twenty feet high," Nashe said. "We're going to need a scaffold, won't we?"

"When the time comes," Murks said.

"And who's supposed to build it? Not us, I hope."

"Don't worry about things that might never happen," Murks said. "We don't have to think about a scaffold until you get to the third row. That's two thousand stones. If you get that far in fifty days, I can build you something real fast. Won't take me longer than a few hours."

"And then there's the cement," Nashe continued. "Are you going to bring in a machine, or do we have to mix it ourselves?"

"I'll get you bags from the hardware store in town. There's a bunch of wheelbarrows out in the tool shed, and you can use one of those to mix it in. You won't need much—just a dab or two in the right places. Those stones are solid. Once they're up, there ain't nothing that's going to knock them down."

Murks rolled up the plans and slipped them back into the tube. Nashe and Pozzi then followed him outside, and the three of them climbed into the jeep and drove to the other end of the meadow. Murks explained that the grass was short because he had mowed it just a few days before, and the fact was that it smelled good, adding a hint of sweetness to the air that reminded Nashe of things from long ago. It put him in a pleasant mood, and by the time the little drive was over, he was no longer fretting about the details of the work. The day was too beautiful for that, and with the warmth of the sun pouring down on his face, it seemed ridiculous to worry about anything. Just take it as it comes, he told himself. Just be glad you're alive.

It had been one thing to look at the stones from a distance, but now that he was there, he found it impossible not to want to touch them, to run his hands along their surfaces and discover what they felt like. Pozzi seemed to respond in the same way, and for the first few minutes the two of them just wandered around the clusters of granite, timidly patting the smooth gray blocks. There was something awesome about them, a stillness that was almost frightening. The stones were so massive, so cool against the skin, it was hard to believe they had once belonged to a castle. They felt too old for that—as if they had been dug out from the deepest layers of the earth, as if they were relics from a time before man had ever been dreamt of.

Nashe saw a stray stone at the edge of one of the piles and bent down to lift it, curious to know how heavy it was. The first tug sent a knot of pressure into his lower back, and by the time he had the thing off the ground, he was grunting from the strain of it, feeling as though the muscles in his legs were about to cramp. He took three or four steps and then put it down. "Jesus," he said. "Not very cooperative, is it?"

"They weigh somewhere between sixty and seventy pounds," Murks said. "Just enough to make you feel each one."

"I felt it," Nashe said. "There's no doubt about that."

"So what's the scoop, old-timer?" Pozzi said, turning to Murks. "Do we move these pebbles with the jeep, or are you going to give us something else? I'm looking around for a truck, but I don't see one in the vicinity."

Murks smiled and slowly shook his head. "You don't think they're stupid, do you?"

"What's that supposed to mean?" Nashe said.

"If we give you a truck, you'll just use it to sneak out of here. That's pretty obvious, isn't it? No sense in giving you an opportunity to escape."

"I didn't know we were in prison," Nashe said. "I thought we'd been hired to do some work."

"That's it," Murks said. "But they don't want you welshing on the deal."

"So how do we move them?" Pozzi said. "They're not sugar cubes, you know. We can't just stuff them in our pockets."

"No need to get worked up about it," Murks said. "We've got a wagon in the shed, and it'll do the job just fine."

"It will take forever that way," Nashe said.

"So what? As long as you put in your hours, you boys are home free. Why should you care how long it takes?"

"God dang it," Pozzi said, snapping his fingers and talking in a dumb hick's voice. "Thanks for setting me straight, Calvin. I mean, hell, what's to complain about? We've got our wagon now, and when you consider how much help it'll be with the work— and the Lord's work it is, too, Brother Calvin—I guess we should be feeling pretty happy. I just wasn't looking at it in the right way. Why Jim and me here, we've got to be about the luckiest fellas that ever walked the earth."

They drove back to the trailer after that and unloaded Nashe's things from the jeep, depositing the suitcases and the bags of books and tapes on the living room floor. Then they sat down at the kitchen table again and drew up a shopping list. Murks did the writing, and he formed his letters so slowly and painstakingly that it took them close to an hour to cover everything: the various foods and drinks and condiments, the work clothes, the boots and gloves, the extra clothes for Pozzi, the sunglasses, the soaps and garbage bags, the flyswatters. Once they had taken care of the essentials, Nashe added a portable radio-tape-player to the list, and Pozzi asked for a number of small items: a deck of cards, a newspaper, a copy of *Penthouse* magazine. Murks told them he would be back by midafternoon, and then, suppressing a yawn, he stood up from the table and began to leave. Just as he was on his way out, however, Nashe remembered a question he had meant to ask before.

"I wonder if I could make a phone call," he said.

"There's no phone here," Murks said. "You can see that for yourself."

"Maybe you could drive me back to the house, then."

"What do you want to make a phone call for?"

"I doubt that's any of your business, Calvin."

"No, I don't suppose it is. But I can't just take you to the house without knowing why."

"I want to call my sister. She's expecting me in a few days, and I don't want her to worry when I don't show up."

Murks thought about it for a moment and then shook his head. "Sorry. I'm not allowed to take you there. They gave me special instructions."

"How about a telegram? If I wrote down the message, you could call it in yourself."

"No, I couldn't do that. The bosses wouldn't like it. But you can send a postcard if you want to. I'd be happy to mail it for you."

"Make it a letter. You can buy me some paper and envelopes in town. If I send it tomorrow, I suppose it will reach her in time."

"Okay, paper and envelopes. You got it."

After Murks had driven off in the jeep, Pozzi turned to Nashe and said, "Do you think he'll mail it?"

"I have no idea. If I had to bet on it, I'd say there's a good chance. But it's hard to be sure."

"One way or another, you'll never know. He'll tell you he sent it, but that doesn't mean you can trust him."

"I'll ask my sister to write back. If she doesn't, then we'll know our friend Murks was lying."

Pozzi lit a cigarette and then pushed the pack of Marlboros across the table to Nashe, who debated for a moment before accepting. Smoking the cigarette made him realize how tired he was, how utterly drained of energy. He snubbed it out after three or four puffs and said, "I think I'm going to take a nap. There's nothing to do now anyway, so I might as well try out my new bed. Which room do you want, Jack? I'll take the other one."

"I don't care," Pozzi answered. "Take your pick."

As Nashe stood up, he moved in such a way that the wooden figures in his pocket were disturbed. They pressed uncomfortably against his leg, and for the first time since stealing them, he remembered they were there. "Look at this," he said, pulling out Flower and Stone and standing them on the table. "Our two little friends."

Pozzi scowled, then slowly broke into a smile as he examined the minuscule, lifelike men. "Where the hell did they come from?"

"Where do you think?"

Pozzi looked up at Nashe with an odd, disbelieving expression on his face. "You didn't steal them, did you?"

"Of course I did. How else do you think they wound up in my pocket?"

"You're nuts, you know that? You're even nuttier than I thought you were."

"It didn't seem right to walk off without taking a souvenir," Nashe said, smiling as though he had just received a compliment.

Pozzi smiled back, clearly impressed by Nashe's audacity. "They're not going to be too happy when they find out," he said.

"Too bad for them."

"Yeah," Pozzi said, picking up the two tiny men from the table and studying them more closely, "too bad for them."

Nashe shut the blinds in his room, stretched out on the bed, and fell asleep as the sounds of the meadow washed over him. Birds sang in the distance, the wind passed through the trees, a cicada clicked in the grass below his window. His last thought before losing consciousness was of Juliette and her birthday. October twelfth was forty-six days away, he told himself. If he had to spend the next fifty nights sleeping in this bed, he wasn't going to make it. In spite of what he had promised her, he would still be in Pennsylvania on the day of her party.

The next morning, Nashe and Pozzi learned that building a wall was not as simple as they had imagined. Before the actual construction could get underway, all sorts of preparations had to be attended to. Lines had to be drawn, a trench had to be dug, a flat surface had to be created. "You can't just plop down stones and hope for the best," Murks said. "You've got to do things right."

Their first job was to roll out two parallel lengths of string and stretch them between the corners of the meadow, marking off the space to be occupied by the wall. Once those lines had been established, Nashe and Pozzi fastened the string to small wooden stakes and then drove the stakes into the ground at five-foot intervals. It was a laborious process that entailed constant measuring and remeasuring, but Nashe and Pozzi were in no particular rush, since they knew that each hour spent with the string would mean one less hour they would have to spend lifting stones. Considering that there were eight hundred stakes to be planted, the three days it took them to finish this task did not seem excessive. Under different circumstances, they might have dragged it out a bit longer, but Murks was never very far away, and his pale blue eyes did not miss a trick.

The next morning they were handed shovels and told to dig a shallow trench between the two lines of string. The fate of the wall hinged on making the bottom of that trench as level as possible, and they therefore proceeded with caution, advancing by only the smallest of increments. Since the meadow was not perfectly flat, they were obliged to eliminate the various bumps and hillocks they encountered along the way, uprooting grass and weeds with their shovels, then turning to picks and crowbars to extract any stones that were lodged beneath the surface. Some of these stones turned out to be fiercely resistant. They refused to unlock themselves from the earth, and Nashe and Pozzi spent the better part of six days doing battle with them, struggling to wrench each one of these impediments from the stubborn soil. The larger stones left behind holes, of course, which subsequently had to be filled in with dirt; then all the excess matter disgorged by the excavation had to be carted off in wheelbarrows and dumped in the woods that surrounded the meadow. The work was slow going, but neither one of them found it especially difficult. By the time they came to the finishing touches, in fact, they were almost beginning to enjoy it. For an entire afternoon they did nothing but smooth out the bottom of the trench, then pound it flat with hoes. For the space of those few hours, the job felt no more strenuous than working in a garden.

It did not take them long to settle into their new life. After three or four days in the meadow, the routine was already familiar to them, and by the end of the first week they no longer had to think about it. Every morning, Nashe's alarm clock would wake them at six. Then, after taking turns in the bathroom, they would go into the kitchen and cook breakfast (Pozzi handling the orange juice, toast, and coffee, Nashe preparing the scrambled eggs and sausages). Murks would show up promptly at seven, give a little knock at the trailer door, and then they would step out into the meadow to begin the day's work. After doing a five-hour shift in the morning, they would return to the trailer for lunch (an hour off without pay), and then put in another five hours in the afternoon. Quitting time came at six o'clock, and that was always a good moment for both of them, a prelude to the comforts of a warm shower and a quiet beer in the living room. Nashe would then withdraw to the kitchen and prepare dinner (simple concoctions for the most part, the old American standbys: steaks and chops, chicken casseroles, mounds of potatoes and vegetables, puddings and ice cream for dessert), and once they had filled their stomachs, Pozzi would do his bit by cleaning up the mess. After that, Nashe would stretch out on the

living room sofa, listening to music and reading books, and Pozzi
would sit down at the kitchen table and play solitaire. Sometimes
they talked, sometimes they said nothing. Sometimes they went
outside and played a form of basketball that Pozzi had invented:
throwing pebbles into a garbage can from a distance of ten feet.
And once or twice, when the evening air was especially beautiful,
they sat on the steps of the trailer and watched the sun go down
behind the woods.

Nashe was not nearly as restless as he had thought he would
be. Once he accepted the fact that the car was gone, he felt little
or no desire to be back on the road, and the ease with which he
adjusted to his new circumstances left him somewhat bewildered.
It made no sense that he should be able to abandon it all so quickly.
But Nashe discovered that he liked working out in the open air,
and after a while the stillness of the meadow seemed to have a
tranquilizing effect on him, as if the grass and the trees had brought
about a change in his metabolism. That did not mean he felt entirely
at home there, however. An atmosphere of suspicion and mistrust
continued to hover around the place, and Nashe resented the implication that he and the kid were not going to keep their end of
the bargain. They had given their word, they had even put their
signatures on a contract, and yet the whole setup was built on the
assumption that they would try to escape. Not only were they not
allowed to work with machines, but Murks now came to the meadow
every morning on foot, proving that even the jeep was considered
too dangerous a temptation, as if its presence would make it impossible to resist stealing it. These precautions were bad enough,
but even more sinister was the chain-link fence that Nashe and
Pozzi discovered on the evening that followed their first full day
of work. After dinner, they had decided to explore some of the
wooded areas that surrounded the meadow. They went to the far
end first, entering the woods along a dirt path that appeared to
have been cut quite recently. Felled trees lay on either side of it,

and from the tire tracks embedded in the soft, loamy earth, they gathered that this was where the trucks had driven in to deliver their cargo of stones. Nashe and Pozzi kept on walking, but before they reached the highway that marked the northern edge of the property, they were stopped by the fence. It was eight or nine feet tall, crowned by a menacing tangle of barbed wire. One section looked newer than the rest, which seemed to indicate that a piece of it had been removed to allow the trucks in, but other than that, all traces of entry had been eliminated. They continued walking alongside the fence, wondering if they would find any break in it, and by the time darkness fell an hour and a half later, they had returned to the same spot where they had begun. At one point, they passed the stone gate they had driven through on the day of their arrival, but that was the only interruption. The fence went everywhere, encompassing the entire extent of Flower and Stone's domain.

They did their best to laugh it off, saying that rich people always lived behind fences, but that did not erase the memory of what they had seen. The barrier had been erected to keep things out, but now that it was there, what was to prevent it from keeping things in as well? All sorts of threatening possibilities were buried in that question. Nashe tried not to let his imagination run away from him, but it was not until a letter from Donna arrived on the eighth day that he was able to put his fears to rest. Pozzi found it reassuring that someone knew where they were now, but as far as Nashe was concerned, the important thing was that Murks had kept his promise. The letter was a demonstration of good faith, tangible proof that no one had been out to deceive them.

All during those early days in the meadow, Pozzi's conduct was exemplary. He seemed to have made up his mind to stick by Nashe, and no matter what was asked of him, he did not complain. He went about his work with stolid goodwill, he pitched in with the household chores, he even pretended to enjoy the classical music that Nashe played every night after dinner. Nashe had not expected the kid to be so obliging, and he was grateful to him for making the effort. But the truth was that he was merely getting back what he had already earned. He had gone the full distance for Pozzi on the night of the poker match, pushing on past any reasonable limit, and even though he had been wiped out in the process, he had won himself a friend. That friend now seemed prepared to do anything for him, even if it meant living in a godforsaken meadow for the next fifty days, busting his chops like some convict sentenced to a term at hard labor.

Still, loyalty was not the same thing as belief. From Pozzi's point of view, the whole situation was absurd, and just because he had chosen to support his friend, that did not mean he felt that Nashe was in his right mind. The kid was indulging him, and once Nashe understood that, he did everything in his power to keep his thoughts to himself. The days passed, and even though there was rarely a moment when they were not together, he continued to say nothing about what truly concerned him—nothing about the struggle to put his life together again, nothing about how he saw the wall as a chance to redeem himself in his own eyes, nothing about how he welcomed the hardships of the meadow as a way to atone for his recklessness and self-pity—for once he got started, he knew that all the wrong words would come tumbling from his mouth, and he didn't want to make Pozzi any more nervous than he already was. The point was to keep him in good spirits, to get him through the fifty days as painlessly as possible. Much better to speak of things only in the most superficial terms—the debt, the contract, the hours they put in—and to bluster along with funny remarks and ironic shrugs of the shoulders. It was sometimes a lonely business for Nashe, but he didn't see what else he could do. If he ever bared his soul to the kid, all hell would break loose. It would be like opening a can of worms, like asking for the worst kind of trouble.

Pozzi continued on his best behavior with Nashe, but with Murks it was another story, and not a day went by when he didn't tease him and insult him and verbally attack him. In the beginning, Nashe interpreted it as a good sign, thinking that if the kid could return to his old rambunctious self, then perhaps that meant he was coping with the situation fairly well. The abuse was delivered with such sarcasm, with such an assortment of smiles and sympathetic nods of the head, that Murks barely seemed to know he was being made fun of. Nashe, who had no particular liking for Murks himself, did not blame Pozzi for letting off a little steam at the foreman's expense. But as time went on, he began to feel that the kid was carrying it too far—not just acting out of innate subversiveness, but responding to panic, to pent-up fears and confusion. The kid made Nashe think of a cornered animal, waiting to strike at the first thing that approached it. As it happened, that thing was always Murks, but no matter how obnoxious Pozzi became, no matter how provocative he tried to be, old Calvin never flinched. There was something so deeply imperturbable about the man, so fundamentally oblique and humorless, that Nashe could never decide if he was inwardly laughing at them or just plain dumb. He simply went about his job, plodding along at the same slow and thorough pace, never offering a word about himself, never asking any questions of Nashe or Pozzi, never showing the slightest hint of anger or curiosity or pleasure. He came punctually every morning at seven, delivering whatever groceries and provisions had been ordered the day before, and then he was all business for the next eleven hours. It was difficult to know what he thought about the wall, but he supervised the work with meticulous attention to detail, leading Nashe and Pozzi through each step of the construction as though he knew what he was talking about. He kept his distance from them, however, and never lent a hand or involved himself in any of the physical aspects of the work. His job was to oversee the building of the wall, and he adhered to that role with strict and absolute superiority over the men in his charge. Murks had the smugness of someone content with his place in the hierarchy, and as with most of the sergeants and crew chiefs of this world, his loyalties were firmly on the side of the people who told him what to do. He never ate lunch with Nashe and Pozzi, for example, and when the workday was done, he never lingered to chat. Work stopped precisely at six, and that was always the end of it. "See you tomorrow, boys," he would say, and then he would shuffle off into the woods, disappearing from sight within a matter of seconds.

It took them nine days to finish the preliminaries. Then they started in on the wall itself, and the world suddenly changed again. As Nashe and Pozzi discovered, it was one thing to lift a sixty-pound stone, but once that stone had been lifted, it was quite another thing to lift a second sixty-pound stone, and still another thing to take on a third stone after lifting the second. No matter how strong they felt while lifting the first, much of that strength would be gone by the time they came to the second, and once they had lifted the second, there would be still less of that strength to call upon for the third. So it went. Every time they worked on the wall, Nashe and Pozzi came up against the same bewitching conundrum: all the stones were identical, and yet each stone was heavier than the one before it.

They spent the mornings hauling stones across the meadow in a little red wagon, depositing each one along the side of the trench and then going back for another. In the afternoons, they worked with trowels and cement, carefully putting the stones into place. Of the two jobs, it was difficult to know which one was worse: the endless lifting and lowering that went on in the mornings, or the pushing and shoving that started in after lunch. The first took more out of them, perhaps, but there was a hidden reward in having to move the stones over such great distances. Murks had instructed them to begin at the far end of the trench, and each time they dropped off another stone, they had to go back empty-handed for the next one—which gave them a small interval in which to catch their breath. The second job was less taxing, but it was also more relentless. There were the brief pauses to slap on the cement, but they were not nearly as long as the return walks across the meadow, and when it came right down to it, it was probably harder to move a stone several inches than to raise it off the ground and put it in a wagon. When all the other variables were taken into consideration—the fact that they usually felt stronger in the morning, the fact that the weather was usually hotter in the afternoon, the fact that their disgust inevitably mounted as the day wore on—it was probably a wash. Six of one, half a dozen of another.

They carted the stones in a Fast Flyer, the same kind of children's wagon that Nashe had bought for Juliette on her third birthday. It seemed like a joke at first, and both he and Pozzi had laughed when Murks wheeled it out and presented it to them. "You're not serious, are you?" Nashe said. But Murks was very serious, and in the long run the toy wagon proved more than adequate for the job: its metal body could support the loads, and its rubber tires were sturdy enough to withstand any bumps and divots in the terrain. Still, there was something ridiculous about having to use such a thing, and Nashe resented the weird, infantilizing effect it had on him. The wagon did not belong in the hands of a grown man. It was an object fit for the nursery, for the trivial, make-believe worlds of children, and every time he pulled it across the meadow, he felt ashamed of himself, afflicted by a sense of his own helplessness.

The work advanced slowly, by almost imperceptible degrees. On a good morning, they could move twenty-five or thirty stones over to the trench, but never more than that. If Pozzi had been a little stronger, they could have doubled their progress, but the kid wasn't up to lifting the stones by himself. He was too small and frail, too unaccustomed to manual work. He could get the stones off the ground, but once he had them there, he was incapable of carrying them for any distance. As soon as he tried to walk, the weight would throw him off balance, and by the time he had taken two or three steps, the thing would start to slip out of his hands. Nashe, who had eight inches and seventy pounds on the kid, did not experience any of these difficulties. It wouldn't have been fair for him to do all the work, however, and so they wound up lifting the stones in tandem. Even then, it still would have been possible to load the wagon with two stones (which would have upped their progress by roughly a third), but Pozzi did not have it in him to pull over a hundred pounds. He could handle sixty or seventy without much strain, and since they had agreed to split the work down the middle—which meant that they took turns pulling the wagon—they kept each load to a single stone. In the end, that was probably for the best. The work was grueling enough anyway, and there was no point in letting it crush them.

Little by little, Nashe settled into it. The first few days were the hardest, and there was rarely a moment when he was not dragged down by an almost intolerable exhaustion. His muscles ached, his mind was clouded over, his body called out constantly for sleep. He had been softened by all those months of sitting in the car, and the relatively light work of the first nine days had done nothing to prepare him for the shock of real exertion. But Nashe was still young, still strong enough to recover from his long bout of inactivity, and as time went on, he began to notice that he was becoming tired a bit later in the day, that whereas previously a morning's work had been enough to bring him to the limit of his endurance, he was now able to get through a large part of the afternoon before that happened. Eventually, he found that it was no longer necessary to crawl into bed straight after dinner. He started reading books again, and by the middle of the second week, he understood that the worst of it was behind him.

Pozzi, on the other hand, did not adjust so well. The kid had been reasonably happy during the early days of digging the trench, but once they moved on to the next stage of the work, he grew more and more miserable. There was no question that the stones took more out of him than they took out of Nashe, but his irritability and moroseness seemed to have less to do with physical suffering than with a sense of moral outrage. The work was appalling to him, and the longer it went on, the more obvious it became to him that he was the victim of a terrible injustice, that his rights had been abused in some monstrous, unspeakable way. He kept going over the poker game with Flower and Stone, again and again replaying the hands out loud to Nashe, unable to accept the fact that he had lost. By the time he had been working on the wall for ten days, he was convinced that he had been cheated, that Flower and Stone had stolen the money by using marked cards or some other illegal trick. Nashe did his best to steer clear of the subject, but the truth was that he was not entirely convinced Pozzi was wrong. The same thought had already occurred to him, but without any evidence to support the accusation, he saw no point in encouraging the kid. Even if he was right, there wasn't a damned thing they could do about it.

Pozzi kept waiting for a chance to have it out with Flower and Stone, but the millionaires never showed up. Their absence was inexplicable, and as time went on, Nashe became more and more perplexed by it. He had assumed that they would come poking around the meadow every day. The wall was their idea, after all, and it seemed only natural that they should want to know how the work was coming along. But the weeks passed, and still there was no sign of them. Whenever Nashe asked Murks where they were, Calvin would shrug his shoulders, look down at the ground, and say that they were busy. It didn't make any sense. Nashe tried talking to Pozzi about it, but the kid was off in another orbit by then, and he always had a ready answer for him. "It means they're guilty," he would say. "The fuckers know I'm on to them, and they're too scared to show their faces."

One night, Pozzi drank five or six beers after dinner and got himself good and drunk. He was in a foul mood, and after a while he began to stagger around the trailer, spouting all kinds of gibberish about the raw deal he was getting. "I'm going to fix those shitbirds," he told Nashe. "I'm going to make that gumbo-gut confess." Without stopping to explain what he had in mind, he grabbed a flashlight off the kitchen counter, opened the door of the trailer, and plunged out into the darkness. Nashe scrambled to his feet and went after him, shouting at the kid to come back. "Get off my case, fireman," Pozzi said, waving the flashlight wildly around the grass. "If those turds won't come out here to talk to us, then we'll just have to go to them."

Short of punching him in the face, Nashe realized, there wasn't any way he could stop him. The kid was juiced, utterly beyond the pull of words, and trying to talk him out of it wasn't going to help. But Nashe had no desire to hit Pozzi. The thought of beating up a desperate, drunken kid was hardly his idea of a solution, and so he made up his mind to do nothing—to play along and see that Pozzi kept himself out of trouble.

They walked through the woods together, guiding themselves by the beam of the flashlight. It was close to eleven o'clock, and the sky was overcast, obscuring the moon and whatever stars there might have been. Nashe kept expecting to see a light from the house, but all was dark over in that direction, and after a while he wasn't sure if they would ever find it. It seemed to be taking a long time, and what with Pozzi tripping over stones and knocking into thorny bushes, the whole expedition began to feel rather pointless. But then they were there, stepping onto the edge of the lawn and approaching the house. It seemed too early for Flower and Stone to be in bed, but not a single window was lit. Pozzi walked around to the front door and pushed the bell, which again played the opening bars of Beethoven's Fifth Symphony. The kid muttered something under his breath, not half as amused as he had been the first time, and waited for someone to open the door. But nothing happened, and after fifteen or twenty seconds he rang again.

"It looks like they're out for the night," Nashe said.

"No, they're in there," Pozzi said. "They're just too chicken to answer."

But no lights went on after the second ring, and the door remained closed.

"I think it's time to give it up," Nashe said. "If you want to, we'll come back tomorrow."

"What about the maid?" Pozzi said. "You figure she's got to be in. We could leave a message with her."

"Maybe she's a heavy sleeper. Or maybe they gave her the night off. It looks pretty dead in there to me."

Pozzi kicked the door in frustration, then suddenly began to curse at the top of his voice. Instead of ringing a third time, he stepped back into the driveway and continued shouting at one of the upstairs windows, venting his rage at the empty house. "Hey, Flower!" he boomed. "That's right, fat man, I'm talking to you! You're a creep, mister, you know that? You and your little friend, you're both creeps, and you're going to pay for what you did to me!" It went on like that for a good three or four minutes, a belligerent outpouring of wild and useless threats, and even as it grew in intensity, it became progressively more pathetic, more dismal in the shrillness of its despair. Nashe's heart filled with pity for the kid, but there wasn't much he could do until Pozzi's anger burned itself out. He stood in the darkness, watching the bugs swarm in the beam of the flashlight. Off in the distance an owl hooted once, twice, and then stopped.

"Come on, Jack," Nashe said. "Let's head back to the trailer and get some sleep."

But Pozzi wasn't quite finished. Before leaving, he bent down in the driveway, scooped up a handful of pebbles, and threw them at the house. It was a stupid gesture, the petty wrath of a twelve-year-old. The gravel splattered like buckshot off the hard surface, and then, almost as an echo, Nashe heard the faint treble sound of breaking glass.

"Let's call it a night," he said. "I think we've had enough."

Pozzi turned and started walking toward the woods. "Assholes," he said to himself. "The whole world is run by assholes."

After that night, Nashe understood that he would have to keep a closer watch over the kid. Pozzi's inner resources were being used up, and they hadn't even come to the halfway point of their term. Without making an issue of it, Nashe began doing more than his share of the work, lifting and carting stones by himself while Pozzi rested, figuring that a little more sweat on his part might help to keep things under control. He didn't want any more outbursts or drunken binges, he didn't want to be constantly worrying that the kid was about to crack up. He could take the extra work, and in the long run it seemed simpler than trying to lecture Pozzi on the virtues of patience. It would all be over in thirty days, he told himself, and if he couldn't manage to see it through until then, what kind of a man was he?

He gave up reading books after dinner and spent those hours with Pozzi instead. The evening was a dangerous time, and it didn't help matters to let the kid sit there brooding alone in the kitchen, working himself into a frenzy of murderous thoughts. Nashe tried to be subtle about it, but from then on he put himself at Pozzi's disposal. If the kid felt like playing cards, he would play cards with him; if the kid felt like having a few drinks, he would open a bottle and match him glass for glass. As long as they were talking to each other, it didn't matter how they filled the time. Every now and then, Nashe would tell stories about the year he had spent on the road, or else he would talk about some of the big fires he had fought in Boston, dwelling on the most ghastly details for Pozzi's benefit, thinking it might get the kid's mind off his own troubles if he heard about what other people had gone through. For a short time at least, Nashe's strategy seemed to work. The kid became noticeably calmer, and the vicious talk about confronting Flower and Stone suddenly stopped, but it wasn't long before new obsessions rose up to replace the old ones. Nashe could handle most of them without much difficulty—girls, for example, and Pozzi's growing preoccupation with getting laid—but others were not so easy to dismiss. It wasn't as though the kid were threatening anyone, but every once in a while, right in the middle of a conversation, he would come out with such schizy, crackpot stuff, it would scare Nashe just to hear it.

"It was going along just the way I'd planned it," Pozzi said to him one night. "You remember that, Jim, don't you? Real smooth it was, as good as you could possibly want it. I'd just about tripled our stake, and there I was, getting ready to zero in for the kill. Those shits were finished. It was just a matter of time before they went belly-up, I could feel it in my bones. That's the feeling I always wait for. It's like a switch turns on inside me, and my whole body starts to hum. Whenever I get that feeling, it means I'm home free, I can coast all the way to the end. Do you follow what I'm saying, Jim? Until that night, I'd never been wrong about it, not once."

"There's a first time for everything," Nashe said, still not sure what the kid was driving at.

"Maybe. But it's hard to believe that's what happened to us. Once your luck starts to roll, there's not a damn thing that can stop it. It's like the whole world suddenly falls into place. You're kind of outside your body, and for the rest of the night you sit there watching yourself perform miracles. It doesn't really have anything to do with you anymore. It's out of your control, and as long as you don't think about it too much, you can't make a mistake."

"It looked good for a while, Jack, I'll admit that. But then it started to turn around. Those are the breaks, and there's nothing to be done about it. It's like a batter who goes four for four, and then the game goes into the bottom of the ninth, and the next time up he strikes out with the bases loaded. His team loses, and maybe you can say he's responsible for the loss. But that doesn't mean he had a bad night."

"No, you're not listening to me. I'm telling you there's no way I can strike out in that situation. The ball looks as big as a fucking watermelon to me by then. I just step into the batter's box, wait for my pitch, and then swat it up the gap for the game-winning hit."

"All right, you hit a line drive into the gap. But the center fielder is after it like a shot, and just when the ball is about to go past him, he leaps up and snags it in the webbing of his glove. It's an impossible catch, one of the great catches of all time. But it's still an out, isn't it, and there's no way you can fault the batter for not doing his best. That's all I'm trying to tell you, Jack. You did your best, and we lost. Worse things have happened in the history of the world. It's not something to worry about anymore."

"Yeah, but you still don't understand what I'm talking about. I'm just not getting through to you."

"It sounds fairly simple to me. For most of the night, it looked like we were going to win. But then something went wrong, and we didn't."

"Exactly. Something went wrong. And what do you think it was?"

"I don't know, kid. You tell me."

"It was you. You broke the rhythm, and after that everything went haywire."

"As I remember it, you were the one playing cards. The only thing I did was sit there and watch."

"But you were a part of it. Hour after hour, you sat there right behind me, breathing down my neck. At first it was a little distracting to have you so close, but then I got used to it, and after a while I knew you were there for a reason. You were breathing life into me, pal, and every time I felt your breath, good luck came pouring into my bones. It was all so perfect. We had everything balanced, all the wheels were turning, and it was beautiful, man, really beautiful. And then you had to get up and leave."

"A call of nature. You didn't expect me to piss in my pants, did you?"

"Sure, fine, go to the bathroom. I don't have any problem with that. But how long does it take? Three minutes? Five minutes? Sure, go ahead and take a leak. But Christ, Jim, you were gone for a whole fucking hour!"

"I was worn out. I had to lie down and take a nap."

"Yeah, but you didn't take any nap, did you? You went upstairs and started prowling around that dumb-ass City of the World. Why the hell did you have to do a crazy thing like that? I'm sitting downstairs waiting for you to come back, and little by little I start to lose my concentration. Where is he? I keep saying to myself, what the hell happened to him? It's getting worse now, and I'm not winning as many hands as I was before. And then, just at the moment when things get really bad, it pops into your head to steal a chunk of the model. I can't believe what a mistake that was. No class, Jim, an amateurish stunt. It's like committing a sin to do a thing like that, it's like violating a fundamental law. We had everything in harmony. We'd come to the point where everything was turning into music for us, and then you have to go upstairs and smash all the instruments. You tampered with the universe, my friend, and once a man does that, he's got to pay the price. I'm just sorry I have to pay it with you."

"You're starting to sound like Flower, Jack. The guy wins the lottery, and all of a sudden he thinks he was chosen by God."

"I'm not talking about God. God has nothing to do with it."

"It's just another word for the same thing. You want to believe in some hidden purpose. You're trying to persuade yourself there's a reason for what happens in the world. I don't care what you call it—God or luck or harmony—it all comes down to the same bullshit. It's a way of avoiding the facts, of refusing to look at how things really work."

"You think you're smart, Nashe, but you don't know a goddamn thing."

"That's right, I don't. And neither do you, Jack. We're just a pair of know-nothings, you and I, a couple of dunces who got in over our heads. Now we're trying to square the account. If we don't mess up, we'll be out of here in twenty-seven days. I'm not saying it's fun, but maybe we'll learn something before it's over."

"You shouldn't have done it, Jim. That's all I'm trying to tell you. Once you stole those little men, things went out of whack."

Nashe let out a sigh of exasperation, stood up from his chair, and pulled the model of Flower and Stone from his pocket. Then he walked over to where Pozzi was sitting and held the figures in front of his eyes. "Take a good look," he said, "and tell me what you see."

"Christ," Pozzi said. "What do you want to be playing games for?"

"Just look," Nashe said sharply. "Come on, Jack, tell me what I'm holding in my hand."

Pozzi stared up at Nashe with a wounded expression in his eyes, then reluctantly obeyed him. "Flower and Stone," he said.

"Flower and Stone? I thought Flower and Stone were bigger than this. I mean, look at them, Jack, these two guys aren't more than an inch and a half tall."

"Okay, so they're not really Flower and Stone. It's what you call a replica."

"It's a piece of wood, isn't it? A stupid little piece of wood. Isn't that right, Jack?"

"If you say so."

"And yet you believe this little scrap of wood is stronger than we are, don't you? You think it's so strong, in fact, that it made us lose all our money."

"That's not what I said. I just meant you shouldn't have pinched it. Some other time, maybe, but not when we were playing poker."

"But here it is. And every time you look at it, you get a little scared, don't you? It's like they're casting an evil spell over you."

"Sort of."

"What do you want me to do with them? Should I give them back? Would that make you feel better?"

"It's too late now. The damage has already been done."

"There's a remedy for everything, kid. A good Catholic boy like you should know that. With the proper medicine, any illness can be cured."

"You've lost me now. I don't know what the fuck you're talking about."

"Just watch. In a few minutes, all your troubles will be over."

Without saying another word, Nashe went into the kitchen and retrieved a baking tin, a book of matches, and a newspaper. When he returned to the living room, he put the baking tin on the floor, positioning it just a few inches in front of Pozzi's feet. Then he crouched down and placed the figures of Flower and Stone in the center of the tin. He tore out a sheet of newspaper, tore that sheet into several strips, and wadded each strip into a ball. Then, very delicately, he put the balls around the wooden statue in the tin. He paused for a moment at that point to look into Pozzi's eyes, and when the kid didn't say anything, he went ahead and lit a match. One by one, he touched the flame to the paper wads, and by the time they were fully ignited, the fire had caught hold of the wooden figures, producing a bright surge of crackling heat as the colors burned and melted away. The wood below was soft and porous, and it could not resist the onslaught. Flower and Stone turned black, shrinking as the fire ate into their bodies, and less than a minute later, the two little men were gone.

Nashe pointed to the ashes at the bottom of the tin and said, "You see? There's nothing to it. Once you know the magic formula, no obstacle is too great."

The kid finally pulled his eyes away from the floor and looked at Nashe. "You're out of your mind," he said. "I hope you realize that."

"If I am, then that makes two of us, my friend. At least you won't have to suffer alone anymore. That's something to be thankful for, isn't it? I'm with you every step of the way, Jack. Every damned step, right to the end of the road."

By the middle of the fourth week, the weather started to turn. The warm, humid skies gave way to the chill of early fall, and on most mornings now they went off to work wearing sweaters. The bugs had disappeared, the battalions of gnats and mosquitoes that had plagued them for so long, and with the leaves beginning to change color in the woods, dying into a profusion of yellows and oranges and reds, it was hard not to feel a little better about things. The rain could be nasty at times, it was true, but even rain seemed preferable to the rigors of the heat, and they did not let it stop them from going on with their work. They were provided with rubber ponchos and baseball caps, and those served reasonably well to protect them from the downpours. The essential thing was to push on, to put in their ten hours every day and wrap up their business on schedule. Since the beginning, they had not taken any time off, and they weren't about to let a little rain intimidate them now. On this point, curiously enough, Pozzi was the more determined of the two. But that was because he was more eager than Nashe to finish, and even on the stormiest, most gloomy days, he trudged off to work without protesting. In some sense, the more violent the weather, the happier he was—for Murks had to be out there with them, and nothing pleased Pozzi more than the sight of the grim, bowlegged foreman decked out in his yellow raingear, standing under a black umbrella for all those hours as his boots sank deeper and deeper into the mud. He loved to see the old guy suffer like that. It was a form of consolation, somehow, a small payback for all the suffering he had gone through himself.

The rain caused problems, however. One day in the last week of September it came down so hard that nearly a third of the trench was destroyed. They had put in approximately seven hundred stones by then, and they were figuring to complete the bottom row in another ten or twelve days. But a huge storm blew up overnight, pummeling the meadow with ferocious, windswept rain, and when they went out the next morning to begin work, they discovered that the exposed portion of the trench had filled up with several inches of water. Not only would it be impossible to put in any more stones until the dirt dried, but all the exacting, meticulous labor of leveling the bottom of the trench had been ruined. The foundation for the wall had turned into an oozing mess of rivulets and mud. They spent the next three days carting stones in the afternoon as well as the morning, filling in the time as best they could, and then, when the water finally evaporated, they abandoned the stones for a couple of days and set about rebuilding the bottom of the trench. It was at this juncture that things finally exploded between Pozzi and Murks. Calvin was suddenly involved in the work again, and instead of standing off to the side and watching them from a safe distance (as he was wont to do), he now spent his days hovering around them, fussing and nagging with constant little comments and instructions to make sure the repairs were done correctly. Pozzi bore up to it on the first morning, but when the interference continued through the afternoon, Nashe could see that it was starting to get under his skin. Another three or four hours went by, and then the kid finally lost his temper.

"All right, big mouth," he said, throwing down his shovel and glaring at Murks in disgust, "if you're such an expert at all this, then why the fuck don't you do it yourself!"

Murks paused for a moment, apparently caught off guard. "Because it's not my job," he finally said, speaking in a very low voice. "You boys are supposed to do the work. I'm just here to see you don't screw up."

"Yeah?" the kid came back at him. "And what makes you so high and mighty, Mr. Potato Head? How come you get to stand there with your goddamn hands in your pockets while we're busting our dicks in this dungheap? Huh? Come on, Mr. Bumpkin, out with it. Give me one good reason."

"That's simple," Murks said, unable to suppress the smile that was forming on his lips. "Because you play cards and I don't."

It was the smile that did it, Nashe felt. A look of deep and genuine contempt flashed across Murks's face, and a moment later Pozzi was charging toward him with clenched fists. At least one blow landed cleanly, for by the time Nashe managed to pull the kid away, blood was dribbling from a corner of Calvin's mouth. Pozzi, still seething with unspent rage, bucked wildly in Nashe's arms for close to a minute after that, but Nashe held on for all he was worth, and eventually the kid settled down. Meanwhile, Murks had backed off a few feet and was dabbing the cut with a handkerchief. "It don't matter," he finally said. "The little squirt can't handle the pressure, that's all. Some guys got what it takes, others don't. The only thing I'm going to say is this: Just don't let it happen again. Next time I won't be so nice about it." He looked down at the watch on his wrist and said, "I think we'll knock off early today. It's getting on close to five now, and there's no sense in starting up again with tempers so hot." Then, giving them his customary little wave, he walked off across the meadow and vanished into the woods.

Nashe could not help admiring Murks for his composure. Most men would have struck back after an assault like that, but Calvin hadn't even raised his hands to defend himself. There was a certain arrogance to it, perhaps—as if he were telling Pozzi that he couldn't hurt him, no matter how hard he tried—but the fact was that the incident had been defused with astonishing quickness. Considering what could have happened, it was a miracle that no greater damage had been done. Even Pozzi seemed aware of that, and while he scrupulously avoided talking about the subject that night, Nashe could tell that he was embarrassed, glad that he had been stopped before it was too late.

There was no reason to think there would be any repercussions. But the next morning at seven o'clock, Murks showed up at the trailer carrying a gun. It was a thirty-eight policeman's revolver, and it was strapped into a leather holster than hung from a cartridge belt around Murks's waist. Nashe noticed that six bullets were missing from the belt—almost certain proof that the weapon was loaded. It was bad enough that things had come to such a pass, he thought, but what made it even worse was that Calvin acted as though nothing had happened. He did not mention the gun, and that silence was finally more troubling to Nashe than the gun itself. It meant that Murks felt he had a right to carry it—and that he had felt that right from the very beginning. Freedom, therefore, had never been an issue. Contracts, handshakes, goodwill—none of that had meant a thing. All along, Nashe and Pozzi had been working under the threat of violence, and it was only because they had chosen to cooperate with Murks that he had left them alone. Bitching and grumbling were apparently allowed, but once their discontent moved beyond the realm of words, he was more than ready to take drastic, intimidating measures against them. And given the way things had been set up, there was no question that he was acting on orders from Flower and Stone.

Still, it didn't seem likely that Murks was planning to use the gun. Its function was symbolic, and just having it there in front of them was enough to make the point. As long as they didn't provoke him, Calvin wouldn't do much more than strut around with the weapon on his hip, doing some half-assed impersonation of a town marshal. When it came right down to it, Nashe felt, the only real danger was Pozzi. The kid's behavior had become so erratic, it was hard to know if he would do something foolish or not. As it turned out, he never did, and eventually Nashe was forced to admit that he had underestimated him. Pozzi had been expecting trouble all along, and when he saw the gun that morning, it did not surprise him so much as confirm his deepest suspicions. Nashe was the one who was surprised, Nashe was the one who had tricked himself into a false reading of the facts, but Pozzi had always known what they were up against. He had known it since the first day in the meadow, and the implications of that knowledge had scared him half to death. Now that everything was finally out in the open, he almost looked relieved. The gun did not change the situation for him, after all. It merely proved that he had been right.

"Well, old buddy," he said to Murks as the three of them walked across the grass, "it looks like you've finally put your cards on the table."

"Cards?" Murks said, confused by the reference. "I told you yesterday I don't play cards."

"Just a figure of speech," Pozzi said, smiling pleasantly. "I'm talking about that funny lollypop you've got there. That dingdong hanging from your waist."

"Oh, that," Murks said, patting the gun in its holster. "Yeah, well, I figured I shouldn't take no more chances. You're a crazy son of a bitch, little guy. No telling what you might do."

"It kind of narrows the possibilities, though, doesn't it?" Pozzi said. "I mean, a thing like that can seriously hamper a man's ability to express himself. Curtail his First Amendment rights, if you know what I'm talking about."

"You don't have to be cute, mister," Murks said. "I know what the First Amendment is."

"Of course you do. That's why I like you so much, Calvin. You're a sharp customer, a real whiz and a half. No one can put anything over on you."

"Like I said yesterday, I'm always willing to give a man a break. But only one. After that, you've got to take appropriate action."

"Like laying your cards out on the table, huh?"

"If that's how you want to put it."

"It's just good to keep things straight, that's all. In fact, I'm kind of glad you put on your dress-up belt today. It gives my friend Jim here a better picture of things."

"That's the idea," Murks said, patting the gun once again. "It does have a way of adjusting the focus, don't it?"

They finished repairing the trench by the end of the morning, and after that work returned to normal. Except for the gun (which Murks continued to wear every day), the outward circumstances of their life did not seem to change much. If anything, Nashe sensed that they were actually beginning to improve. The rain had stopped, for one thing, and instead of the wet, clammy days that had bogged them down for more than a week, they entered a period of superb fall weather: crisp, shimmering skies; firm ground underfoot; the crackle of leaves scudding past them in the wind. But Pozzi seemed to have improved as well, and it was no longer such a strain for Nashe to be with him. The gun had been a turning point, somehow, and since then he had managed to recover much of his bounce and spirit. The crazy talk had stopped; he kept his anger under control; the world was beginning to amuse him again. That was real progress, but there was also the progress of the calendar, and perhaps that meant more than anything else. They had made it into October now, and all of a sudden the end was in sight. Just knowing that was enough to awaken some hope in them, some flicker of optimism that had not been there before. There were sixteen days to go, and not even the gun could take that away from them. As long as they kept on working, the work was going to make them free.

They put in the thousandth stone on October eighth, polishing off the bottom row with more than a week to spare. In spite of everything, Nashe could not help feeling a sense of accomplishment. They had made a mark somehow, they had done something that would remain after they were gone, and no matter where they happened to be, a part of this wall would always belong to them. Even Pozzi looked happy about it, and when the last stone was finally cemented into place, he stepped back for a moment and said to Nashe, "Well, my man, get a load of what we just did." Uncharacteristically, the kid then hopped up onto the stones and started prancing down the length of the row, holding out his arms like a tightrope walker. Nashe was glad to see the kid respond in that way, and as he watched the small figure tiptoe off into the distance, following the pantomime of the high-wire stunt (as though he were in danger, as though he were about to fall from a great height), something suddenly choked up inside him, and he felt himself on the verge of tears. A moment later, Murks came up beside him and said, "It looks like the little bugger is feeling pretty proud of himself, don't it?"

"He deserves to," Nashe said. "He's worked hard."

"Well, it hasn't been easy, I'll grant you that. But it looks like we're coming along now. It looks like this thing is finally going up."

"Little by little, one stone at a time."

"That's the way it's done. One stone at a time."

"I guess you'll have to start looking for some new workers. The way Jack and I figure it, we're due to leave here on the sixteenth."

"I know that. It's kind of a shame, though. I mean, just when you boys are getting the hang of it and all."

"Those are the breaks, Calvin."

"Yeah, I guess so. But if nothing better comes along, you might consider coming back. I know that sounds crazy to you right now, but give it a little thought anyway."

"Thought?" Nashe said, not knowing if he was about to laugh or cry.

"It's really not such bad work," Murks continued. "At least it's all there in front of you. You put down a stone, and something happens. You put down another stone, and something more happens. There's no big mystery to it. You can see the wall going up, and after a while it starts to give you a good feeling. It's not like mowing the grass or chopping wood. That's work, too, but it don't ever amount to much. When you work on a wall like this, you've always got something to show for it."

"I suppose it has its points," Nashe said, a little dumbfounded by Murks's venture into philosophy, "but I can think of other things I'd rather be doing."

"Suit yourself. But just remember we've got nine rows left. You could earn yourself some good money if you stuck with it."

"I'll bear that in mind. But if I were you, Calvin, I wouldn't hold my breath."

# 7

There was a problem, however. It had been there all along, a small thing in the back of their minds, but now that the sixteenth was only a week away, it suddenly grew larger, attaining such proportions as to dwarf everything else. The debt would be paid off on the sixteenth, but at that point they would only be back to zero. They would be free, perhaps, but they would also be broke, and how far would that freedom take them if they had no money? They wouldn't even be able to afford the price of a bus ticket. The moment they walked out of there, they would be turned into bums, a pair of penniless drifters trying to make their way in the dark.

For a few minutes, it looked as though Nashe's credit card might rescue them, but when he pulled it out of his wallet and showed it to Pozzi, the kid discovered that it had expired at the end of September. They talked about writing to someone to ask for a loan, but the only people they could think of were Pozzi's mother and Nashe's sister, and that didn't sit too well with either of them. It wasn't worth the embarrassment, they said, and besides, it was probably too late anyway. By the time they sent off their letter and received an answer, it would already be past the sixteenth.

Then Nashe told Pozzi about the conversation he had had with Murks that afternoon. It was a terrible prospect (at one point, it even looked as though the kid was about to start crying), but little by little they came around to the idea that they would have to stay with the wall a bit longer. There just wasn't any choice. Unless they built up some cash for themselves, there would only be more trouble after they left, and neither one of them felt equal to it. They were too worn out, too shaken to run that risk now. One or two extra days ought to do it, they said, just a couple of hundred dollars apiece to get them going. In the long run, maybe it wouldn't be as bad as all that. At least they would be working for themselves, and that was bound to make a difference. Or so they said—but what else could they say to each other at that moment? They had drunk close to a fifth of bourbon by then, and dwelling on the truth only would have made things worse than they already were.

They talked to Calvin about it the next morning, just to make sure he had been serious about his offer. He didn't see why not, he said. In fact, he'd already talked to Flower and Stone about it last night, and they hadn't raised any objections. If Nashe and Pozzi wanted to go on working after the debt had been squared, they were free to do so. They could earn the same ten dollars an hour they had been earning all along, and the offer would stand until the wall was finished.

"We're just talking about two or three extra days," Nashe said.

"Sure, I understand," Murks said. "You want to set aside a little nest egg before you leave. I figured you'd get around to my way of thinking sooner or later."

"It has nothing to do with that," Nashe said. "We're staying because we have to, not because we want to."

"One way or the other," Murks said, "it comes down to the same thing, don't it? You need money, and this here job is the way to get it."

Before Nashe could answer, Pozzi broke in and said, "We're not going to stay unless we have it in writing. The exact terms, everything spelled out."

"What you call a rider to the contract," Murks said. "Is that what you mean?"

"Yeah, that's it," Pozzi said. "A rider. If we don't get that, then we walk out of here on the sixteenth."

"Fair enough," Murks said, looking more and more pleased with himself. "But you don't have to worry. It's already been taken care of." The foreman then popped open the snaps of his blue down jacket, reached into the inner pocket with his right hand, and pulled out two sheets of folded paper. "Read these over and tell me what you think," he said.

It was the original and a duplicate of the new clause: a brief, simply stated paragraph setting out the conditions for "labor subsequent to the discharge of the debt." Both copies had already been signed by Flower and Stone, and as far as Nashe and Pozzi could tell, everything was in order. That was what was so strange about it. They hadn't even come to a decision until last night, and yet here were the results of that decision already waiting for them, boiled down into the precise language of contracts. How was that possible? It was as if Flower and Stone had been able to read their thoughts, as if they had known what they would do before they knew it themselves. For one short paranoid moment, Nashe wondered if the trailer had been bugged. It was a gruesome thought, but nothing else seemed to explain it. What if there were listening devices in the walls? Flower and Stone could easily have picked up their conversations then—they could have been following every word he and the kid had spoken to each other for the past six weeks. Maybe that was their nighttime entertainment, Nashe thought. Turn on the radio and listen to Jim and Jack's Comedy Hour. Fun for the whole family, a guaranteed laugh riot.

"You're awfully sure of yourself, Calvin, aren't you?" he said.

"Just common sense," Murks replied. "I mean, it was only a matter of time before you asked me about it. Ain't no other way it could have gone. So I figured I'd get ready for you and have the bosses draw up the papers. It didn't take but a minute."

So they put their signatures on both copies of the rider, and the business was settled. Another day went by. When they sat down to dinner that evening, Pozzi said that he thought they should plan a celebration for the night of the sixteenth. Even if they weren't going to leave then, it seemed wrong to let the day slip by without doing something special. They should whoop it up a little, he said, throw a shindig of some kind to welcome in the new era. Nashe assumed he was talking about a cake or a bottle of champagne, but Pozzi had bigger plans than that. "No," he said, "I mean let's really do it right. Lobsters, caviar, the whole works. And we'll bring in some girls, too. You can't have a party without girls."

Nashe couldn't help smiling at the kid's enthusiasm. "And what girls would those be, Jack?" he said. "The only girl I've ever seen around here is Louise, and somehow she doesn't strike me as your type. Even if we invited her, I doubt she'd want to come."

"No, no, I'm talking about real broads. Hookers. You know, juicy babes. Girls we can fuck."

"And where do we find these juicy babes? Out there in the woods?"

"We bring them in. Atlantic City's not far from here, you know. That burg is crawling with female flesh. There's pussy for sale on every corner down there."

"Fine. And what makes you think Flower and Stone will agree to it?"

"They said we could have anything we want, didn't they?"

"Food is one thing, Jack. A book, a magazine, even a bottle of bourbon or two. But don't you think this is pushing it a bit far?"

"Anything means anything. There's no harm in asking, anyway."

"Sure, you can ask all you want. Just don't be surprised when Calvin laughs at you."

"I'll bring it up with him first thing tomorrow morning."

"You do that. But just ask for one girl, all right? Old grandpa here doesn't know if he's up for that kind of celebrating."

"Well, this little boy is up for it, I can tell you that. It's been so long now, my pecker's about ready to explode."

Contrary to what Nashe had predicted, Murks didn't laugh at Pozzi the next morning. But the look of confusion and embarrassment that swept across his face was almost as good as a laugh, perhaps even better. He had been prepared for their questions the day before, but this time he was stumped, could scarcely even take in what the kid was talking about. After the second or third go-through, he finally caught on, but that only seemed to add to his embarrassment. "You mean a hoor?" he said. "Is that what you're trying to tell me? You want us to get you a hoor?"

Murks did not have the authority to handle such an unorthodox request, but he promised to take it up with the bosses that night. Unbelievably, when he came back with the answer the next morning, he told Pozzi it would be taken care of, he would have his girl on the sixteenth. "That was the deal," he said. "Whatever you want, you can get. I can't say they looked too happy about it, but a deal's a deal, they said, and there you have it. If you ask me, it was kind of big of them. They're nice fellas, those two, and once they give their word about something, they'll bend over backwards to make it good."

It felt all wrong to Nashe. Flower and Stone weren't the kind of men who threw away their money on parties for other people, and the fact that they had gone along with Pozzi's request immediately put him on his guard. For their own sakes, he thought, it would have been better to push on with the work and then creep out of there as quickly and quietly as possible. The second row was proving less difficult than the first, and the work was advancing steadily, perhaps more steadily than ever before. The wall was higher now, and they no longer had to put their backs through the multiple contortions of bending and squatting to push the stones into place. A single, economical gesture was all that was required, and once they had mastered the finer points of this new rhythm, they were able to increase their output to as many as forty stones a day. How simple it would have been to go on like that to the end. But the kid had his heart set on a party, and now that the girl was coming, Nashe realized there was nothing he could do to prevent it. If he spoke up, it would only sound as if he were trying to spoil Pozzi's fun, and that was the last thing he wanted. The kid deserved to have his little romp, and even if it led to more trouble than it was worth, Nashe felt a moral obligation to play along with him.

Over the next few nights, he assumed the role of caterer, sitting in the living room with a pencil and jotting down notes as he helped Pozzi work out the details of the celebration. There were endless decisions to be made, and Nashe was determined that the kid be satisfied on every point. Should the meal begin with shrimp cocktail or French onion soup? Should the main course consist of steak or lobster or both? How many bottles of champagne should they order? Should the girl be there for dinner, or should they eat alone and have her join them for dessert? Were decorations necessary, and if so, what color balloons did they want? They handed the completed list to Murks on the morning of the fifteenth, and that same night the foreman made a special trip to the meadow to deliver the packages. For once he came in the jeep, and Nashe wondered if that wasn't an encouraging sign, a token of their impending freedom. Then again, it could have meant nothing. There were many packages, after all, and he could have driven there simply because the load was too big to carry in his arms. For if they were about to become free men, why would Murks bother to go on wearing the gun?

They put in forty-seven stones on the last day, surpassing their previous record by five. It took an enormous effort to pull it off, but they both wanted to end with a flourish, and they worked as if they were out to prove something, never once slackening their pace, wielding the stones with an assurance that bordered on contempt, as if the only thing that mattered now was to show they had not been defeated, that they had triumphed over the whole rotten business. Murks called them to a halt at six sharp, and they put down their tools with the cold autumn air still burning in their lungs. Darkness came earlier now, and when Nashe looked up at the sky, he saw that evening was already upon them.

For several moments he was too stunned to know what to think. Pozzi came over to him and pounded him on the back, chattering with excitement, but Nashe's mind remained curiously empty, as if he were unable to absorb the magnitude of what he had done. I'm back to zero, he finally said to himself. And all of a sudden he knew that an entire period of his life had just ended. It wasn't just the wall and the meadow, it was everything that had put him there in the first place, the whole crazy saga of the past two years: Thérèse and the money and the car, all of it. He was back to zero again, and now those things were gone. For even the smallest zero was a great hole of nothingness, a circle large enough to contain the world.

The girl was supposed to be chauffeured up by limousine from Atlantic City. Murks had told them to expect her at around eight o'clock, but it was closer to nine when she finally walked through the door of the trailer. Nashe and Pozzi had polished off a bottle of champagne by then, and Nashe was fussing over the lobster pot in the kitchen, watching the water as it approached the boiling point for the third or fourth time that evening. The three lobsters in the bathtub were barely alive, but Pozzi had chosen to include the girl for dinner ("It makes a better impression that way"), and so there was nothing to do but hang around until she showed up. Neither one of them was used to drinking champagne, and the bubbles had quickly gone to their heads, leaving them both a bit punchy by the time the celebration finally got started.

The girl called herself Tiffany, and she couldn't have been more than eighteen or nineteen years old. She was one of those pale, skinny blondes with sloped shoulders and a sunken chest, and she tottered around on her three-inch heels as if she were trying to walk on ice skates. Nashe noted the small, yellowing bruise on her left thigh, the overdone makeup, the dismal miniskirt that exposed her thin, shapeless legs. Her face was almost pretty, he felt, but in spite of her pouting, childlike expression, there was a worn-out quality to her, a sullenness that glowed through the smiles and apparent gaiety of her manner. It didn't matter how young she was. Her eyes were too hard, too cynical, and they bore the look of someone who had already seen too much.

The kid popped open another bottle of champagne, and the three of them sat down for a pre-dinner drink—Pozzi and the girl on the couch, Nashe in a chair several feet away.

"So what's the story, fellas?" she said, sipping daintily from her glass. "Is this going to be a threesome, or do I take you on one at a time?"

"I'm just the cook," Nashe said, a little thrown by the girl's bluntness. "Once dinner is over, I'm finished for the night."

"Old Jeeves here is a wizard in the kitchen," Pozzi said, "but he's scared of the ladies. It's just one of those things. They make him nervous."

"Yeah, sure," the girl said, studying Nashe with a cold, appraising look. "What's the matter, big guy, not in the mood to-night?"

"It's not that," Nashe said. "It's just that I have a lot of reading to catch up on. I've been trying to learn a new recipe, and some of the ingredients are pretty complicated."

"Well, you can always change your mind," the girl said. "That fat guy shelled out plenty for this, and I came here thinking I was going to fuck you both. It's no skin off my back. For that kind of money, I'd fuck a dog if I had to."

"I understand," Nashe said. "But I'm sure you'll have your hands full with Jack anyway. Once he gets started, he can be a real savage."

"That's right, babe," Pozzi said, squeezing the girl's thigh and pulling her toward him for a kiss. "My appetite's insatiable."

It promised to be a sad and lugubrious dinner, but Pozzi's high spirits turned it into something else—something buoyant and memorable, a free-for-all of slithering lobster shells and drunken laughter. The kid was a whirlwind that night, and neither Nashe nor the girl could resist his happiness, the manic energy that kept pouring out from him and flooding the room. It seemed that he knew exactly what to say to the girl at every moment, how to flatter her and to tease her and to make her laugh, and Nashe was astonished to see how she slowly gave in to the assault of his charms, how her face softened and her eyes grew steadily brighter. Nashe had never had this talent with girls, and he watched Pozzi's performance with a mounting sense of wonder and envy. It was all a matter of treating everyone the same, he realized, of giving as much care and attention to a sad, unattractive prostitute as you would to the girl of your dreams. Nashe had always been too fussy for that, too self-contained and serious, and he admired the kid for making the girl laugh so hard, for loving life so much at that moment that he was able to draw out what was still alive in her.

The best bit of improvisation came halfway through the meal, when Pozzi suddenly began to talk about their work. He and Nashe were architects, he explained, and they had come to Pennsylvania a couple of weeks ago to oversee the construction of a castle they had designed. They were specialists in the art of "historical reverberation," and because so few people could afford to hire them, they invariably wound up working for eccentric millionaires. "I don't know what the fat man in the house told you about us," he said, "but you can forget it right now. He's a great kidder, that one, and he'd just as soon wet his pants in public as give you a straight answer about anything." A crew of thirty-six masons and carpenters came to the meadow every day, but he and Jim were living on the construction site because they always did that. Atmosphere meant everything, and the job always turned out better if they lived the life they'd been hired to create. This job was a "medieval reverberation," so for the time being they had to live like monks. Their next job would be taking them to Texas, where an oil baron had asked them to build a replica of Buckingham Palace in his backyard. That might sound easy, but once you realized that every stone had to be numbered in advance, you could begin to understand how complicated it was. If the stones weren't put together in the right order, the whole thing would come tumbling down. Imagine building the Brooklyn Bridge in San Jose, California. Well, they had done that for someone just last year. Think about designing a life-size Eiffel Tower to fit over a ranch house in the New Jersey suburbs. That was on their résumé as well. Sure, there were times when they felt like packing it in and moving to a condo in West Palm Beach, but the work was finally too damned interesting to stop, and what with all the American millionaires who wanted to live in European castles, they didn't have the heart to turn everyone down.

All this nonsense was accompanied by the noise of cracking lobster shells and the slurping of champagne. When Nashe stood up to clear the table, he stumbled against a leg of his chair and dropped two or three dishes to the floor. They broke with a great clattering din, and because one of them happened to be a bowl containing the remnants of the melted butter, the mess on the linoleum ran riot. Tiffany made a move to help Nashe clean it up, but walking had never been her strong point, and now that the champagne bubbles were percolating in her bloodstream, she could manage no more than two or three steps before she fell into Pozzi's lap, overcome by a fit of laughter. Or perhaps it was Pozzi who grabbed hold of her before she could get away from him (by then, Nashe could no longer keep track of such nuances), but however it may have happened, by the time Nashe stood up with the shards of broken crockery in his hand, the two young people were sitting on the chair together, locked in a passionate kiss. Pozzi started to rub one of the girl's breasts, and a moment later Tiffany was reaching out for the bulge in his crotch, but before things could go any further, Nashe (not knowing what else to do) cleared his throat and announced that it was time for dessert.

They had ordered one of those chocolate layer cakes you find in the frozen-food department of the A&P, but Nashe carried it out with all the pomp and ceremony of a lord high chamberlain about to place a crown on the head of a queen. In keeping with the solemnity of the occasion, he suddenly and unexpectedly found himself singing a hymn from his boyhood. It was "Jerusalem," with words by William Blake, and although he hadn't sung it in over twenty years, all the verses came back to him, rolling off his tongue as though he had spent the past two months rehearsing for this moment. Hearing the words as he sang them, the *burning gold* and the *mental fight* and the *dark satanic mills*, he understood how beautiful and painful they were, and he sang them as though to express his own longing, all the sadness and joy that had welled up in him since the first day in the meadow. It was a difficult melody, but except for a few false notes in the opening stanza, his voice did not betray him. He sang as he had always dreamed of singing, and he knew that he was not deluding himself from the way Pozzi and the girl looked at him, from the stunned expressions on their faces when they realized that the sounds were coming from his mouth. They listened in silence to the end, and then, when Nashe sat down and forced an embarrassed smile in their direction, they both began to clap, and they did not stop until he finally agreed to stand up again and take a bow.

They drank the last bottle of champagne with the cake, telling stories about their childhoods, and then Nashe realized it was time to back off. He didn't want to be in the kid's way anymore, and now that the food was gone, he had run out of excuses for being there. This time, the girl didn't ask him to reconsider, but she gave him a big hug anyway and said she hoped they would run into each other again. He thought that was nice of her and said he hoped so too, and then he winked at the kid and stumbled off to bed.

Still, it wasn't easy lying there in the dark, listening to their laughter and thumping out in the other room. He tried not to imagine what was going on, but the only way he could do that was by thinking about Fiona, and that only seemed to make matters worse. Luckily, he was too drunk to keep his eyes open for very long. Before he could begin to feel truly sorry for himself, he was already dead to the world.

They planned to take the next day off. It seemed only appropriate after working for seven straight weeks, and what with the hangovers that were bound to follow their night of carousing, they had arranged this respite with Murks several days in advance. Nashe awoke shortly past ten, head cracking in both temples, and started off toward the shower. On the way, he glanced into Pozzi's room and saw that the kid was still asleep, alone in his bed with his arms flung out on both sides. Nashe stood under the water for a good six or seven minutes, then stepped out into the living room with a towel around his waist. A lacy black bra sat tangled on a cushion of the sofa, but the girl herself was gone. The room looked as though a marauding army had camped there for the night, and the floor was a chaos of empty bottles and overturned ashtrays, of fallen streamers and shriveled balloons. Picking his way through the debris, Nashe went into the kitchen and made himself a pot of coffee.

He drank three cups, sitting at the table and smoking cigarettes from a pack the girl had left behind. When he felt sufficiently awake to start moving again, he stood up and began cleaning the trailer, working as quietly as possible so as not to wake the kid. He took care of the living room first, systematically attacking each category of refuse (ashes, balloons, broken glasses), and then headed into the kitchen, where he scraped plates, discarded lobster shells, and washed the dishes and silverware. It took him two hours to put the little house in order, and Pozzi slept through it, never once stirring from his room. Once the cleanup was finished, Nashe made himself a ham and cheese sandwich and a fresh pot of coffee, and then he tiptoed back into his own room to retrieve one of his unread books—*Our Mutual Friend*, by Charles Dickens. He ate the sandwich, drank another cup of coffee, and then carried one of the kitchen chairs outside, positioning it so as to prop up his legs on the steps of the trailer. It was an unusually warm and sunny day for mid-October, and as Nashe sat there with the book in his lap, lighting up one of the cigars they had ordered for the party, he suddenly felt so tranquil, so profoundly at peace with himself, that he decided not to open the book until he had smoked the cigar to the end.

He had been at it for nearly twenty minutes when he heard a sound of thrashing leaves off in the woods. He rose from his chair, turned in the direction of the sound, and saw Murks walking toward him, emerging from the foliage with the holster cinched around his blue jacket. Nashe was so accustomed to the gun by then that he failed to notice it, but he was surprised to see Murks, and since there was no question of doing any work that day, he wondered what this unexpected visit could mean. They made small talk for the first three or four minutes, referring vaguely to the party and the mild weather. Murks told him that the chauffeur had driven off with the girl at five thirty, and from the way the kid was sleeping in there, he said, it looked like he'd had a busy night. Yes, Nashe said, he hadn't been disappointed, the whole thing had worked out well.

There was a long pause after that, and for the next fifteen or twenty seconds, Murks looked at the ground, poking the dirt with the tip of his shoe. "I'm afraid I've got some bad news for you," he said at last, still not daring to look Nashe in the eye.

"I know that," Nashe said. "You wouldn't have come out here today unless you did."

"Well, I'm awful sorry," Murks said, taking a sealed envelope from his pocket and handing it to Nashe. "It kind of confused me when they told me about it, but I suppose they're within their rights. It all depends on how you look at it, I guess."

Seeing the envelope, Nashe automatically assumed it was a letter from Donna. No one else would bother to write to him, he thought, and the moment this thought entered his consciousness, he was overwhelmed by a sudden attack of nausea and shame. He had forgotten Juliette's birthday. The twelfth had come and gone five days ago, and he hadn't even noticed.

Then he looked at the envelope and saw that it was blank. It couldn't have come from Donna without stamps, he told himself, and when he finally tore it open, he found a single sheet of typed paper inside—words and numbers arranged in perfect columns with a heading that read, NASHE AND POZZI: EXPENSES.

"What's this supposed to be?" he asked.

"The bosses' figures," Murks said. "Credits and debits, the balance sheet of money spent and money earned."

When Nashe examined the page more closely, he saw that it was precisely that. It was an accountant's statement, the meticulous work of a bookkeeper, and if nothing else it proved that Flower had not forgotten his old profession since striking it rich seven years ago. The pluses were itemized in the left-hand column, all duly noted according to Nashe and Pozzi's calculations, with no quibbles or discrepancies: 1000 hours of work at $10 per hour = $10,000. But then there were the minuses in the right-hand column, a list of sums that amounted to an inventory of everything that had happened to them in the past fifty days:

| | |
|---|---|
| Food | $1628.41 |
| Beer, liquor | 217.36 |
| Books, newspapers, magazines | 72.15 |
| Tobacco | 87.48 |
| Radio | 59.86 |
| Broken window | 66.50 |
| Entertainment (10/16) | 900.00 |
| —hostess $400 | |
| —car $500 | |
| Miscellaneous | 41.14 |

($3072.90)

"What's this," Nashe said, "some kind of prank?"

"I'm afraid not," Murks said.

"But all these things were supposed to be included."

"I thought so, too. But I guess we were wrong."

"What do you mean, wrong? We all shook hands on it. You know that as well as I do."

"Maybe so. But if you look at the contract, you'll see there's no mention of food. Lodging, yes. Work clothes, yes. But there's not a word in there about food."

"This is a dark and dirty thing, Calvin. I hope you understand that."

"It's not for me to say. The bosses have always treated me fair, and I've never had any reason to complain. The way they figure it, a job means earning money for the work you do, but how you spend that money is your own business. That's how it is with me. They give me my salary and a house to live in, but I buy my own food. It's a nice arrangement as far as I'm concerned. Nine-tenths of the folks that work ain't half so lucky. They got to pay for everything. Not just food, but lodging as well. That's the way it is the world over."

"But these are special circumstances."

"Well, maybe they're not so special, after all. When you come right down to it, you should be glad they didn't charge you for rent and utilities."

Nashe saw that the cigar he was smoking had gone out. He studied it for a moment without really seeing it, then tossed it to the ground and crushed it underfoot. "I think it's time I went over to the main house and had a talk with your bosses," he said.

"Can't do that now," Murks said. "They're gone."

"Gone? What are you talking about?"

"That's right, they're gone. They left for Paris, France, about three hours ago, and they won't be back until after Christmas."

"It's hard to believe they'd just take off like that—without bothering to look at the wall. It doesn't make any sense."

"Oh, they saw it all right. I took them out here early this morning when you and the kid were still asleep. They thought it was coming along real nice. Good job, they said, keep up the good work. They couldn't have been happier."

"Shit," Nashe said. "Shit on them and their goddamned wall."

"No sense in getting angry, friend. It's only another two or three weeks. If you cut out the parties and such, you'll be out of here before you know it."

"Three weeks from now, it will be November."

"That's all right. You're a tough one, Nashe, you can handle it."

"Sure, I can handle it. But what about Jack? Once he sees this paper, it's going to kill him."

Ten minutes after Nashe went back into the trailer, Pozzi woke up. The kid looked so touseled and swollen-eyed that Nashe didn't have the heart to spring the news on him, and for the next half hour he allowed the conversation to drift along with aimless, inconsequential remarks, listening to Pozzi's blow-by-blow description of what he and the girl had done to each other after Nashe had gone to bed. It seemed wrong to interrupt such a story and spoil the kid's pleasure in telling it, but once a decent interval had elapsed, Nashe finally changed the subject and pulled out the envelope that Murks had given him.

"It's like this, Jack," he said, barely giving the kid a chance to look at the paper. "They've pulled a fast one on us, and now we're sunk. We thought we were even, but the way they've worked it out, we're still three thousand dollars in the hole. Food, magazines, even the goddamned broken window—they've charged us for all of it. Not to speak of Miss Hot Pants and her chauffeur, which probably goes without saying. We just took it for granted that those things were covered by the contract, but the contract doesn't say anything about them. Fine. So we made a mistake. The point is: What do we do now? As far as I'm concerned, you're not in it anymore. You've done enough, and from now on this thing is my problem. So I'm going to get you out of here. We'll dig a hole under the fence, and once it gets dark, you'll crawl through that hole and be on your way."

"And what about you?" Pozzi said.

"I'm going to stay and finish the job."

"Not a chance. You're crawling through that hole with me."

"Not this time, Jack. I can't."

"And why the hell not? You afraid of holes or something? You've already been living in one for the past two months—or haven't you noticed?"

"I promised myself I'd see it through to the end. I'm not asking you to understand it, but I'm just not going to run away. I've done too much of that already, and I don't want to live like that anymore. If I sneak out of here before the debt is paid off, I won't be worth a goddamned thing to myself."

"Custer's last stand."

"That's it. The old put-up-or-shut-up routine."

"It's the wrong battle, Jim. You'll just be wasting your time, fucking yourself over for nothing. If the three grand is so important to you, why don't you send them a check? They don't care how they get their money, and they'll have it a whole lot sooner if you leave with me tonight. Shit, I'll even go half-and-half with you. I know a guy in Philly who can get us into a game tomorrow night. All we have to do is hitch a ride, and we'll have the dough in less than forty-eight hours. Simple. We'll send it to them special delivery, and that will be that."

"Flower and Stone aren't here. They left for Paris this morning."

"Jesus, you're a stubborn son of a bitch, aren't you? Who the fuck cares where they are?"

"Sorry, kid. No dice. You can talk yourself blue in the face, but I'm not going."

"It will take you twice as long working by yourself, asshole. Did you ever think of that? Ten dollars an hour, not twenty. You'll be lugging around those stones until Christmas."

"I know that. Just don't forget to send me a card, Jack, that's all I ask. I usually get kind of sentimental around that time of year."

They kept it up for another forty-five minutes, arguing back and forth until Pozzi finally slammed down his fist on the kitchen table and left the room. He was so angry at Nashe that he wouldn't talk to him for the next three hours, hiding behind the closed door of his bedroom and refusing to come out. At four o'clock, Nashe went to the door and announced that he was going outside to start digging the hole. Pozzi didn't respond, but not long after Nashe put on his jacket and left the trailer, he heard the door slam again, and a moment later the kid was trotting across the meadow to catch up with him. Nashe waited, and then they walked to the tool shed together in silence, neither one of them daring to reopen the argument.

"I've been thinking it over," Pozzi said, as they stood before the locked door of the shed. "What's the point of going through all this escape business? Wouldn't it be simpler if we just went to Calvin and told him I'm leaving? As long as you're still here to honor the contract, what difference could it make?"

"I'll tell you why," Nashe said, picking up a small stone from the ground and smashing it against the door to break the lock. "Because I don't trust him. Calvin isn't as stupid as he looks, and he knows your name is on that contract. With Flower and Stone gone, he'll say he doesn't have the authority to make any changes, that we can't do anything until they get back. That's his line, isn't it? I just work here, boys, and I do what the bosses tell me. But he knows what's going on, he's been part of it from the beginning. Otherwise, Flower and Stone wouldn't have taken off and left him in charge. He pretends to be on our side, but he belongs to them, he doesn't give a rat's ass about us. As soon as we told him you wanted to leave, he'd figure out you were going to escape. That's the next step, isn't it? And I don't want to give him any advance warning. Who knows what kind of trick he'd pull on us then?"

So they broke open the door of the shed, took out two shovels, and carried them down the dirt path that led through the woods. It was a longer walk to the fence than they had remembered, and by the time they started digging, the light had already begun to fade. The ground was hard and the bottom of the fence ran deep, and they both grunted each time they struck their shovels into the dirt. They could see the road right before them, but only one car passed in the half hour they spent there, a battered station wagon with a man, a woman, and a small boy inside it. The boy waved to them with a startled expression on his face as the car drove by, but neither Nashe nor Pozzi waved back. They dug on in silence, and when they had finally carved out a hole large enough for Pozzi's body to fit through, their arms were aching with exhaustion. They flung down their shovels at that point and headed back to the trailer, crossing into the meadow as the sky grew purple around them, glowing thinly in the mid-October dusk.

They ate their last meal together as if they were strangers. They didn't know what to say to each other anymore, and their attempts at conversation were awkward, at times even embarrassing. Pozzi's departure was too near to allow them to think of anything else, and yet neither one of them was willing to talk about it, so for long stretches they sat there locked in silence, each one imagining what would become of him without the other. There was no point in reminiscing about the past, in looking back over the good times they had spent together, for there hadn't been any good times, and the future was too uncertain to be anything but a shadow, a formless, unarticulated presence that neither one of them wished to examine very closely. It was only after they stood up from the table and began clearing their plates that the tension spilled over into words again. Night had come, and suddenly they had reached the moment of last-minute preparations and farewells. They exchanged addresses and telephone numbers, promising to stay in touch with each other, but Nashe knew that it would never happen, that this was the last time he would ever see Pozzi. They packed a small bag of provisions—food, cigarettes, road maps of Pennsylvania and New Jersey—and then Nashe handed Pozzi a twenty-dollar bill, which he had found at the bottom of his suitcase earlier that afternoon.

"It's not much," he said, "but I suppose it's better than nothing."

The air was cold that night, and they bundled up in sweatshirts and jackets before leaving the trailer. They walked across the meadow carrying flashlights, moving along the length of the unfinished wall as a way to guide them in the darkness. When they came to the end and saw the immense piles of stones standing at the edge of the woods, they played their beams along the surfaces for a moment as they passed by. It produced a ghostly effect of weird shapes and darting shadows, and Nashe could not help thinking that the stones were alive, that the night had turned them into a colony of sleeping animals. He wanted to make a joke about it, but he couldn't come up with anything fast enough, and a moment later they were walking down the dirt path in the woods. When they reached the fence, he saw the two shovels they had left on the ground and realized that it wouldn't look right if Murks found both of them. One shovel would mean that Pozzi had planned his escape alone, but two shovels would mean that Nashe had been a part of it as well. As soon as Pozzi was gone, he would have to pick one up and carry it back to the shed.

Pozzi struck a match, and as he lifted the flame to his cigarette, Nashe noticed that his hand was trembling. "Well, Mr. Fireman," he said, "it looks like we've come to a parting of the ways."

"You'll be fine, Jack," Nashe said. "Just remember to brush your teeth after every meal, and nothing bad can happen to you."

They grasped each other by the elbows, squeezing hard for a moment or two, and then Pozzi asked Nashe to hold the cigarette while he crawled through the hole. A moment later he was standing on the other side of the fence, and Nashe handed the cigarette back to him.

"Come with me," Pozzi said. "Don't be a jerk, Jim. Come with me now."

He said it with such earnestness that Nashe almost gave in, but then he waited too long before giving an answer, and in that interval the temptation passed. "I'll catch up with you in a couple of months," he said. "You'd better get moving."

Pozzi backed off from the fence, dragged once on the cigarette, and then flicked it away from him, causing a small shower of sparks to flare up briefly on the road. "I'll call your sister tomorrow and tell her you're okay," he said.

"Just beat it," Nashe said, rattling the fence with an abrupt, impatient gesture. "Go as fast as you can."

"I'm already out of here," Pozzi said. "By the time you count to a hundred, you won't even remember who I am."

Then, without saying good-bye, he turned on his heels and started running down the road.


Lying in bed that night, Nashe rehearsed the story he was planning to tell Murks in the morning, going over it several times until it began to sound like the truth: how he and Pozzi had gone to sleep at around ten o'clock, how he hadn't heard a sound for the next eight hours ("I always sleep like a log"), and how he had come out of his room at six to prepare breakfast, had knocked on the kid's door to wake him up, and had discovered that he was gone. No, Jack hadn't talked about running away, and he hadn't left a note or any clue as to where he might be. Who knows what happened to him? Maybe he got up early and decided to take a walk. Sure, I'll help you look for him. He's probably wandering around in the woods somewhere, trying to catch a glimpse of the migrating geese.

But Nashe never had a chance to tell any of those lies. When his alarm rang at six o'clock the next morning, he went into the kitchen to boil a pot of water for coffee, and then, curious to know what the temperature was, he opened the door of the trailer and stuck his head outside to test the air. That was when he saw Pozzi— although it took several moments before he realized who it was. At first he saw no more than an indistinguishable heap, a bundle of blood-spattered clothing sprawled out on the ground, and even after he saw that a man was in those clothes, he did not see Pozzi so much as he saw a hallucination, a thing that could not have been there. He noticed that the clothes were remarkably similar to the ones that Pozzi had been wearing the night before, that the man was dressed in the same windbreaker and hooded sweatshirt, the same blue jeans and mustard-colored boots, but even then Nashe could not put those facts together and say to himself: *I am looking at Pozzi*. For the man's limbs were oddly tangled and inert, and from the way his head was cocked to one side (twisted at an almost impossible angle, as if the head were about to separate itself from the body), Nashe felt certain that he was dead.

He started down the steps a moment later, and at that point he finally understood what he was seeing. As he walked across the grass toward the kid's body, Nashe felt a series of small gagging sounds escape from his throat. He fell to his knees, took Pozzi's battered face in his hands, and discovered that a pulse was still fluttering weakly in the veins of the kid's neck. "My God," he said, only half-aware that he was talking out loud. "What have they done to you, Jack?" Both the kid's eyes were swollen shut, ugly gashes had been opened on his forehead, temples, and mouth, and several teeth were gone: it was a pulverized face, a face beaten beyond recognition. Nashe heard the gagging sounds escape from his throat again, and then, almost whimpering, he gathered Pozzi into his arms and carried him up the steps of the trailer.

It was impossible to know how serious the injuries were. The kid was unconscious, perhaps even in a coma, but lying out there in the frigid autumn weather for God knows how many hours had only made matters worse. In the end, that had probably done as much damage as the beating itself. Nashe laid the kid out on the sofa and then rushed into both bedrooms and stripped the blankets off the beds. He had seen several people die of shock after being rescued from fires, and Pozzi had all the symptoms of a bad case: the dreadful pallor, the blueness of the lips, the icy, corpselike hands. Nashe did everything he could to keep him warm, rubbing his body under the blankets and tilting his legs to get the blood flowing again, but even after the kid's temperature began to rise a little, he showed no signs of waking up.

Things happened quickly after that. Murks arrived at seven, tramping up the steps of the trailer and giving his customary knock on the door, and when Nashe called for him to come in, his first response on seeing Pozzi was to laugh. "What's the matter with him?" he said, gesturing at the sofa with his thumb. "Did he tie one on again last night?" But once he stepped into the room and was close enough to see Pozzi's face, his amusement turned to alarm. "Christ almighty," he said. "This boy's in trouble." "You're damn right he's in trouble," Nashe said. "If we don't get him to a hospital in the next hour, he's not going to make it."

So Murks ran back to the house to fetch the jeep, and in the meantime Nashe dragged out the mattress from Pozzi's bed and leaned it against the wall of the trailer, keeping it there to be used for their makeshift ambulance. The ride was going to be hard enough anyway, but perhaps the cushion would prevent the kid from being jolted around too much. When Murks finally returned, there was another man sitting with him in the front of the jeep. "This here is Floyd," he said. "He can help us carry the kid." Floyd was Murks's son-in-law, and he looked to be somewhere in his mid to late twenties—a large, solidly built young man who stood at least six four or six five, with a smooth reddish face and a woolen hunting cap on his head. He seemed no more than moderately intelligent, however, and when Murks introduced him to Nashe he extended his hand with a clumsy, earnest cheerfulness that was entirely inappropriate for the situation. Nashe was so disgusted that he refused to offer his hand in return, merely staring at Floyd until the big man dropped his arm to his side.

Nashe maneuvered the mattress into the back of the jeep, and then the three of them went into the trailer and lifted Pozzi off the sofa, carrying him outside with the blankets still wrapped around his body. Nashe tucked him in, trying to make him as comfortable as possible, but every time he looked down at the kid's face, he knew there was no hope. Pozzi didn't have a chance anymore. By the time they got him to the hospital, he would already be dead.

But worse was still to come. Murks clapped his hand on Nashe's shoulder at that point and said, "We'll be back as soon as we can," and when it finally dawned on Nashe that they weren't planning to take him along, something in him snapped, and he turned on Murks in a sudden fit of rage. "Sorry," Murks said. "I can't let you do that. There's been enough commotion around here for one day, and I don't want things getting out of hand. You don't have to worry, Nashe. Floyd and me can manage on our own."

But Nashe was beside himself, and instead of backing off, he lunged at Murks and grabbed hold of his jacket, calling him a liar and a goddamn son of a bitch. Before he could bring his fist into Calvin's face, however, Floyd was all over him, wrapping his arms around him from behind and yanking him off the ground. Murks took two or three steps back, pulled his gun out of the holster, and pointed it at Nashe. But not even that was enough to put an end to it, and Nashe went on yelling and kicking in Floyd's arms. "Shoot me, you son of a bitch!" he said to Murks. "Come on, go ahead and shoot me!"

"He don't know what he's saying anymore," Murks said calmly, glancing over at his son-in-law. "The poor bugger's lost it."

Without warning, Floyd threw Nashe violently to the ground, and before Nashe could get up to resume the assault, a foot came crashing into his stomach. It knocked the wind out of him, and as he lay there gasping for breath, the two men broke for the jeep and climbed in. Nashe heard the engine kick over, and by the time he was able to stand up again, they were already driving off, disappearing with Pozzi into the woods.

He did not hesitate after that. He went inside, put on his jacket, stuffed the pockets with as much food as they would hold, and immediately left the trailer again. His only thought was to get out of there. He would never have a better chance to escape, and he wasn't going to squander the opportunity. He would crawl through the hole he had dug with Pozzi the night before, and that would be the end of it.

He walked across the meadow at a quick pace, not even bothering to look at the wall, and when he reached the woods on the other side, he suddenly started to run, charging down the dirt path as if his life depended on it. He came to the fence a few minutes later, breathing hard from the exertion, staring out at the road before him with his arms pressed against the barrier for support. For a moment or two, it didn't even occur to him that the hole had vanished. But once he began to recover his breath, he looked down at his feet and saw that he was standing on level ground. The hole had been filled in, the shovel was gone, and what with the leaves and twigs scattered around him, it was almost impossible to know that a hole had ever been there.

Nashe gripped the fence with all ten fingers and squeezed as hard as he could. He held on like that for close to a minute, and then, opening his hands again, he brought them to his face and began to sob.

# 8

---

For several nights after that, he had the same recurring dream. He would imagine that he was waking up in the darkness of his own room, and once he understood that he was no longer asleep, he would put on his clothes, leave the trailer, and start walking across the meadow. When he came to the tool shed at the other end, he would kick down the door, grab a shovel, and continue on into the woods, running down the dirt path that led to the fence. The dream was always vivid and exact, less a distortion of the real than a simulacrum, an illusion so rich in the details of waking life that Nashe never suspected that he was dreaming. He would hear the faint crackling of the earth underfoot, he would feel the chill of the night air against his skin, he would smell the pungent autumn decay wafting through the woods. But every time he came to the fence with the shovel in his hand, the dream would suddenly stop, and he would wake up to discover that he was still lying in his own bed.

The question was: Why didn't he get up at that point and do what he had just done in the dream? There was nothing to prevent him from trying to escape, and yet he continued to balk at it, refused even to consider it as a possibility. At first, he attributed this reluctance to fear. He was convinced that Murks was responsible for what had happened to Pozzi (with a helping hand from Floyd, no doubt), and there was every reason to believe that something similar would be in store for him if he tried to run out on the contract. It was true that Murks had looked upset when he saw Pozzi that morning in the trailer, but who was to say he hadn't been putting on an act? Nashe had seen Pozzi running down the road, and how could he have wound up in the meadow again if Murks hadn't put him there? If the kid had been beaten by someone else, his attacker would have left him on the road and run away. And even if Pozzi had still been conscious then, he wouldn't have had the strength to crawl back through the hole, let alone cross the entire meadow by himself. No, Murks had put him there as a warning, to show Nashe what happened to people who tried to escape. His story was that he had driven Pozzi to the Sisters of Mercy Hospital in Doylestown, but why couldn't he have been lying about that as well? They could just as easily have dumped the kid in the woods somewhere and buried him. What difference would it make if he had still been alive? Cover a man's face with dirt, and he'll smother to death before you can count to a hundred. Murks was a master at filling in holes, after all. Once he got through with one of them, you couldn't even tell if it had been there or not.

Little by little, however, Nashe understood that fear had nothing to do with it. Every time he imagined himself running away from the meadow, he saw Murks pointing a gun at his back and slowly pulling the trigger—but the thought of the bullet ripping through his flesh and rupturing his heart did not frighten him so much as make him angry. He deserved to die, perhaps, but he did not want to give Murks the satisfaction of killing him. That would be too easy, too predictable a way for things to end. He had already caused Pozzi's death by forcing him to escape, but even if he let himself die as well (and there were times when this thought became almost irresistible to him), it wasn't going to undo the wrong he had done. That was why he continued working on the wall—not because he was afraid, not because he felt obliged to pay off the debt anymore, but because he wanted revenge. He would finish out his time there, and once he was free to go, he would call in the cops and have Murks arrested. That was the least he could do for the kid now, he felt. He had to keep himself alive long enough to see that the son of a bitch got what was coming to him.

He sat down and wrote a letter to Donna, explaining that his construction job was taking longer than expected. He had thought they would be finished by now, but it looked like the work was going to last another six to eight weeks. He felt certain that Murks would open the letter and read it before sending it off, and so he made sure not to mention anything about what had happened to Pozzi. He tried to keep the tone light and cheerful, adding a separate page for Juliette with a drawing of a castle and several riddles he thought would amuse her, and when Donna wrote back a week later, she said that she was happy to hear him sounding so well. It didn't matter what kind of work he was doing, she added. As long as he was enjoying it, that was reward enough in itself. But she did hope he would think about settling down after the job was over. They all missed him terribly, and Juliette couldn't wait to see him again.

It pained Nashe to read this letter, and for many days afterward he cringed whenever he thought of how thoroughly he had deceived his sister. He was more cut off from the world now than ever before, and there were times when he could feel something collapsing inside him, as if the ground he stood on were gradually giving way, crumbling under the pressure of his loneliness. The work continued, but that was a solitary business as well, and he avoided Murks as much as possible, refusing to speak to him except when it was absolutely necessary. Murks maintained the same placid demeanor as before, but Nashe would not be lulled by it, and he resisted the foreman's apparent friendliness with barely hidden contempt. At least once a day he went through an elaborate scene in which he imagined himself turning on Murks in a sudden outburst of violence—jumping on top of him and wrestling him to the ground, then freeing the gun from its holster and pointing it straight between his eyes. Work was the only escape from this tumult, the mindless labor of lifting and carting stones, and he threw himself into it with a grim and relentless passion, doing more on his own each day than he and Pozzi had ever managed together. He finished the second row of the wall in less than a week, loading up the wagon with three or four stones at once, and every time he made another journey across the meadow, he would inexplicably find himself thinking about Stone's miniature world in the main house, as if the act of touching a real stone had called forth a memory of the man who bore that name. Sooner or later, Nashe thought, there would be a new section to represent where he was now, a scale model of the wall and the meadow and the trailer, and once those things were finished, two tiny figures would be set down in the middle of the field: one for Pozzi and one for himself. The idea of such extravagant smallness began to exert an almost unbearable fascination over Nashe. Sometimes, powerless to stop himself, he even went so far as to imagine that he was already living inside the model. Flower and Stone would look down on him then, and he would suddenly be able to see himself through their eyes—as if he were no larger than a thumb, a little gray mouse darting back and forth in his cage.

It was worst at night, however, after the work had ended and he went back to the trailer alone. That was when he missed Pozzi the most, and in the beginning there were times when his sorrow and nostalgia were so acute that he could barely muster the strength to cook a proper meal for himself. Once or twice, he did not eat anything at all, but sat down in the living room with a bottle of bourbon and spent the hours until bedtime listening to requiem masses by Mozart and Verdi with the volume at full blast, literally weeping as he sat there amid the uproar of the music, remembering the kid through the onrushing wind of human voices as though he were no more than a piece of earth, a brittle clot of earth scattering into the dust he was made of. It soothed him to indulge in these histrionics of grief, to sink to the depths of a lurid, imponderable sadness, but even after he caught hold of himself and began to adjust to his solitude, he never fully recovered from Pozzi's absence, and he went on mourning the kid as though a part of himself had been lost forever. His domestic routines became dry and meaningless, a mechanical drudgery of preparing food and shoveling it into his mouth, of making things dirty and cleaning them up, the clockwork of animal functions. He tried to fill the emptiness by reading books, remembering how much pleasure they had given him on the road, but he found it difficult to concentrate now, and no sooner would he begin to read the words on the page than his head would swarm with images from his past: an afternoon he had spent in Minnesota five months ago, blowing bubbles with Juliette in the backyard; watching his friend Bobby Turnbull fall through a burning floor in Boston; the precise words he had spoken to Thérèse when he asked her to marry him; his mother's face when he walked into the hospital room in Florida for the first time after her stroke; Donna jumping up and down as a cheerleader in high school. He didn't want to remember any of these things, but without the stories in the books to take him away from himself, the memories kept pouring through him whether he liked it or not. He endured these assaults every night for close to a week, and then, not knowing what else to do, he broke down one morning and asked Murks if he could have a piano. No, it didn't have to be a real piano, he said, he just needed something to keep himself busy, a distraction to steady his nerves.

"I can understand that," Murks said, trying to sound sympathetic. "It must get lonely out here all by yourself. I mean, the kid had some peculiar ways about him, but at least he was company. It'll cost you, though. Not that you don't know that already."

"I don't care," Nashe said. "I'm not asking for a real piano. It can't come to that much."

"First time I ever heard of a piano that's not a piano. What kind of instrument are we talking about?"

"An electronic keyboard. You know, one of those portable things you plug into a socket in the wall. It comes with speakers and funny little plastic keys. You've probably seen them around in the stores."

"I can't say that I have. But that don't mean nothing. You just tell me what you want, Nashe, and I'll see that you get it."

Fortunately, he still had his books of music, and there was no shortage of material for him to play. Once he had sold his piano, there had seemed little reason to hold onto them, but he hadn't been able to throw them out, and so they had spent the whole year traveling around in the trunk of his car. There were about a dozen books in all: selections from a variety of composers (Bach, Couperin, Mozart, Beethoven, Schubert, Bartok, Satie), a couple of Czerny exercise books, and a fat volume of popular jazz and blues numbers transcribed for piano. Murks showed up with the instrument the next evening, and although it was a bizarre and ridiculous piece of technology—scarcely better than a toy, in fact—Nashe happily removed the thing from its box and set it on the kitchen table. For a couple of nights he spent the hours between dinner and bedtime teaching himself how to play again, going through countless finger exercises to limber up his rusty joints as he learned the possibilities and limitations of the curious machine: the oddness of the touch, the amplified sounds, the lack of percussive force. In that respect, the keyboard functioned more like a harpsichord than a piano, and when he finally started to play real pieces on the third night, he discovered that older works—pieces written before the invention of the piano—tended to sound better than the new ones. This led him to concentrate on works by pre-nineteenth-century composers: *The Notebook of Anna Magdalena Bach, The Well-Tempered Clavier*, "The Mysterious Barricades." It was impossible for him to play this last piece without thinking about the wall, and he found himself returning to it more often than any of the others. It took just over two minutes to perform, and at no point in its slow, stately progress, with all its pauses, suspensions, and repetitions, did it require him to touch more than one note at a time. The music started and stopped, then started again, then stopped again, and yet through it all the piece continued to advance, pushing on toward a resolution that never came. Were those the mysterious barricades? Nashe remembered reading somewhere that no one was certain what Couperin had meant by that title. Some scholars interpreted it as a comical reference to women's underclothing—the impenetrability of corsets—while others saw it as an allusion to the unresolved harmonies in the piece. Nashe had no way of knowing. As far as he was concerned, the barricades stood for the wall he was building in the meadow, but that was quite another thing from knowing what they meant.

He no longer looked upon the hours after work as a blank and leaden time. Music brought oblivion, the sweetness of no longer having to think about himself, and once he had finished practicing for the night, Nashe usually felt so languorous and empty of emotion that he was able to fall asleep without much trouble. Still, he despised himself for allowing his feelings to soften toward Murks, for remembering the foreman's kindness to him with such gratitude. It wasn't just that Murks had gone out of his way to buy the keyboard—he had positively jumped at the chance, acting as though his single desire in life were to restore Nashe's good opinion of him. Nashe wanted to hate Murks totally, to turn him into something less than human by the sheer force of that hatred, but how was that possible when the man refused to act like a monster? Murks began showing up at the trailer with little presents (pies baked by his wife, woolen scarves, extra blankets), and at work he was never less than indulgent, always telling Nashe to slow down and not to push so hard. Most troubling of all, he even seemed to be worried about Pozzi, and several times a week he would give Nashe a progress report on the kid's condition, talking as though he were in constant touch with the hospital. What was Nashe to make of this solicitude? He sensed it was a trick, a smoke screen to cover up the true danger that Murks posed to him—and yet how could he be sure? Little by little, he felt himself weakening, gradually giving in to the foreman's quiet persistence. Every time he accepted another gift, every time he paused to chat about the weather or smiled at one of Calvin's remarks, he felt that he was betraying himself. And yet he kept on doing it. After a while, the only thing that prevented him from capitulating was the continued presence of the gun. That was the ultimate sign of how things stood between them, and he had only to look at the weapon on Murks's waist to remind himself of their fundamental inequality. Then one day, just to see what would happen, he turned to Murks and said, "What's with the gun, Calvin? Are you still expecting trouble?" And Murks glanced down at the holster with a puzzled look on his face and said, "I don't know. I just got into the habit of wearing it, I guess." And when he came out to the meadow the next morning to begin work, the gun was gone.

Nashe didn't know what to think anymore. Was Murks telling him that he was free now, or was this simply another twist in an elaborate strategy of deception? Before Nashe could begin to decide, yet another element was thrown into the maelstrom of his uncertainty. It came in the form of a small boy, and for several days after that, Nashe felt that he was standing on the edge of a precipice, staring into the bowels of a private hell that he had never even known was there: a fiery underworld of clamoring beasts and dark, unimaginable impulses. On October thirtieth, just two days after Murks stopped wearing the gun, he came to the meadow holding the hand of a four-year-old boy whom he introduced as his grandson, Floyd Junior.

"Floyd Senior lost his job in Texas this summer," he said, "and now him and my daughter Sally are back here trying to make a fresh start. They're both out looking for work and a place to live, and since Addie's feeling a bit under the weather this morning, she thought it might be a good idea if little Floyd tagged along with me. I hope you don't mind. I'll keep an eye on him and make sure he doesn't get in your way."

He was a scrawny child with a long, narrow face and a runny nose, and he stood there beside his grandfather bundled up in a thick red parka, gazing at Nashe with both curiosity and detachment, as if he had been plunked down in front of an odd-looking bird or shrub. No, Nashe didn't mind, but even if he had, how could he have dared to say it? For the better part of the morning, the boy scrambled among the piles of stones in the corner of the meadow, cavorting like some strange and silent monkey, but every time Nashe returned to that area to load up the wagon again, the boy would stop what he was doing, squat down on his perch, and study Nashe with those same rapt and expressionless eyes. It began to make Nashe feel uncomfortable, and after it had happened five or six times, he was so unnerved by it that he forced himself to look up at the boy and smile—simply as a way to break the spell. Unexpectedly, the boy smiled back at him and waved, and just then, as if remembering something from another century, Nashe understood that this was the same boy who had waved to him and Pozzi that night from the back of the station wagon. Was that how they had been found out? he wondered. Had the boy told his mother and father that he had seen two men digging a hole under the fence? Had the father then gone to Murks and reported what the boy had said? Nashe could never quite grasp how it happened, but an instant after this thought occurred to him, he looked up at Murks's grandson again and realized that he hated him more than he had ever hated anyone in his life. He hated him so much, he felt he wanted to kill him.

That was when the horror began. A tiny seed had been planted in Nashe's head, and before he even knew it was there, it was already sprouting inside him, proliferating like some wild, mutant flower, an ecstatic burgeoning that threatened to overrun the entire field of his consciousness. All he had to do was snatch the boy, he thought, and everything would change for him: he would suddenly know what he had to know. The boy for the truth, he would say to Murks, and at that point Calvin would have to talk, he would have to tell him what he had done with Pozzi. There wouldn't be any choice. If he didn't talk, his grandson would be dead. Nashe would make sure of that. He would strangle the kid right in front of his eyes.

Once Nashe allowed that thought to enter his head, it was succeeded by others, each one more violent and repulsive than the last. He slit the boy's throat with a razor. He kicked him to death with his boots. He took his head and smashed it against a stone, beating in his little skull until his brains turned to pulp. By the end of the morning, Nashe was in a frenzy, a delirium of homicidal lust. No matter how desperately he tried to erase those images, he would begin to hunger for them the moment they disappeared. That was the true horror: not that he could imagine killing the boy, but that even after he had imagined it, he wanted to imagine it again.

The worst part of it was that the boy kept coming back to the meadow—not just the next day, but the day after that as well. The first hours had been bad enough, but then the boy took it into his head to become infatuated with Nashe, responding to their exchange of smiles as if they had sworn an oath to each other and were now friends for life. Even before lunch, Floyd Junior had crawled down from his mountain of stones and was trotting after Nashe as his new hero pulled the wagon back and forth across the meadow. Murks made a move to stop him, but Nashe, already dreaming of how he was going to kill the child, waved him off and said it was all right. "I don't mind," he said. "I like kids." By then, Nashe had already begun to sense that something was wrong with the boy—some dullness or simplemindedness that made him appear subnormal. He was barely able to talk, and the only thing he said as he ran along behind him through the grass was *Jim! Jim! Jim!* pronouncing the name over and over again in a kind of moronic incantation. Except for his age, he seemed to have nothing in common with Juliette, and when Nashe compared the sad pallor of this little boy with the brightness and sparkle of his curly-headed daughter, his darling dervish with her crystal laugh and chubby knees, he felt nothing but contempt for him. With every hour that passed, his urge to attack him became stronger and more uncontrollable, and when six o'clock finally rolled around, it seemed almost a miracle to Nashe that the boy was still alive. He put away his tools in the shed, and just as he was about to shut the door, Murks came up to him and patted him on the shoulder. "I have to hand it to you, Nashe," he said. "You've got the magic touch. The little fella ain't never taken to anyone like he did to you today. If I hadn't seen it with my own eyes, I wouldn't have believed it."

The next morning, the boy came to the meadow dressed in his Halloween costume: a black-and-white skeleton outfit with a mask that looked like a skull. It was one of those crude, flimsy things you buy in a box at Woolworth's, and because the weather was cold that day, he wore it over his outer garments, which gave him an oddly bloated appearance, as if he had doubled his weight overnight. According to Murks, the boy had insisted on wearing the costume so that Nashe could see how he looked in it, and in his demented state at that moment, Nashe immediately began to wonder if the boy wasn't trying to tell him something. The costume stood for death, after all, death in its purest and most symbolic form, and perhaps that meant the boy knew what Nashe was planning, that he had  ome to the meadow dressed as death because he knew he was going to die. Nashe could not help seeing it as a message written in code. The boy was telling him that it was all right, that as long as Nashe was the one who killed him, everything was going to be all right.

He warred against himself for the whole of that day, devising any number of ruses to keep the skeleton boy at a safe distance from his murderous hands. In the morning, he told him to watch a particular stone at the back of one of the piles, instructing him to guard it so that it would not disappear, and in the afternoon Nashe let him play with the wagon while he went off and busied himself with masonry work at the other end of the meadow. But inevitably there were lapses, moments when the boy's concentration broke down and he came running toward Nashe, or else, even from a distance, those times when Nashe had to endure the litany of his name, the endless *Jim, Jim, Jim*, resounding like an alarm from the depths of his own fear. Again and again, he wanted to tell Murks not to bring him around anymore, but the struggle to keep his feelings under control took so much out of him, brought him so close to the point of mental collapse, that he could no longer trust himself with the words he wanted to say. He drank himself into a stupor that night, and the next morning, as if waking into the fullness of a nightmare, he opened the door of the trailer and saw that the boy was back—clutching a bag of Halloween candies against his chest, and then, without saying a word, solemnly handing it over to Nashe like a young brave delivering the spoils of his first hunt to the tribal chief.

"What's this for?" Nashe said to Murks.

"Jim," the boy said, answering the question himself. "Sweeties for Jim."

"That's right," Murks said. "He wanted to share his candy with you."

Nashe opened the bag a crack and peered down at the jumble of candy bars, apples, and raisins inside. "This is taking it a bit far, don't you think, Calvin? What's the kid trying to do, poison me?"

"He don't mean nothing by it," Murks said. "He just felt sorry for you—missing out on the trick-or-treating and all. It's not like you have to eat it."

"Sure," Nashe said, staring at the boy and wondering how he was going to live through another day of this. "It's the thought that counts, right?"

But he couldn't stand it anymore. The moment he stepped out into the meadow, he knew that he had reached his limit, that the boy would be dead within the next hour if he did not find a way to stop himself. He put one stone into the wagon, started to lift another, and then let it fall from his hands, listening to the thud as it crashed against the ground.

"There's something wrong with me today," he said to Murks. "I don't feel like myself."

"Maybe it's that flu bug that's been going around," Murks said.

"Yeah, that must be it. I'm probably coming down with the flu."

"You work too hard, Nashe, that's the problem. You're all worn out."

"If I lie down for an hour or two, maybe I'll feel better this afternoon."

"Forget this afternoon. Take the whole day off. There's no sense in pushing too hard, no sense at all. You need to get your strength back."

"All right, then. I'll take a couple of aspirins and crawl into bed. I hate to lose the day, though. But I guess it can't be helped."

"Don't worry about the money. I'll give you credit for the ten hours anyway. We'll call it a baby-sitting bonus."

"There's no need for that."

"No, I don't suppose there is, but that don't mean I can't do it. It's probably just as well, anyway. The weather's too cold out here for little Floyd. He'd catch his death standing around in this meadow all day."

"Yeah, I think you're right."

"Of course I'm right. The kid would catch his death on a day like this."

Nashe's head buzzed with these strangely omniscient words as he walked back to the trailer with Murks and the boy, and by the time he opened the door, he discovered that he was actually feeling ill. His body ached, and his muscles had become inexpressibly weak with exhaustion, as if he were suddenly burning up with a high fever. It was odd how quickly it had come over him: no sooner had Murks mentioned the word *flu* than he seemed to have caught it. Perhaps he had used himself up, he thought, and there was nothing left inside him. Perhaps he was so empty now that even a word could make him sick.

"Oh my gosh," Murks said, slapping himself against the forehead just as he was about to leave. "I almost forgot to tell you."

"Tell me?" Nashe said. "Tell me what?"

"About Pozzi. I called the hospital last night to see how he was, and the nurse said he was gone."

"Gone. Gone in what sense?"

"Gone. As in gone good-bye. He just got himself up out of bed, put on his clothes, and walked out of the hospital."

"You don't have to make up stories, Calvin. Jack's dead. He died two weeks ago."

"No, sir, he ain't dead. It looked pretty bad there for a while, I'll grant you that, but then he pulled through. The little runt was tougher than we thought. And now he's got himself all better. At least better enough to stand up and walk out of the hospital. I thought you'd want to know."

"I only want to know the truth. Nothing else interests me."

"Well, that's the truth. Jack Pozzi's gone, and you don't have to worry about him no more."

"Then let me call the hospital myself."

"I can't do that, son, you know that. No calls allowed until you finish paying off the debt. At the rate you're going, it won't be long now. Then you can make all the calls you want. As far as I'm concerned, you can go on calling till kingdom come."

It was three days before Nashe was able to work again. For the first two days he slept, rousing himself only when Murks entered the trailer to deliver aspirin and tea and canned soup, and when he was sufficiently conscious to realize that those two days had been lost to him, he understood that sleep had not only been a physical necessity, it had been a moral imperative as well. The drama with the little boy had changed him, and if not for the hibernation that followed, those forty-eight hours in which he had temporarily vanished from himself, he might never have woken up into the man he had become. Sleep was a passage from one life into another, a small death in which the demons inside him had caught fire again, melting back into the flames they were born of. It wasn't that they were gone, but they had no shape anymore, and in their formless ubiquity they had spread themselves through his entire body—invisible yet present, a part of him now in the same way that his blood and chromosomes were, a fire awash in the very fluids that kept him alive. He did not feel that he was any better or worse than he had been before, but he was no longer frightened. That was the crucial difference. He had rushed into the burning house and pulled himself out of the flames, and now that he had done it, the thought of doing it again no longer frightened him.

On the third morning he woke up hungry, instinctively climbing out of bed and heading for the kitchen, and although he was remarkably unsteady on his feet, he knew that hunger was a good sign, that it meant he was getting well. Rummaging around in one of the drawers for a clean spoon, he came upon a slip of paper with a telephone number written on it, and as he studied the childish, unfamiliar penmanship, he suddenly found himself thinking of the girl. She had written down her number for him at some point during the party on the sixteenth, he remembered, but several minutes passed before he could bring back her name. He ran through an inventory of near misses (Tammy, Kitty, Tippi, Kimberly), went blank for thirty or forty seconds after that, and then, just when he was about to give up, he found it: Tiffany. She was the only person who could help him, he realized. It would cost him a fortune to get that help, but what did it matter if his questions were finally answered? The girl had liked Pozzi, she seemed to have been crazy about him in fact, and once she heard the story of what had happened to him after the party, chances were that she would be willing to call the hospital. That was all it would take—one telephone call. She would ask them if Jack Pozzi had ever been a patient there, and then she would write to Nashe—a short letter telling him what she had found out. There might be a problem with the letter, of course, but that was a risk he'd have to take. He didn't think the letters from Donna had been opened. At least the envelopes hadn't looked tampered with, and why shouldn't Tiffany's letter get through to him as well? It was worth a try in any case. The more Nashe thought about this plan, the more promising it felt to him. What did he have to lose except money? He sat down at the kitchen table and began to drink his tea, trying to imagine what would happen when the girl came to visit him in the trailer. Before he could think of any of the words he would say to her, he discovered that he had an erection.

It took some doing to get Murks to go along with it, however.

When Nashe explained that he wanted to see the girl, Calvin reacted with surprise, and then, almost immediately afterward, a look of profound disappointment. It was as though Nashe had let him down, as though he had reneged on some tacit understanding between them, and he wasn't about to let it happen without putting up a fight.

"It don't make sense," Murks said. "Nine hundred dollars for a roll in the hay. That's nine days' work, Nashe, ninety hours of sweat and toil for nothing. It just don't add up. A little taste of girlie flesh against all that. Anybody can see it don't add up. You're a smart fella, Nashe, it's not like you don't know what I'm talking about."

"I don't ask you how you spend your money," Nashe said. "And it's none of your business how I spend mine."

"I just hate to see a man make a fool of himself, that's all. Especially when there's no need for it."

"Your needs are not my needs, Calvin. As long as I do the work, I'm entitled to any damned thing I want. It's written in the contract, and it's not your place to say a word about it."

So Nashe won the argument, and even though Murks continued to grumble about it, he went ahead and arranged for the girl's visit. She was due to come on the tenth, less than a week after Nashe had found her telephone number in the drawer, and it was a good thing he didn't have to wait any longer than that, for once he had convinced Murks to call her, he found it impossible to think about anything else. Long before the girl showed up, therefore, he knew that his reasons for inviting her were only partly connected to Pozzi. The erection had proved that (along with the others that followed), and he spent the next few days alternating between fits of dread and excitement, skulking around the meadow like some hormone-crazed adolescent. But he had not been with a woman since the middle of the summer—not since that day in Berkeley when he had held the sobbing Fiona in his arms—and it was probably inevitable that the girl's impending visit should fill his head with thoughts about sex. That was her business, after all. She fucked men for money, and since he was already paying for it, what was the harm in fulfilling his end of the exchange? It wouldn't prevent him from asking for her help, but that was only going to take twenty or thirty minutes, and in order to get her there to spend that time with him, he had to buy her services for the whole evening. There would be no point in wasting those hours. They belonged to him, and just because he wanted the girl for one thing, that didn't mean it was wrong to want her for another thing as well.

The tenth turned out to be a cold night, more like winter than fall, with strong winds gusting across the meadow and a sky full of stars. The girl arrived in a fur coat, cheeks red and eyes tearing from the chill, and Nashe felt that she was prettier than he had remembered, although it could have been the color in her face that made him think that. Her clothes were less provocative than the last time—white turtleneck sweater, blue jeans with woolen leg warmers, the ever-present spike heels—and all in all it was an improvement over the gaudy costume she had worn in October. She seemed more her age now, and for whatever it was worth, Nashe decided that he preferred her this way, that it made him feel less uncomfortable to look at her.

It helped that she smiled at him when she entered the trailer, and even though he found it a somewhat florid and theatrical smile, there was enough warmth in it to persuade him that she was not unhappy to be seeing him again. He realized that she had expected Pozzi to be there as well, and when she glanced around the room and did not find him, it was only natural that she should ask Nashe where he was. But Nashe couldn't quite bring himself to tell the truth—at least not yet. "Jack was called away on another job," he said. "Remember the Texas project he told you about last time? Well, our oilman had some questions about the drawings, and so he flew Jack down to Houston last night on his private jet. It was one of those spur-of-the-moment things. Jack was real sorry about it, but that's how it is with our work. We have to keep our clients happy."

"Geez," the girl said, making no attempt to hide her disappointment. "I liked that little guy a whole lot. I was looking forward to seeing him again."

"He's one in a million," Nashe said. "They don't make them any better than Jack."

"Yeah, he's a terrific guy. You get a john like that, and it doesn't feel like work anymore."

Nashe smiled at the girl, and then he reached out tentatively and touched her shoulder. "I'm afraid you'll have to settle for me tonight," he said.

"Well, worse things have happened," she replied, recovering quickly with a playful, down-from-under look. To emphasize the point, she moaned softly and began running her tongue over her lips. "I might be wrong," she said, "but I seem to remember that we had some unfinished business to take care of anyway."

Nashe had half a mind to tell her to take off her clothes right then, but he suddenly felt self-conscious, tongue-tied by his own arousal, and instead of taking her in his arms, he just stood where he was, wondering what to do next. He wished that Pozzi could have left behind a couple of jokes for him to use then, a few wisecracks to lighten up the atmosphere.

"How about a little music?" he suggested, seizing on the first thing that popped into his head. Before the girl could answer, he was already down on the floor, digging through the piles of cassettes he kept under the coffee table. After clattering among the operas and classical pieces for close to a minute, he finally pulled out his tape of Billie Holiday songs, *Billie's Greatest Hits*.

The girl frowned at what she called the "old-fashioned" music, but when Nashe asked her to dance, she seemed touched by the quaintness of the proposal, as if he had just asked her to partake of some prehistoric rite—a taffy pull, for example, or bobbing for apples in a wooden bucket. But the fact was that Nashe liked to dance, and he thought the movement might help to steady his nerves. He took hold of her with a firm grip, guiding her in small circles around the living room, and after a few minutes she seemed to settle into it, following him more gracefully than he would have expected. In spite of the high heels, she was impressively light on her feet.

"I've never known anyone named Tiffany before," he said. "I think it's very nice. It makes me think of beautiful and expensive things."

"That's the idea," she said. "It's supposed to make you see diamonds."

"Your parents must have known you'd turn out to be a beautiful girl."

"My parents had nothing to do with it. I picked the name myself."

"Oh. Well, that makes it even better. There's no point in being stuck with a name you don't like, is there?"

"I couldn't stand mine. As soon as I got away from home, I changed it."

"Was it really that bad?"

"How would you like to be called Dolores? It's about the worst name I can think of."

"That's funny. My mother's name was Dolores, and she never liked it either."

"No shit? Your old lady was a Dolores?"

"Honest. She was Dolores from the day she was born until the day she died."

"If she didn't like being Dolores, why didn't she change it?"

"She did. Not in a big way like you, but she used to go by a nickname. In fact, I never knew her real name was Dolores until I was about ten years old."

"What did she call herself?"

"Dolly."

"Yeah, I tried that for a while, too, but it wasn't much better. It only works if you're fat. Dolly. It's a name for a fat woman."

"Well, my mother was pretty fat, now that you mention it. Not always, but in the last few years of her life, she put on a lot of weight. Too much booze. It does that to some people. It has something to do with how the alcohol metabolizes in your blood."

"My old man drank like a fish for years, but he was always a skinny bastard. The only way you could tell was by looking at the veins around his nose."

The conversation went back and forth like that for a while, and when the tape ran out, they sat down on the sofa and opened a bottle of Scotch. Almost predictably, Nashe imagined that he was falling for her, and now that the ice had been broken, he began to ask her all sorts of questions about herself, trying to create an intimacy that would somehow mask the nature of their transaction and turn her into someone real. But the talk was part of the transaction, too, and even though she went on at great length about herself, at bottom he understood that she was only doing her job, talking because he was one of those customers who liked to talk. Everything she said seemed plausible, but at the same time he felt that she had been through it all before, that her words were not false so much as untrue, a delusion that she had little by little convinced herself to believe in, much as Pozzi had deluded himself with his dreams about the World Series of Poker. At one point, she even told him that hooking was only a temporary solution for her. "Once I get enough cash together," she said, "I'm going to quit the life and go into show business." It was impossible not to feel sorry for her, impossible not to feel saddened by her childish banality, but Nashe was too far gone by then to let that stand in his way.

"I think you'll make a wonderful actress," he said. "The minute I started dancing with you, I could tell you were the real thing. You move like an angel."

"Fucking keeps you in shape," she said seriously, announcing it as though it were a medical fact. "It's good for the pelvis. And if there's one thing I've done a lot of in the past couple of years, it's fuck. I must be as limber as a goddamn contortionist by now."

"It so happens that I know a few agents in New York," Nashe said, unable to stop himself anymore. "One of them has a big operation, and I'm sure he'd be interested in taking a look at you. A fellow by the name of Sid Zeno. If you like, I can call him tomorrow and set up an appointment."

"We're not talking about skin flicks, are we?"

"No, no, nothing like that. Zeno's strictly on the up-and-up. He handles some of the best young talent in the movies today."

"It's not that I wouldn't do it, you understand. But once you get into that biz, it's hard to get out. They typecast you, and then you never get a chance to play any parts with your clothes on. I mean, my bod's okay, but it's nothing to get worked up about. I'd rather do something where I can really act. You know, land a part in one of the daytime soaps, or maybe even try out for a sitcom. It might not be obvious to you, but once I get going, I can be pretty funny."

"No problem. Sid has good contacts with television, too. That's how he got started in fact. Back in the fifties, he was one of the first agents to work exclusively in television."

Nashe hardly knew what he was saying anymore. Filled with desire, and yet half dreading what would come of that desire, he blathered on as if he thought the girl might actually believe the nonsense he was telling her. But once they adjourned to the bedroom, she did not disappoint him. She began by letting him kiss her on the mouth, and because Nashe hadn't dared to hope for such a thing, he instantly imagined that he was falling in love with her. It was true that her naked body was less than beautiful, but now that he understood that she wasn't going to rush him through it or humiliate him by acting bored, he didn't care what she looked like. It had been so long, after all, and once they moved onto the bed, she demonstrated the talents of her overworked pelvis with such pride and abandon, it never occurred to him that the pleasure he seemed to be giving her could be anything but authentic. After a while, his brains became so scrambled that he lost his head, and he wound up saying a number of idiotic things to her, things so stupid and inappropriate, in fact, that if he hadn't been the one who was saying them, he would have thought he was insane.

What he proposed was that she stay there and live with him while he worked on the wall. He would take care of her, he said, and once the work was finished, they would go to New York together and he would manage her career. Forget Sid Zeno. He would do a better job because he believed in her, because he was crazy about her. They wouldn't be in the trailer more than a month or two, and she wouldn't have to do anything but rest and take it easy. He would do all the cooking, all the household chores, and it would be like a vacation for her, a way of getting the past two years out of her system. It wasn't a bad life in the meadow. It was calm and simple and good for the soul. He just needed to share it with someone now. He had been alone for too long, and he didn't think he could go on by himself anymore. It was too much to ask of anyone, he said, and the loneliness was beginning to drive him crazy. Just last week, he had almost killed someone, an innocent little boy, and he was afraid that worse things would happen to him if he didn't make some changes in his life very soon. If she agreed to stay there with him, he would do anything for her. He would give her anything she wanted. He would love her until she exploded with happiness.

Fortunately, he delivered this speech with such passion and sincerity that he left her with no alternative but to think it was a joke. No one could say such things with a straight face and expect to be believed, and the very foolishness of Nashe's confession was what saved him from total embarrassment. The girl took him for a prankster, an oddball with a gift for making up wild stories, and instead of telling him to drop dead (which she might have done if she had taken him seriously), she smiled at the trembling supplication in his voice and played along as if it were the funniest thing he had said all night. "I'll be happy to live here with you, honey," she said. "All you have to do is take care of Regis, and I'll move in with you first thing tomorrow morning."

"Regis?" he said.

"You know, the guy who handles my appointments. My pimp."

Hearing that response, Nashe understood how ridiculous he must have sounded. But her sarcasm had given him a second chance, an escape from impending disaster, and rather than let his feelings show (the hurt, the wretchedness, the misery her words had caused), he bounced up naked from the bed and clapped his hands together in mock exuberance. "Great!" he said. "I'll kill the bastard tonight, and then you'll be mine forever."

She started laughing then, as though a part of her actually enjoyed hearing him say those things, and the moment he became conscious of what that laughter meant, he felt a strange and powerful bitterness surge up inside him. He started laughing himself, joining in with her to keep the taste of that bitterness in his mouth, to revel in the comedy of his own abjection. Then, out of nowhere, he suddenly remembered Pozzi. It came like an electric shock, and the jolt of it nearly threw him to the floor. He hadn't given Jack a single thought in the past two hours, and the selfishness of that neglect mortified him. He stopped laughing with almost terrifying abruptness, and then he started climbing into his clothes, yanking on his pants as if a bell had just sounded in his head.

"There's only one problem," the girl said through her subsiding laughter, still bent on prolonging the game. "What happens when

Jack comes back from his trip? I mean, it could get a little crowded around here, don't you think? He's a cute guy, too, you know, and maybe there'll be nights when I feel like sleeping with him. What would you do then? Would you be jealous or what?"

"That's just it," Nashe said, his voice suddenly grim and hard. "Jack's not coming back. He disappeared almost a month ago."

"What do you mean? I thought you said he was in Texas."

"I was just making that up. There's no job in Texas, there's no oilman, there's no nothing. The day after you came here for the party, Jack tried to escape. I found him lying outside the trailer the next morning. His skull was bashed in, and he was unconscious—just lying there in a pool of his own blood. Chances are he's dead by now, but I'm not sure. That's what I want you to find out for me."

He told her everything then, going through the whole story about Pozzi and the card game and the wall, but he had already told her so many lies that night, it was hard to make her believe a word he said. She just looked at him as though he were mad, a lunatic foaming at the mouth with tales of little purple men in flying saucers. But Nashe kept hammering away, and after a while his vehemence began to frighten her. If she hadn't been sitting naked on the bed, she probably would have made a run for it, but as it was she was trapped, and eventually Nashe managed to wear her down, describing the results of Pozzi's beating in such ugly and elaborate detail that the full horror of it finally sank in, and by the time that happened, she was sobbing there on the bed, her face buried in her hands and her thin back shaking in fierce, uncontrollable spasms.

Yes, she said. She would call the hospital. She promised she would. Poor Jack. Of course she would call the hospital. Jesus Christ poor Jack. Jesus Christ poor Jack sweet mother of God. She would call the hospital, and then she would write him a letter.

Goddamn them. Of course she would do it. Poor Jack. Goddamn them to hell. Sweet Jack oh Jesus poor Jesus poor mother of God. Yes, she would do it. She promised she would. The moment she got home, she would pick up the phone and do it. Yes, he could count on her. God God God God God. She promised. She promised she would do it.

# 9

---

Crazy with loneliness. Every time Nashe thought of the girl, those were the first words that entered his head: *crazy with loneliness*. Eventually, he repeated that phrase so often to himself, it began to lose its meaning.

He never held it against her that the letter did not come. He knew that she had kept her promise, and because he continued to believe that, he did not despair. If anything, he began to feel encouraged. He was at a loss to explain this change of heart, but the fact was that he was growing optimistic, perhaps more optimistic than at any time since the first day in the meadow.

There was no point in asking Murks what he had done with the girl's letter. He only would have lied to him, and Nashe didn't want to expose his suspicions if nothing could be gained by it. Eventually, he was going to learn the truth. He knew that now, and the certainty of that knowledge comforted him, kept him going from one day to the next. "Things happen in their own sweet time," he told himself. Before you could learn the truth, you had to learn patience.

Meanwhile, work on the wall advanced. After the third row was completed, Murks built a wooden platform for him, and Nashe now had to mount the steps of this little structure each time he put another stone in place. It slowed his progress somewhat, but that meant nothing compared to the pleasure he felt in being able to work off the ground. Once he started on the fourth row, the wall began to change for him. It was taller than a man now, taller even than a big man like himself, and the fact that he could no longer see past it, that it blocked his view to the other side, made him feel as though something important had begun to happen. All of a sudden, the stones were turning into a wall, and in spite of the pain it had cost him, he could not help admiring it. Whenever he stopped and looked at it now, he felt awed by what he had done.

For several weeks he read almost nothing. Then one night in late November he picked up a book by William Faulkner (*The Sound and the Fury*), opened it at random, and came across these words in the middle of a sentence: " . . . until someday in very disgust he risks everything on the single blind turn of a card . . ."

Sparrows, cardinals, chickadees, blue jays. Those were the only birds left in the woods now. And crows. Those best of all, Nashe felt. Every now and then, they would come swooping down over the meadow, letting out their strange, throttled cries, and he would interrupt what he was doing to watch them pass overhead. He loved the suddenness of their comings and goings, the way they would appear and disappear, as if for no reason at all.

Standing out by his trailer in the early morning, he could look through the bare trees and see the outlines of Flower and Stone's house. On some mornings, however, the fog was too thick for him to see that far. Even the wall could vanish then, and he would have to scan the meadow a long time before he could tell the difference between the gray stones and the gray air around them.

He had never thought of himself as a man destined for great things. All his life, he had assumed that he was just like everyone else. Now, little by little, he was beginning to suspect that he had been wrong.

Those were the days when he thought most about Flower's collection of objects: the handkerchiefs, the spectacles, the rings, the mountains of absurd memorabilia. Every couple of hours, it seemed, another one of them would appear in his head. He was not disturbed by this, however, merely astonished.

Every night before going to bed, he would write down the number of stones he had added to the wall that day. The figures themselves were unimportant to him, but once the list had grown to ten or twelve entries, he began to take pleasure in the simple accumulation, studying the results in the same way he had once read the box scores in the morning paper. At first, he imagined it was a purely statistical pleasure, but after a while he sensed that it was fulfilling some inner need, some compulsion to keep track of himself and not lose sight of where he was. By early December, he began to think of it as a journal, a logbook in which the numbers stood for his most intimate thoughts.

Listening to *The Marriage of Figaro* in the trailer at night. Sometimes, when a particularly beautiful aria came on, he would imagine that Juliette was singing to him, that it was her voice he was hearing.

The cold weather bothered him less than he thought it would. Even on the bitterest days, he would shed his jacket within an hour of starting work, and by midafternoon he would often be down to his shirtsleeves. Murks would stand there in his heavy coat, shivering against the wind, and yet Nashe would feel almost nothing. It made so little sense to him, he wondered if his body hadn't caught fire.

One day, Murks suggested that they begin using the jeep to cart the stones. They could increase the loads that way, he said, and the wall could go up more quickly. But Nashe turned him down. The noise of the engine would distract him, he said. And besides, he was used to the old way of doing things. He liked the slowness of the wagon, the long walks across the meadow, the odd little rumbling sound of the wheels. "If it ain't broke," he said, "why fix it?"

Some time in the third week of November, Nashe realized that it would be possible to bring himself back to zero on his birthday, which fell on December thirteenth. It would mean making several small adjustments in his habits (spending a bit less on food, for example, cutting out newspapers and cigars), but the symmetry of the plan appealed to him, and he decided it would be worth the effort. If all went well, he would win back his freedom on the day he turned thirty-four. It was an arbitrary ambition, but once he put his mind to it, he found that it helped him to organize his thoughts, to concentrate on what had to be done.

He went over his calculations with Murks every morning, toting up the pluses and minuses to make sure there were no discrepancies, checking and rechecking until their figures matched. On the night of the twelfth, therefore, he knew for certain that the debt would be paid off by three o'clock the next day. He wasn't planning to stop, then, however. He had already told Murks that he wanted to make use of the contract rider to earn some traveling money, and since he knew exactly how much he was going to need (enough to pay for cabs, a plane ticket to Minnesota, and Christmas presents for Juliette and her cousins), he had resigned himself to staying on for another week. That would take him up to the twentieth. The first thing he would do after that was get a cab to drive him to the hospital in Doylestown, and once he found out that Pozzi had never been there, he would call another cab and go to the police. He would probably have to hang around for a while to help with the investigation, but no more than a few days, he thought, perhaps only one or two. If he was lucky, he might even get back to Minnesota in time for Christmas Eve.

He didn't tell Murks it was his birthday. He felt oddly out of sorts that morning, and even as the day wore on and three o'clock approached, an overwhelming sadness continued to drag down his spirits. Until then, Nashe had assumed that he would want to celebrate—to light up an imaginary cigar, perhaps, or merely to shake Murks's hand—but the memory of Pozzi weighed too heavily on him, and he couldn't rouse himself into the proper mood. Each time he picked up another stone, he felt as if he were carrying Pozzi in his arms again, lifting him off the ground and looking into his poor, annihilated face, and when two o'clock came round and the time had dwindled to a matter of minutes, he suddenly found himself thinking back to that day in October when he and the kid had reached this point together, working their heads off in a manic burst of happiness. He missed him so much, he realized. He missed him so much, it ached just to think about him.

The best way to handle it was to do nothing, he decided, just go on working and ignore the whole business, but at three o'clock he was jolted by a strange piercing noise—a whoop or a shriek or a cry of distress—and when Nashe looked up to see what the trouble was, he saw Murks waving his hat at him from across the meadow. *You did it!* Nashe heard him say. *You're a free man now!* Nashe stopped for a moment and waved back with a casual flip of his hand, and then he immediately bent down over his work again, fixing his attention on the wheelbarrow in which he was stirring cement. Very briefly, he fought off an impulse to start crying, but it didn't last more than a couple of seconds, and by the time Murks had walked over to congratulate him, he was fully in control of himself again.

"I figured maybe you'd like to go out for a drink with me and Floyd tonight," Calvin said.

"What for?" Nashe answered, barely looking up from his work.

"I don't know. Just to get out and see what the world looks like again. You've been cooped up here a long time, son. It might not be a bad idea to do a little celebrating."

"I thought you were against celebrations."

"Depends on what kind of celebrating you mean. I'm not talking about anything fancy here. Just a few drinks over at Ollie's in town. A workingman's night out."

"You forget that I don't have any money."

"That's all right. The drinks are on me."

"Thanks, but I think I'll pass. I was planning on writing a few letters tonight."

"You can always write them tomorrow."

"That's true. But then again, I could be dead tomorrow. You never know what's going to happen."

"All the more reason not to worry about it."

"Maybe some other time. It's nice of you to offer, but I'm just not in the mood tonight."

"I'm just trying to be friendly, Nashe."

"I know you are, and I appreciate it. But you don't have to worry about me. I can take care of myself."

Cooking dinner alone in the trailer that night, however, Nashe regretted his stubbornness. There was no question that he had done the right thing, but the truth was that he was desperate for a chance to leave the meadow, and the moral correctness he had shown in refusing Murks's invitation felt like a paltry triumph to him now. He spent ten hours a day in the man's company, after all, and just because they sat down together and had a drink, it wasn't going to stop him from turning the son of a bitch over to the police. As it happened, Nashe got precisely what he wanted anyway. Just after he finished dinner, Murks and his son-in-law came around to the trailer to ask him if he had changed his mind. They were going out now, they said, and it didn't seem fair that he should miss out on the fun.

"It's not like you're the only one who's been set free today," Murks said, blowing his nose into a large white handkerchief. "I've been out there in that field same as you, freezing my butt off seven days a week. It's about the worst damned job I've ever had. I've got nothing personal against you, Nashe, but it's been no picnic. No sir, no picnic at all. Maybe it's about time we sat down and buried the hatchet."

"You know," Floyd said, smiling at Nashe as if to encourage him, "let bygones be bygones."

"You guys don't give up, do you?" Nashe said, still trying to sound reluctant.

"We're not twisting your arm or anything," Murks said. "Just trying to enter into the Christmas spirit."

"Like Santa's helpers," Floyd said. "Spreading good cheer wherever we go."

"All right," Nashe said, studying their expectant faces. "I'll go out for a drink with you. Why the hell not?"

Before they could drive to town, they had to stop off at the main house to get Murks's car. Murks's car meant his car, of course, but in the excitement of the moment Nashe had forgotten all about that. He sat in the back of the jeep as they bounced along through the dark and icy woods, and it wasn't until this first little journey was over that he realized his mistake. He saw the red Saab parked in the driveway, and the moment he understood what he was looking at, he felt himself go numb with grief. The thought of riding in it again made him sick, but there was no way he could back out of it now. They were set to go, and he had already caused enough fuss for one night.

He didn't say a word. He took his place in the backseat and closed his eyes, trying to make his mind go blank, listening to the familiar sound of the engine as the car moved along the road. He could hear that Murks and Floyd were talking in the front, but he didn't pay attention to what they said, and after a while their voices blurred with the sound of the engine, producing a low, continuous hum that vibrated in his ears, a lulling music that sang along his skin and dug down into the depths of his body. He didn't open his eyes again until the car stopped, and then he found himself standing in a parking lot at the edge of a small, deserted town, listening to a traffic sign rattle in the wind. Christmas decorations blinked in the distance down the street, and the cold air was red with the pulsing reflections, the throbs of light that bounced off the shop windows and glowed on the frozen sidewalks. Nashe had no idea where he was. They could still be in Pennsylvania, he thought, but then again, they could have crossed the river and gone into New Jersey. For a brief moment, he considered asking Murks which state they were in, but then he decided that he didn't care.

Ollie's was a dark and noisy place, and he took an immediate dislike to it. Country-and-western songs thundered out of a jukebox in one corner, and the bar was thronged with a crush of beer-drinkers—men in flannel shirts, for the most part, decked out in fancy baseball caps and wearing belts with large, elaborate buckles. They were farmers and mechanics and truck drivers, Nashe supposed, and the few women scattered among them looked like regulars—puffy, dough-faced alcoholics who sat on the barstools and laughed as loudly as the men. Nashe had been in a hundred places like this before, and it didn't take thirty seconds for him to realize that he wasn't up to it tonight, that he had been away from crowds for too long. Everyone was talking at once, it seemed, and the ruckus of loud voices and blaring music was already hurting his head.

They drank several rounds at a table in the far corner of the room, and after the first couple of bourbons Nashe began to feel somewhat revived. Floyd did most of the talking, addressing nearly all his remarks to Nashe, and after a while it became hard not to notice how little Murks was contributing to the conversation. He looked more under the weather than usual, Nashe thought, and every so often he would turn away and cough violently into his handkerchief, hawking up nasty gobs of phlegm. These fits seemed to take a lot out of him, and afterward he would sit there in silence, pale and shaken from the effort to still his lungs.

"Granddad hasn't been feeling too well lately," Floyd said to Nashe (he always referred to Murks as Granddad). "I've been trying to talk him into taking a couple of weeks off."

"It's nothing," Murks said. "Just a touch of the ague, that's all."

"The ague?" Nashe said. "Where the hell did you learn to talk, Calvin."

"What's wrong with the way I talk?" Murks said.

"No one uses words like that anymore," Nashe said. "They went out about a hundred years ago."

"I learned it from my mother," Murks said. "And she only died six years back. She'd be eighty-eight if she was alive today—which proves that word ain't as old as you think it is."

Nashe found it strange to hear Murks talking about his mother. It was difficult to imagine that he had once been a child, let alone that twenty or twenty-five years ago he had once been Nashe's age—a young man with a life to look forward to, a person with a future. For the first time since they had been thrown together, Nashe realized that he knew next to nothing about Murks. He didn't know where he had been born; he didn't know how he had met his wife or how many children he had; he didn't even know how long he had been working for Flower and Stone. Murks was a creature who existed wholly in the present for him, and beyond that present he was nothing, a being as insubstantial as a shadow or a thought. When all was said and done, however, that was precisely how Nashe wanted it. Even if Murks had turned to him at that moment and offered to tell the story of his life, he would have refused to listen.

Meanwhile, Floyd was telling him about his new job. Since Nashe seemed to have played some part in his finding it, he had to sit through an exhaustive, rambling account of how Floyd had struck up a conversation with the chauffeur who had driven the girl from Atlantic City on the night of her visit last month. The limousine company had apparently been looking for new drivers, and Floyd had gone down the very next day to apply for a job. He was only working on a part-time basis now, just two or three days a week, but he was hoping they'd have more work for him after the first of the year. Just for something to say, Nashe asked him how he liked wearing the uniform. Floyd said it didn't bother him. It was nice to have something special to wear, he said, it made him feel like someone important.

"The main thing is that I love to drive," he continued. "I don't care what kind of car it is. As long as I'm sitting behind the wheel and moving down the road, I'm a happy man. I can't think of a better way to make a living. Imagine getting paid for something you love to do. It almost doesn't feel right."

"Yes," Nashe said, "driving is a good thing. I agree with you about that."

"Well, you ought to know," Floyd said. "I mean, look at Granddad's car. That's a beautiful machine. Isn't that so, Granddad?" he said to Murks. "It's a stunner, isn't it?"

"A fine piece of work," Calvin said. "Handles real good. Takes the curves and hills like nobody's business."

"You must have enjoyed driving around in that thing," Floyd said to Nashe.

"I did," Nashe said. "It was the best car I ever owned."

"There's one thing that puzzles me, though," Floyd said. "How did you ever manage to put so many miles on it? I mean, it's a pretty new model, and the odometer's already showing close to eighty thousand miles. That's an awful lot of driving to do in one year."

"I suppose it is," Nashe said.

"Were you some kind of traveling salesman or something?"

"Yeah, that's it, I was a traveling salesman. They gave me a large territory, and so I had to be on the road a lot. You know, lugging around the samples in the trunk, living out of a suitcase, staying in a different city every night. I moved around so much, I sometimes forgot where I lived."

"I think I'd like that," Floyd said. "It sounds like a good job to me."

"It's not bad. You have to like being alone, but once you've taken care of that, the rest is easy."

Floyd was beginning to get on his nerves. The man was an oaf, Nashe thought, a full-fledged imbecile, and the longer he went on talking, the more he reminded Nashe of his son. They both had that same desperate desire to please, that same fawning timidity, that same lostness in the eyes. To look at him, you would never think he would harm a soul—but he had harmed Jack that night, Nashe was sure of it, and it was precisely that emptiness inside him that had made it possible, that immense chasm of want. It wasn't that Floyd was a cruel or violent person, but he was big and strong and ever so willing, and he loved Granddad more than anyone else in the world. It was written all over his face, and every time he turned his eyes in Murks's direction, it was as though he were looking at a god. Granddad had told him what to do, and he had gone ahead and done it.

After the third or fourth round of drinks, Floyd asked Nashe if he would care to play some pool. There were several tables in the back room, he said, and one of them was bound to be free. Nashe was feeling a little woozy by then, but he accepted anyway, welcoming it as a chance to get up from his seat and end the conversation. It was close to eleven o'clock, and the crowd at Ollie's had become thinner and less boisterous. Floyd asked Murks if he wanted to join them, but Calvin said he'd rather stay where he was and finish his drink.

It was a large, dimly lit room with four pool tables in the center and a number of pinball machines and computer games along the side walls. They stopped by the rack near the door to choose their sticks, and as they walked over to one of the free tables, Floyd asked if it might not be more interesting if they made a friendly little bet on the action. Nashe had never been much of a pool player, but he didn't think twice about saying yes. He wanted to beat Floyd in the worst way, he realized, and there was no question that putting some money on it would help him to concentrate.

"I don't have any cash," he said. "But I'll be good for it as soon as I get paid next week."

"I know that," Floyd said. "If I didn't think you'd be good for it, I wouldn't have asked."

"How much do you want to make it for?"

"I don't know. Depends on what you've got in mind."

"How about ten dollars a game?"

"Ten dollars? All right, sounds good to me."

They played eight-ball on one of those bumpy, quarter-a-rack tables, and Nashe scarcely said a word the whole time they were there. Floyd wasn't bad, but in spite of his drunkenness, Nashe was better, and he wound up playing his heart out, zeroing in on his shots with a skill and precision that surpassed anything he had done before. He felt utterly happy and loose, and once he fell into the rhythm of the clicking, tumbling balls, the stick began to glide through his fingers as if it were moving on its own. He won the first four games by steadily increasing margins (by one ball, by two balls, by four balls, by six balls), and then he won the fifth game before Floyd could even take a turn, sinking two striped balls on the break and going on from there to clear the table, ending with a flourish as he sank the eight-ball on a three-way combination shot in the corner pocket.

"That's enough for me," Floyd said after the fifth game. "I figured you might be good, but this is ridiculous."

"Just luck," Nashe said, struggling to keep a smile off his face. "I'm generally pretty feeble. Things kept falling my way tonight."

"Feeble or not, it looks like I owe you fifty bucks."

"Forget the money, Floyd. It doesn't make any difference to me."

"What do you mean, forget it? You just won yourself fifty bucks. It's yours."

"No, no, I'm telling you to keep it. I don't want your money."

Floyd kept trying to press the fifty dollars into Nashe's hand, but Nashe was just as adamant about refusing it, and after a few moments it finally dawned on Floyd that Nashe meant what he was saying, that he wasn't just putting on an act.

"Buy your little boy a present," Nashe said. "If you want to make me happy, use it on him."

"It's awfully good of you," Floyd said. "Most guys wouldn't let fifty bucks slip through their fingers like that."

"I'm not most guys," Nashe said.

"I guess I owe you one," Floyd said, patting Nashe's back in an awkward show of gratitude. "Any time you need a favor, all you have to do is ask."

It was one of those empty, obliging remarks that people often make at such moments, and under any other circumstances Nashe probably would have let it pass. But he suddenly found himself glowing with the warmth of an idea, and rather than lose the opportunity he had just been given, he looked straight back at Floyd and said, "Well, now that you mention it, maybe there is one thing you can do for me. It's a very small thing really, but your help would mean a lot."

"Sure, Jim," Floyd said. "Just name it."

"Let me drive the car back home tonight."

"You mean Granddad's car?"

"That's right, Granddad's car. The car I used to own."

"I don't think it's for me to say whether you can or not, Jim. It's Granddad's car, and he's the one you'll have to ask. But I'll certainly put in a word for you."

As it turned out, Murks didn't mind. He was feeling pretty tuckered, he said, and he was planning to ask Floyd to drive the car anyway. If Floyd wanted to let Nashe do it, that was all right with him. As long as they got to where they were going, what difference did it make?

When they stepped outside, they discovered that it was snowing. It was the first snow of the year, and it fell in thick, moist flakes, most of it melting the instant it touched the ground. The Christmas decorations had been turned off down the street, and the wind had stopped blowing. The air was still now, so still that the weather felt almost warm. Nashe took a deep breath, glanced up at the sky, and stood there for a moment as the snow fell against his face. He was happy, he realized, happier than he had been in a long time.

When they came to the parking lot, Murks handed him the keys to the car. Nashe unlocked the front door, but just as he was about to open it and climb in, he pulled back his hand and started to laugh. "Hey, Calvin," he said. "Where the hell are we?"

"What do you mean where are we?" Murks said.

"What town?"

"Billings."

"Billings? I thought that was in Montana."

"Billings, New Jersey."

"So we're not in Pennsylvania anymore?"

"No, you have to cross the bridge to get back there. Don't you remember?"

"I don't remember anything."

"Just take Route Sixteen. It carries you right on through."

He hadn't thought it would be so important to him, but once he positioned himself behind the wheel, he noticed that his hands were trembling. He started the engine, flicked on the headlights and windshield wipers, and then backed out slowly from the parking space. It hadn't been so long, he thought. Just three and a half months, and yet it took a while before he felt any of the old pleasure again. He was distracted by Murks coughing beside him in the front seat, by Floyd rattling on about how he had lost at pool in the back, and it was only when Nashe turned on the radio that he was able to forget they were there with him, that he was not alone as he had been for all those months when he had driven back and forth across America. He never wanted to do that again, he realized, but once he left the town behind him and could accelerate on the empty road, it was hard not to pretend for a little while, to imagine that he was back in those days before the real story of his life had begun. This was the only chance he would have, and he wanted to savor what had been given to him, to push the memory of who he had once been as far as it would go. The snow whirled down onto the windshield before him, and in his mind he saw the crows swooping down over the meadow, calling out with their mysterious cries as he watched them pass overhead. The meadow would look beautiful under the snow, he thought, and he hoped it would go on falling through the night so he could wake up to see it that way in the morning. He imagined the immensity of the white field, and the snow continuing to fall until even the mountains of stones were covered, until everything disappeared under an avalanche of whiteness.

He had turned the radio to a classical station, and he recognized the music as something familiar, a piece he had listened to many times before. It was the andante from an eighteenth-century string quartet, but even though Nashe knew every passage by heart, the name of the composer kept eluding him. He quickly narrowed it down to Mozart or Haydn, but after that he felt stuck. For several moments it would sound like the work of one, and then, almost immediately, it would begin to sound like something by the other. It might have been one of the quartets that Mozart dedicated to Haydn, Nashe thought, but it might have been the other way around. At a certain point, the music of both men seemed to touch, and it was no longer possible to tell them apart. And yet Haydn had lived to a ripe old age, honored with commissions and court appointments and every advantage the world of that time could offer. And Mozart had died young and poor, and his body had been thrown into a common grave.

Nashe had the car up to sixty by then, feeling in absolute control as he whipped along the narrow, twisting country road. The music had pushed Murks and Floyd far into the background, and he could no longer hear anything but the four stringed instruments pouring out their sounds into the dark, enclosed space. Then he was doing seventy, and immediately after that he heard Murks shouting at him through another fit of coughing. "You damned fool," Nashe heard him say. "You're driving too fast!" By way of response, Nashe pressed down on the accelerator and pushed the car up to eighty, taking the curve with a light and steady grip on the wheel. What did Murks know about driving? he thought. What did Murks know about anything?

At the precise moment the car hit eighty-five, Murks leaned forward and snapped off the radio. The sudden silence came as a jolt to Nashe, and he automatically turned to the old man and told him to mind his own business. When he looked at the road again a moment later, he could already see the headlight looming up at him. It seemed to come out of nowhere, a cyclops star hurtling straight for his eyes, and in the sudden panic that engulfed him, his only thought was that this was the last thought he would ever have. There was no time to stop, no time to prevent what was going to happen, and so instead of slamming his foot on the brakes, he pressed down even harder on the gas. He could hear Murks and his son-in-law howling in the distance, but their voices were muffled, drowned out by the roar of blood in his head. And then the light was upon him, and Nashe shut his eyes, unable to look at it anymore.